GHOSTS OF THE HEARTLAND

GHOSTS OF THE HEARTLAND

Haunting, Spine-Chilling Stories
from the American Midwest

Edited by
Frank D. McSherry, Jr., Charles G. Waugh,
and Martin H. Greenberg

Rutledge Hill Press
Nashville, Tennessee

Published in Nashville, Tennessee, by Rutledge Hill Press, Inc., 513 Third Avenue South, Nashville, Tennessee 37210.

Typography by Bailey Typography, Nashville, Tennessee
Cover design by Harriette Bateman

Library of Congress Cataloging-in-Publication Data

Ghosts of the heartland : haunting, spine-chilling stories from the
   American Midwest / edited by Frank D. McSherry, Jr., Charles G.
   Waugh, and Martin H. Greenberg.
     p. cm.
   ISBN 1-55853-068-1
    1. Ghost stories, American—Middle West 2. Middle West—Fiction.
 I. McSherry, Frank D. II. Waugh, Charles III. Greenberg, Martin
Harry.
PS648.G48G47 1990   90-30532
813'.08733083277—dc20   CIP

Manufactured in the United States of America
1 2 3 4 5 6 7 8 — 96 95 94 93 92 91 90

Table of Contents

Introduction

Can There Be Such Things? Here?

"This is a beautiful country."
—Rev. John Brown, two minutes
before being hung for treason,
December 2, 1859

Imagine a man in a room.

He's seated comfortably in a leather chair on this quiet summer night, reading the paper by lamplight. His hand drops down to pet his dog. After a moment, he pauses, somewhat puzzled. The fur seems coarser, the head shaped a bit differently than he remembers . . .

Then he recalls: he'd locked the dog out for the night an hour ago . . .

That icy thrill down the spine, that *frisson d'horreur* that we read ghost stories for, always seems to come more effectively when ghosts appear where they're not expected.

And what less likely setting can you find for ghosts than the American heartland? The golden wheat fields of Kansas, limitless under a vast azure dome of summer sky; the wood-lined winding rivers of Wisconsin; the deep, cool lakes of Minnesota; the seas of grass that are the plains of Nebraska . . .

Yet deeds dark indeed were done in this sunny region. Here the half-insane Hells Benders set up the tavern which so many travelers entered and so few left; where John Brown and his abolitionists battled pro-slavery settlers so viciously that the battleground went down in history as Bloody Kansas. It was in Indiana that Belle Guiness ran her murder farm for matrimonial prospects she met through Lonely Hearts columns, writing them to visit her bringing all the cash they had, and adding, "Come prepared to stay forever . . ."

It is not only artistic skill that lets our authors write of ghosts in the Heartlands. Each of the stories presented here tells something of the state it's set in, the history or terrain or towns—a bonus for the reader. Robert Bloch, author of *Psycho,* tells of the veteran who finds that the grandmother he had to leave wasn't as alone as he feared; it's just that her new friends all seem to visit at night and that they all seem to come from the direction of the graveyard . . . Action-adventure writer Robert Adams of the Horseclans tells of a terrible vengeance wreaked on the children of buffalo hunters as a herd of bison roam the North Dakota plains again. Ghosts move with the times in Fritz Leiber's "Smoke Ghost," when big cities and pollution create a new and horrible kind of ghost . . . Manly Wade Wellman, winner of the World Fantasy Award (1980), tells of a terrifying school that taught its pupils more than its principal ever dreamed. "Professor Kate" learns that there are things more frightening than Indian raids.

But while all ghosts are eerie, they are not all horrifying. Nor should they be, as these stories point out. If there are such things (and there are a few unsettling cases that are difficult to explain otherwise), then they are evidence that something of us does not die and may even return, under the right circumstances, to the people and places we love.

Perhaps it is well that we have ghost stories and that we are all reminded from time to time that, despite our impressive advances, there are things in nature that we do not understand . . . and that even in Eden there fell a shadow of supernatural horror, a thing whose eyes glowed red out of the darkness.

—Frank D. McSherry, Jr.
McAlester, Oklahoma

Acknowledgments

GHOSTS OF THE
HEARTLAND

A college professor has to be wary of what he says to his students—and what the students think they hear.

But at My Back I Will Always Hear

David Morrell

She phoned again last night. At 3 A.M. the way she always does. I'm scared to death. I can't keep running. On the hotel's register downstairs, I lied about my name, address, and occupation, hoping to hide from her. My real name's Charles Ingram. Though I'm here in Johnstown, Pennsylvania, I'm from Iowa City, Iowa. I teach—or used to teach until three days ago—creative writing at the University. I can't risk going back there. But I don't think I can hide much longer. Each night, she comes closer.

From the start, she scared me. I came to school at eight to prepare my classes. Through the side door of the English building I went up a stairwell to my third-floor office, which was isolated by a fire door from all the other offices. My colleagues used to joke that I'd been banished, but I didn't care, for in my far-off corner I could concentrate. Few students interrupted me. Regardless of the busy noises past the fire door, I sometimes felt there was no one else inside the building. And indeed at 8 A.M. I often *was* the only person in the building.

That day I was wrong, however. Clutching my heavy briefcase, I trudged up the stairwell. My scraping footsteps echoed off the walls of pale-red cinderblock, the stairs of pale-green imitation marble. First floor. Second floor. The neon lights glowed coldly. Then the stairwell angled toward the third floor, and I saw her waiting on a chair outside my office. Pausing, I frowned up at her. I felt uneasy.

1

Eight A.M., for you, is probably not early. You've been up for quite a while so you can get to work on time or get your children off to school. But 8 A.M., for college students, is the middle of the night. They don't like morning classes. When their schedules force them to attend one, they don't crawl from bed until they absolutely have to, and they don't come stumbling into class until I'm just about to start my lecture.

I felt startled, then, to find her waiting ninety minutes early. She sat tensely: lifeless dull brown hair, a shapeless dingy sweater, baggy faded jeans with patches on the knees and frays around the cuffs. Her eyes seemed haunted, wild, and deep and dark.

I climbed the last few steps and, puzzled, stopped before her. "Do you want an early conference?"

Instead of answering, she nodded bleakly.

"You're concerned about a grade I gave you?"

This time, though, in pain she shook her head from side to side.

Confused, I fumbled with my key and opened the office, stepping in. The room was small and narrow: a desk, two chairs, a wall of bookshelves, and a window. As I sat behind the desk, I watched her slowly come inside. She glanced around uncertainly. Distraught, she shut the door.

That made me nervous. When a female student shuts the door, I start to worry that a colleague or a student might walk up the stairs and hear a female voice and wonder what's so private I want to keep the door closed. Though I should have told her to reopen it, her frantic eyes aroused such pity in me that I sacrificed my principle, deciding her torment was so personal she could talk about it only in strict secrecy.

"Sit down." I smiled and tried to make her feel at ease, though I myself was not at ease. "What seems to be the difficulty, Miss . . . ? I'm sorry, but I don't recall your name."

"Samantha Perry. I don't like 'Samantha', though." She fidgeted. "I've shortened it to—"

"Yes? To what?"

"To 'Sam'. I'm in your Tuesday-Thursday class." She bit her lip. "You spoke to me."

I frowned, not understanding. "You mean what I taught seemed vivid to you? I inspired you to write a better story?"

"Mr. Ingram, no. I mean you *spoke* to me. You stared at me while you were teaching. You ignored the other students. You directed what you said to *me*. When you talked about Hemingway, how Frederic Henry wants to go to bed with Catherine—" She swallowed. "—you were asking me to go to bed with you."

I gaped. To disguise my shock, I quickly lit a cigarette. "You're mistaken."

"But I *heard* you. You kept staring straight at *me*. I felt all the other students knew what you were doing."

"I was only lecturing. I often look at students' faces to make sure they pay attention. You received the wrong impression."

"You weren't asking me to go to bed with you?" Her voice sounded anguished.

"No. I don't trade sex for grades."

"But I don't care about a grade!"

"I'm married. Happily. I've got two children. Anyway, suppose I did intend to proposition you. Would I do it in the middle of a class? I'd be foolish."

"Then you never meant to—" Ske kept biting her lip.

"I'm sorry."

"But you speak to me! Outside class I hear your voice! When I'm in my room or walking down the street! You talk to me when I'm asleep! You say you want to go to bed with me!"

My skin prickled. I felt frozen. "You're mistaken. Your imagination's playing tricks."

"But I hear your voice so clearly! When I'm studying or—"

"How? If I'm not there."

"You send your thoughts! You concentrate and put your voice inside my mind!"

Adrenaline scalded my stomach. I frantically sought an argument to disillusion her. "Telepathy? I don't believe in it. I've never tried to send my thoughts to you."

"Unconsciously?"

I shook my head from side to side. I couldn't bring myself

to tell her: of all the female students in her class, she looked so plain, even if I wasn't married I'd never have wanted sex with her.

"You're studying too hard. You want to do so well you're preoccupied with me. That's why you think you hear my voice when I'm not there. I try to make my lectures vivid. As a consequence, you think I'm speaking totally to you."

"Then you shouldn't teach that way!" she shouted. "It's not fair! It's cruel! It's teasing!" Tears streamed down her face. "You made a fool of me!"

"I didn't mean to."

"But you did! You tricked me! You misled me!"

"No."

She stood so quickly I flinched, afraid she'd lunge at me or scream for help and claim I'd tried to rape her. That damned door. I cursed myself for not insisting she leave it open.

She rushed sobbing toward it. She pawed the knob and stumbled out, hysterically retreating down the stairwell.

Shaken, I stubbed out my cigarette, grabbing another. My chest tightened as I heard the dwindling echo of her wracking sobs, the awkward scuffle of her dimming footsteps, then the low deep rumble of the outside door.

The silence settled over me.

An hour later I found her waiting in class. She'd wiped her tears. The only signs of what had happened were her red and puffy eyes. She sat alertly, pen to paper. I carefully didn't face her as I spoke. She seldom glanced up from her notes.

After class I asked my graduate assistant if he knew her.

"You mean Sam? Sure, I know her. She's been getting Ds. She had a conference with me. Instead of asking how to get a better grade, though, all she did was talk about you, pumping me for information. She's got quite a thing for you. Too bad about her."

"Why?"

"Well, she's so plain, she doesn't have many friends. I doubt she goes out much. There's a problem with her father. She was vague about it, but I had the sense her three sisters are so beautiful that Daddy treats her as the ugly duckling. She wants very much to please him. He ignores her, though. He's practically disowned her. You remind her of him."

"Who? Of her father?"

"She admits you're ten years younger than him, but she says you look exactly like him."

I felt heartsick.

Two days later, I found her waiting for me—again at 8 A.M. —outside my office.

Tense, I unlocked the door. As if she heard my thought, she didn't shut it this time. Sitting before my desk, she didn't fidget. She just stared at me.

"It happened again," she said.

"In class I didn't even look at you."

"No, afterward, when I went to the library." She drew an anguished breath."And later—I ate supper in the dorm. I heard your voice so clearly, I was sure you were in the room."

"What time was that?"

"Five-thirty."

"I was having cocktails with the Dean. Believe me, Sam, I wasn't sending messages to you. I didn't even *think* of you."

"I couldn't have imagined it! You wanted me to go to bed with you!"

"I wanted research money from the Dean. I thought of nothing else. My mind was totally involved in trying to convince him. When I didn't get the money, I was too annoyed to concentrate on anything but getting drunk."

"Your voice—"

"It isn't real. If I sent thoughts to you, wouldn't I admit what I was doing? When you asked me, wouldn't I confirm the message? Why would I deny it?"

"I'm afraid."

"You're troubled by your father."

"*What?*"

"My graduate assistant says you identify me with your father."

She went ashen. "That's supposed to be a secret!"

"Sam, I asked him. He won't lie to me."

5

"If you remind me of my father, if I want to go to bed with you, then I must want to go to bed with—"

"Sam—"

"—my father! You must think I'm disgusting!"

"No, I think you're confused. You ought to find some help. You ought to see a—"

But she never let me finish. Weeping again, ashamed, hysterical, she bolted from the room.

And that's the last I ever saw of her. An hour later, when I started lecturing, she wasn't in class. A few days later I received a drop-slip from the registrar, informing me she'd canceled all her classes.

I forgot her.

Summer came. Then fall arrived. November. On a rainy Tuesday night, my wife and I stayed up to watch the close results of the election, worried for our presidential candidate.

At 3 A.M. the phone rang. No one calls that late unless . . .

The jangle of the phone made me bang my head as I searched for a beer in the fridge. I rubbed my throbbing skull and swung alarmed as Jean, my wife, came from the living room and squinted toward the kitchen phone.

"It might be just a friend," I said. "Election gossip."

But I worried about our parents. Maybe one of them was sick or . . .

I watched uneasily as Jean picked up the phone.

"Hello?" She listened apprehensively. Frowning, she put her hand across the mouthpiece. "It's for you. A woman."

"What?"

"She's young. She asked for Mr. Ingram."

"Damn, a student."

"At 3 A.M.?"

I almost didn't think to shut the fridge. Annoyed, I yanked the pop-tab off the can of beer. My marriage is successful. I'll admit we've had our troubles. So has every couple. But we've faced those troubles, and we're happy. Jean is thirty-five, attractive, smart, and patient. But her trust in me was clearly tested at that moment. A woman had to know me awfully well to call at 3 A.M.

"Let's find out." I grabbed the phone. To prove my innocence to Jean, I roughly said, "Yeah, what?"

"I heard you." The female voice was frail and plaintive, trembling.

"Who *is* this?" I said angrily.

"It's me."

I heard a low-pitched crackle on the line.

"Who the hell is *me*? Just tell me what your name is."

"Sam."

My knees went weak. I slumped against the wall.

Jean stared. "What's wrong?" Her eyes narrowed with suspicion.

"Sam, it's 3 A.M. What's do damn important you can't wait to call me during office hours?"

"Three? It can't be. No, it's one."

"It's three. For God sake, Sam, I know what time it is."

"Please, don't get angry. On my radio the news announcer said it was one o'clock."

"Where *are* you, Sam?"

"At Berkeley."

"California? Sam, the time-zone difference. In the Midwest it's two hours later. Here it's three o'clock."

". . . I guess I just forgot."

"But that's absurd. Have you been drinking? Are you drunk?"

"No, not exactly."

"What the hell does *that* mean?"

"Well, I took some pills. I'm not sure what they were."

"Oh, Jesus."

"Then I heard you. You were speaking to me."

"No. I told you your mind's playing tricks. The voice isn't real. You're imagining—"

"You called to me. You said you wanted me to go to bed with you. You wanted me to come to you."

"To Iowa? No. You've got to understand. Don't do it. I'm not sending thoughts to you."

"You're lying! Tell me why you're lying!"

"I don't want to go to bed with you. I'm glad you're in Berkeley. Stay there. Get some help. Lord, don't you realize? Those pills. They make you hear my voice. They make you hallucinate."

"I . . ."

"Trust me, Sam. Believe me. I'm not sending thoughts to you. I didn't even know you'd gone to Berkeley. You're two thousand miles away from me. What you're suggesting is impossible."

She didn't answer. All I heard was low-pitched static.

"Sam—"

The dial tone abruptly droned. My stomach sank. Appalled, I kept the phone against my ear. I swallowed dryly, shaking as I set the phone back on its cradle.

Jean glared. "Who was that? She wasn't any 'Sam.' She wants to go to bed with you? At 3 A.M.? What games have you been playing?"

"None." I gulped my beer, but my throat stayed dry. "You'd better sit. I'll get a beer for you."

Jean clutched her stomach.

"It's not what you think. I promise I'm not screwing anybody. But it's bad. I'm scared."

I handed Jean a beer.

"I don't know why it happened. But last spring, at 8 A.M., I went to school and . . ."

Jean listened, troubled. Afterward she asked for Sam's description, somewhat mollified to learn she was plain and pitiful.

"The truth?" Jean asked.

"I promise you."

Jean studied me. "You did nothing to encourage her?"

"I guarantee it. I wasn't aware of her until I found her waiting for me."

"But unconsciously?"

"Sam asked me that as well. I was only lecturing the best way I know how."

Jean kept her eyes on me. She nodded, glancing toward her beer. "Then she's disturbed. There's nothing you can do for her. I'm glad she moved to Berkeley. In your place, I'd have been afraid."

"I *am* afraid. She spooks me."

At a dinner party the next Saturday, I told our host and hostess what had happened, motivated more than just by need to share my fear with someone else, for while the host was both a friend and colleague, he was married to a clinical psychologist. I needed professional advice.

Diane, the hostess, listened with slim interest until half-way through my story, when she suddenly sat straight and peered at me.

I faltered. "What's the matter?"

"Don't stop. What else?"

I frowned and finished, waiting for Diane's reaction. Instead she poured more wine. She offered more lasagna.

"Something bothered you."

She tucked her long black hair behind her ears. "It could be nothing."

"I need to know."

She nodded grimly. "I can't make a diagnosis merely on the basis of your story. I'd be irresponsible."

"But hypothetically . . ."

"And *only* hypothetically. She hears your voice. That's symptomatic of a severe disturbance. Paranoia, for example. Schizophrenia. The man who shot John Lennon heard a voice. And so did Manson. So did Son of Sam."

"My God," Jean said. "Her name." She set her fork down loudly.

"The parallel occurred to me," Diane said. "Chuck, if she identifies you with her father, she might be dangerous to Jean and to the children."

"Why?"

"Jealousy. To hurt the equivalent of her mother and her rival sisters."

I felt sick; the wine turned sour in my stomach.

"There's another possibility. No more encouraging. If you continue to reject her, she could be dangerous to you. Instead of dealing with her father, she might redirect her rage and jealousy toward you. By killing you, she'd be venting her frustration toward her father."

I felt panicked. "For the *good* news."

"Understand, I'm speaking hypothetically. Possibly she's lying to you, and she doesn't hear your voice. Or, as you guessed, the drugs she takes might make her hallucinate. There could be many explanations. Without seeing her, without the proper tests, I wouldn't dare to judge her symp-

9

toms. You're a friend, so I'm compromising. Possibly she's homicidal."

"Tell me what to do."

"For openers, I'd stay away from her."

"I'm *trying*. She called from California. She's threatening to come back here to see me."

"Talk her out of it."

"I'm no psychologist. I don't know what to say to her."

"Suggest she get professional advice."

"I tried that."

"Try again. But if you find her at your office, don't go in the room with her. Find other people. Crowds protect you."

"But at 8 A.M. there's no one in the building."

"Think of some excuse to leave her. Jean, if she comes to the house, don't let her in."

Jean paled. "I've never seen her. How could I identify her?"

"Chuck described her. Don't take chances. Don't trust anyone who might resemble her, and keep a close watch on the children."

"*How?* Rebecca's twelve. Sue's nine. I can't insist they stay around the house."

Diane turned her wine glass, saying nothing.

". . . Oh, dear Lord," Jean said.

The next few weeks were hellish. Every time the phone rang, Jean and I jerked, startled, staring at it. But the calls were from our friends or from our children's friends or from some insulation/magazine/home-siding salesman. Every day I mustered courage as I climbed the stairwell to my office. Silent prayers were answered. Sam was never there. My tension dissipated. I began to feel she no longer was obsessed with me.

Thanksgiving came—the last day of peace I've known. We went to church. Our parents live too far away for us to share the feast with them. But we invited friends to dinner. We watched football. I helped Jean make the dressing for the turkey. I made both the pumpkin pies. The friends we'd invited were my colleague and his wife, the clinical psychologist. She asked if my student had continued to harass me.

Shaking my head from side to side, I grinned and raised my glass in special thanks.

The guests stayed late to watch a movie with us. Jean and I felt pleasantly exhausted, mellowed by good food, good drink, good friends, when after midnight we washed all the dishes, went to bed, made love, and drifted wearily to sleep.

The phone rang, shocking me awake. I fumbled toward the bedside lamp. Jean's eyes went wide with fright. She clutched my arm and pointed toward the clock. It was 3 A.M.

The phone kept ringing.

"Don't," Jean said.

"Suppose it's someone else."

"You know it isn't."

"If it's Sam and I don't answer, she might come to the house instead of phoning."

"For God's sake, make her stop."

I grabbed the phone, but my throat wouldn't work.

"I'm coming to you," the voice wailed."

"Sam?"

"I heard you. I won't disappoint you. I'll be there soon."

"No. Wait. Listen."

"I've been listening. I hear you all the time. The anguish in your voice. You're begging me to come to you, to hold you, to make love to you."

"That isn't true."

"You say your wife's jealous of me. I'll convince her she isn't being fair. I'll make her let you go. Then we'll be happy."

"Sam, where are you? Still at Berkeley?"

"Yes. I spent Thanksgiving by myself. My father didn't want me to come home."

"You have to stay there, Sam. I didn't send my voice. You need advice. You need to see a doctor. Will you do that for me? As a favor?"

"I already did. But Dr. Campbell doesn't understand. He thinks I'm imagining what I hear. He humors me. He doesn't realize how much you love me."

"Sam, you have to talk to him again. You have to tell him what you plan to do."

11

"I can't wait any longer. I'll be there soon. I'll be with you."

My heart pounded frantically. I heard a roar in my head. I flinched as the phone was yanked away from me.

Jean shouted to the mouthpiece, "Stay away from us! Don't call again! Stop terrorizing—"

Jean stared wildly at me. "No one's there. The line went dead. I hear just the dial tone."

I'm writing this as quickly as I can. I don't have much more time. It's almost three o'clock.

That night, we didn't try to go back to sleep. We couldn't. We got dressed and went downstairs where, drinking coffee, we decided what to do. At eight, as soon as we'd sent the kids to school, we drove to the police.

They listened sympathetically, but there was no way they could help us. After all, Sam hadn't broken any law. Her calls weren't obscene; it was difficult to prove harassment; she'd made no overt threats. Unless she harmed us, there was nothing the police could do.

"Protect us," I insisted.

"How?" the sergeant said.

"Assign an officer to guard the house."

"How long? A day, as week, a month? That woman might not even bother you again. We're overworked and understaffed. I'm sorry—I can't spare an officer whose only duty is to watch you. I can send a car to check the house from time to time. No more than that. But if this woman does show up and bother you, then call us. We'll take care of her."

"But that might be too late."

We took the children home from school. Sam couldn't have arrived from California yet, but what else could we do? I don't own any guns. If all of us stayed together, we had some chance for protection.

That was Friday. I slept lightly. Three A.M., the phone rang. It was Sam, of course.

"I'm coming."

"Sam, where are you?"

"Reno."

"You're not flying."

"No, I can't."

"Turn back, Sam. Go to Berkeley. See that doctor."

"I can't wait to see you."

"Please—"

The dial tone was droning.

I phoned Berkeley information. Sam had mentioned Dr. Campbell. But the operator couldn't find him in the yellow pages.

"Try the University," I blurted. "Student Counseling."

I was right. A Dr. Campbell was a university psychiatrist. On Saturday I couldn't reach him at his office, but a woman answered his home. He wouldn't be available until the afternoon. At four o'clock I finally got through to him.

"You've got a patient named Samantha Perry," I began.

"I did. Not anymore."

"I know. She's left for Iowa. She wants to see me. I'm afraid. I think she might be dangerous."

"Well, you don't have to worry."

"She's not dangerous?"

"Potentially she was."

"But tell me what to do when she arrives. You're treating her. You'll know what I should do."

"No, Mr. Ingram, she won't come to see you. On Thanksgiving night, at 1 A.M., she killed herself. An overdose of drugs."

My vision failed. I clutched the kitchen table to prevent myself from falling. "That's impossible."

"I saw the body. I identified it."

"But she called that night."

"What time?"

"At 3 A.M. Midwestern time."

"Or one o'clock in California. No doubt after or before she took the drugs. She didn't leave a note, but she called you."

"She gave no indication—"

"She mentioned you quite often. She was morbidly attracted to you. She had an extreme, unhealthy certainty that she was telepathic, that you put your voice inside her mind."

"I know that! Was she paranoid or homicidal?"

"Mr. Ingram, I've already said too much. Although she's dead, I can't violate her confidence."

"But I don't think she's dead."

"I beg your pardon?"

"If she died on Thursday night, then tell me how she called again on *Friday* night."

The line hummed. I sensed the doctor's hesitation. "Mr. Ingram, you're upset. You don't know what you're saying. You've confused the nights."

"I'm telling you she called again on Friday!"

"And I'm telling she died on *Thursday.* Either someone's tricking you, or else . . ." The doctor swallowed with discomfort.

"Or?" I trembled. "*I'm* the one who's hearing voices?"

"Mr. Ingram, don't upset yourself. You're honestly confused."

I slowly put the phone down, terrified. "I'm sure I heard her voice."

That night, Sam called again. At 3 A.M. From Salt Lake City. When I handed Jean the phone she heard just the dial tone.

"But you know the goddamn phone rang!" I insisted.

"Maybe a short circuit. Chuck, I'm telling you there was no one on the line."

Then Sunday. Three A.M. Cheyenne, Wyoming. Coming closer.

But she couldn't be if she was dead.

The student paper at the University subscribes to all the other major student papers. Monday, Jean and I left the children with friends and drove to its office. Friday's copy of the Berkeley campus paper had arrived. In desperation I searched its pages. "There!" A two-inch item. Sudden student death. Samantha Perry. Tactfully, no cause was given.

Outside in the parking lot, Jean said, "Now do you believe she's dead?"

"Then tell me why I hear her voice! I've got to be crazy if I think I hear a corpse!"

"You're feeling guilty that she killed herself because of

14

you. You shouldn't. There was nothing you could do to stop her. You've been losing too much sleep. Your imagination's taking over."

"You admit you heard the phone ring!"

"Yes, it's true. I can't explain that. If the phone's broken, we'll have it fixed. To put your mind at rest, we'll get a new, unlisted number."

I felt better. After several drinks, I even got some sleep.

But Monday night, again the phone rang. Three A.M. I jerked awake. Cringing, I insisted Jean answer it. But she heard just the dial tone. I grabbed the phone. Of course, I heard Sam's voice.

"I'm almost there. I'll hurry. I'm in Omaha."

"This number isn't listed!"

"But you told me the new one. Your wife's the one who changed it. She's trying to keep us apart. I'll make her sorry. Darling, I can't wait to be with you."

I screamed. Jean jerked away from me.

"Sam, you've got to stop! I spoke to Dr. Campbell!"

"No. He wouldn't dare. He wouldn't violate my trust."

"He said you were dead!"

"I couldn't live without you. Soon we'll be together."

Shrieking, I woke the children, so hysterical Jean had to call an ambulance. Two interns struggled to sedate me.

Omaha was one day's drive from where we live. Jean came to visit me in the hospital on Tuesday.

"Are you feeling better?" Jean frowned, troubled.

"Please, you have to humor me," I said. "All right? Suspect I've gone crazy, but for God sake, humor me. I can't prove what I'm thinking, but I know you're in danger. I am too. You have to get the children and leave town. You have to hide somewhere. Tonight at 3 A.M. she'll reach the house."

Jean stared with pity.

"Promise me!" I said.

She saw the anguish on my face and nodded.

"Maybe she won't try the house," I said. "She might come here. I have to get away. I'm not sure how, but later, when you're gone, I'll find a way to leave."

Jean peered at me, distressed; her voice sounded totally discouraged. "Chuck."

"I'll check the house when I get out of here. If you're still there, you know you'll make me more upset."

"I promise. I'll take Susan and Rebecca, and we'll drive somewhere."

"I love you."

Jean began to cry. "I won't know where you are."

"If I survive this, I'll get word to you."

"But how?"

"The English department. I'll leave a message with the secretary."

Jean leaned down to kiss me, crying, certain I'd lost my mind.

I reached the house that night. As she'd promised, Jean had left with the children. I got in my sports car and raced to the Interstate.

A Chicago hotel where at 3 A.M. Sam called from Iowa. She'd heard my voice. She said I'd told her where I was, but she was hurt and angry. "Tell me why you're running."

I fled from Chicago in the middle of the night, driving until I absolutely had to rest. I checked in here at 1 A.M. In Johnstown, Pennsylvania. I can't sleep. I've got an awful feeling. Last night Sam repeated, "Soon you'll join me." In the desk I found this stationery.

God, it's 3 A.M. I pray I'll see the sun come up.

It's almost four. She didn't phone. I can't believe I escaped, but I keep staring at the phone.

It's four. Dear Christ, I hear the ringing.

Finally I've realizd. Sam killed herself at one. In Iowa the time-zone difference made it three. But I'm in Pennsylvania. In the East. A different time zone. One o'clock in California would be *four* o'clock, not three, in Pennsylvania.

Now.

The ringing persists. But I've realized something else. This hotel's unusual, designed to seem like a home.

The ringing?
God help me, it's the doorbell.

Famed for his creation of movie hero Rambo, David Morrell was born in Ottawa, Canada, in 1943, and educated at the University of Waterloo and Pennsylvania State University. An English teacher at the University of Iowa since 1970, he sold his first story, "The Dripping," a dark and ominous tale, to Ellery Queen's Mystery Magazine in 1972. His first novel was the bestseller First Blood *(1972), made into the smash hit movie* RAMBO *starring Sylvester Stallone. His five subsequent novels, mostly about the dark world of espionage and treachery, have also been highly successful.*

When the Nicolet Island championship basketball team insisted on driving home over the ice, the coach had tried to talk them out of it. Or had he?

TWO

Death's Door
Robert McNear

I read from the oil company travel guide: "Blackrock is the northernmost community on the peninsula. Here you get the feeling of a true fishing center among the anchored fishing boats and nets reeled out to dry. Off Blackrock lies the Porte des Morts, a strait six miles wide separating mainland Wisconsin and Nicolet Island. In 1679, about 300 Potawatomi Indians drowned in a sudden storm while crossing the water to engage the Winnebagos. The tragedy was witnessed by explorers La Salle and De Tonti, who named the strait Porte des Morts, or Death's Door. Today it is said the strait contains more shipwrecks per square mile than any other area in the Great Lakes."

I folded the travel guide and put it in the glove compartment. Sitting there in my car, on the last leg of my journey, my immediate impression was that the waters were a lure for the local Chamber of Commerce to attract visitors, a thrill for these station wagon travelers at seeing so sinister a place, a pool for skindivers in which to explore old wrecks.

Porte des Morts: Death's door. It seemed very commonplace this late afternoon: a desolate little landing deep in the snow, a weather-beaten smokehouse whose door moved open and shut with the wind, a timber dock where a veteran ferryboat—the R. L. Ostenson, Nicolet Island, Wisconsin—creaked patiently on its hawsers. Beyond that was the bleak strait—sky the color of worn steel and bay the same, hinged by the horizon line and identical except for the dark channel of water out through the ice.

I like forgotten, half-populated places, almost-deserted

18

cubbyholes of the world. I suppose that's one of the reasons I stay on as a reporter for a small town newspaper instead of going to Chicago and becoming a well-known journalist.

I'd been waiting in the car for about five minutes when the hunchbacked deckhand turned up. He came half skipping from the dock, thumb up, to motion me out of the car. I got out in the ankle deep snow, saying, unnecessarily, "You'll take her on?" He swung into the driver's seat and slammed the door for an answer.

Great! I liked every bit of it. Only in some out-of-the-way place like this would you find a hunchbacked deckhand who—I had got a good look at him—had fine, golden hair and an almost-perfect Botticelli face. He took the car carefully across the planking and onto the deck while I, bothered by the usual curiosity, had to walk across the road to the smokehouse and look inside. No fire had burned there for months, but the ghost of smoke and fish possessed the place completely. It was so dark that I could see little except the small drift of snow that had come in through the door. Now, one of my itches is about doors—I can't stand to see them open when they should be shut, or idly swinging, like this one; so I closed it tight, for this winter, at least.

Then I took myself aboard the ferryboat, climbed the stairs, and came to the door of the passenger lounge. I'd felt almost alone until now, but there were about ten people sitting around, smoking, drinking coffee, waiting. It looked like a roadside diner, with plywood booths along the walls and a couple of scarred tables in the center. It looked stifling in there, so I turned away from the door and made my way along the railing to the pilothouse door.

Inside the pilothouse, leaning on the wheel and smoking a cigarette as he gazed at the car deck below, was a youngish, long-jawed man with pepper-and-salt hair, who, in spite of the ordinary windbreaker and dungarees he wore, was obviously the captain. On his head he had an old-fashioned officer's cap with a brass plate above the bill. It read: CAPTAIN. I watched him douse the cigarette, straighten up, and signal down to the hunchback on the deck. A floodlight went on down there.

The hunchback and a teenage boy moved around quickly to cast off. The captain tugged twice at a cord on the compressed-air horn, bouncing two blasts off the snow-shrouded face of Blackrock. Then he pulled the engine tele-graph to reverse and I could feel the deck plates vibrate as the ferry backed away from the wharf. The skin of ice crushed under the black-steel hull as we moved out to swing around slowly into the channel. *Bon voyage*, R. L. Ostenson.

In those few minutes the pale daylight had gone completely; and now, looking out across the strait, I saw an early moon laying a yellow path almost directly alongside the channel through the ice of the Porte des Morts. At the end of the double line I could see the low fishback of Nicolet Island. "Strange place, the island," Ed Kinney had said back in Green Bay. "Isolated, ingrown, maybe two hundred people, fifty families. Swedes, Icelanders, Germans. They don't warm much to strangers. Lots of superstition."

Kinney has been a feature editor for a long time and he can't help talking like that. Still, he used to summer on the island and I didn't doubt the truth of what he said. "Trouble is," he'd added, "there's nothing to be superstitious about. In winter the island's about as exciting as the lobby of the Northland Hotel at two o'clock of a Sunday morning. You'll see 'em all come out of hibernation for that basketball game. Then they go back into it for the rest of the winter."

Blackrock had slowly receded into the distance and the last lonely peninsula pine had faded astern. I realized that the sharp wind had got through my overcoat and that I was beginning to shiver. Just then the wheelhouse door opened and the nasal voice of the captain said, "So softhearted I can't stand to see even a damn fool freeze to death. C'mon in, friend."

I stepped inside. "Thanks, Captain." It was like the fresh and gentle breeze of May. "You are speaking to a man who has covered the Green Bay Packers Sunday in and Sunday out for four winters."

"Hey, a reporter!" he said, smiling. We shook hands. "I'm Axel Ostenson. Now, why d'you figure Vince Lombardi had to go and retire? Those boys ain't been the same since."

"Even the iron men wear out in time," I said. At this point the radio squawked and he went over to say something into a microphone about position and time of arrival. I looked around.

All was neat and newly painted—up front near the window, the wheel and the engine telegraph, the captain's high stool. A padded bench ran the length of the pilothouse. Framed on the walls were some Great Lakes shipping charts, a safety-inspection certificate, and a plaque informing me that the Sturgeon Bay Shipbuilding Company had created this noble vessel. Ostenson finished with the radio.

"You remember Ed Kinney?" I asked. "He's my editor on the *News* down in Green Bay."

"Sure do. Used to have a summer place on the island. I taught his boy Gene how to sail."

"Ed thought I ought to cover the Door County championship game this year. First one on Nicolet Island since 1947. Ed thought there might be a good feature story in it, along with the play-by-play. I thought maybe you could help me, so I thought I'd ask you a few questions—"

"Nuremberg, Germany," he said.

"What's that?"

"Missed it. I was in Nuremberg, Germany, with the Tenth Division in 1947."

"But you must have heard a lot of talk since about—"

"I'm sorry, mister, but you know the Great Lakes maritime regulations say that I'm not supposed to have anybody who don't belong in the pilothouse. I'm gonna have to ask you to go along to the lounge. You get yourself a Coke or a cuppa coffee." He didn't look at me, but kept staring straight ahead as I went out.

Queer how suddenly the Great Lakes maritime regulations got enforced.

I moved along the rail to about midship. The wind was like a cold blade on my face, but I wanted to give myself just a few more minutes before I had to go into the stuffy, smoke-filled saloon where I knew that, in spite of myself, I'd drink at least three or four cups of bad coffee to pass the time. So I'd cut the taste of that with something better. I groped in the inside pocket of my overcoat and found the oblong shape of my flask. The bourbon built a comfortable small fire in my throat and my innards.

I stared down at the black edge of water alongside the hull

and the thick shelf of ice. In the moonlight the strait was one vast skating rink. Every now and then a chunky little berg came scraping along the hull as we passed. I wondered what might happen if the R. L. Ostenson didn't go back and forth from Blackrock to the island twice a day. How long would it take before the channel froze over solid? But, I supposed, even at that, the island could hardly be cut off. With this kind of freeze, the iceboats—those craft with runners and sails or a motor—could make it back and forth without the slightest trouble.

Speak of the Devil, I thought. It was just about then that I heard the motor. I took another sip and peered ahead into the dark. Funny that somebody would be running one of those things this time of evening. There was more spray now than there had been and it stung my forehead and fogged my glasses. There seemed to be an area of low-lying mist on the ice ahead.

I took my glasses off and gave them a good wipe with my handkerchief. The motor noise got no louder; it was still a low chugga-chugga-chugga, like something I remembered out of my boyhood. I leaned over the rail and strained my eyes toward the sound. I saw one red eye in the gray cotton fog.

Then, gradually, as we overtook it, the thing took shape just at the far reach of glimmer from our deck lights. No iceboat, but a black, sign-bedecked Model-A Ford, bumping along at maybe ten or fifteen miles an hour. Running boards, spare tire on the rear, dim yellow headlights on the ice. It looked just like the one my dad used to own back when. Only Dad would never have let anybody violate the glossy black finish with signs like, HOLD ME TIGHT, BABY and BEAT FISH CREEK and THERE AIN'T NO FLIES ON THE N.I.S. Bent backward in the wind was a radio aerial from which flew a green pennant that read in block letters, NICOLET IS-LAND.

I leaned as far over the rail as I could and, as the old car came abreast of me and then gradually began to drop astern, I tried to make out the faces of the kids inside. It was too dark for much more than silhouettes. However, I did raise my arm and wave to them. And I swear that I saw somebody waving back from the rear seat. Then the yellow headlight beams grew dimmer, the chugga-chugga dropped back out of earshot, and we'd lost them.

Funny, I thought. I'd hate to have any kids of mine out on the ice on a freezing night like this one. But I supposed that people up here had different ideas. They probably drove over to Blackrock—when the ice was thick enough—as casually as we'd go down to the drug store in Green Bay.

Anyway, it was an interesting little incident, probably not the usual thing to the average Wisconsin newspaper reader. I thought I'd pin it down a little more and use it somewhere in the feature. "Up around Nicolet Island, some strange things are taken as a matter of course," my lead might go. "As I was crossing over on the ferryboat last night, I saw . . ."

I made my way along the railing until I'd come back to the pilothouse door. Ostenson was still at the wheel, as if he hadn't moved since I'd left. I went on in. He glanced at me.

"Captain, I guess you saw those kids out on the ice in the old car back there just a bit. Heading over to the island. Is that a fairly common thing up here? Couldn't the kids get into trouble?"

He didn't reply. He swung his whole head around toward me, his face perfectly immobile and his gray fish-scale eyes staring. Then he looked back at his course and was silent for nearly a minute.

At last he said quietly, "It happens." Then, in a louder voice, he commanded, "Come here!" I walked over. "Open your mouth and breathe out," he said. He waited a moment. Then he said, "Liquor drinking on this ship is against the law. I could file a complaint against you and get you fined. You hear that?"

"Come off it, Cap," I said. "It's just a drop to keep the old blood flowing."

"Maybe," he said in a cold voice. "But I could testify that you barged into my pilothouse and I had to order you out. Then you spent some time drinking liquor somewhere. Then you came back into the pilothouse against my orders. Mister, this may be just a dinky little Great Lakes ferryboat, but the captain is still the law on it. Now, you go back and sit down in the passenger cabin and shut up."

I made my disconsolate way back to the cabin. What in

the world had gone wrong with that moron in the pilot-house? He'd seemed perfectly friendly until . . . I couldn't figure out what came after the "until." I sat down at one of the tables in the middle of the cabin. A burly man with a blond mustache and wearing a thick mackinaw looked up from across the table. He pointed at a half-full bottle of rye whiskey and a paper cup. "Drink?" he asked.

I looked around. Just about every table had a pint or a fifth on it. Obviously, not a temperance ship. Just when I was going to ask mackinaw-mustache about the captain, I decided better. If Kinney's two paragraphs were any guide to the island, this chap was probably the captain's older brother, or at least a first cousin. Probably just Ostenson's quirk; he must have suddenly decided that he didn't like my face.

I was on deck again to observe our landing. The dark form of the island was very close now and I could see lights farther up the channel. They seemed to outline the dock. We passed a channel buoy frozen in the ice at a drunken tilt and wearing a snowy beard.

The wind swept in from the lake, even harsher and stronger than before, then calmed a little as we came in. The engine went half speed, then silent, and came on loud again in reverse. I saw the wooden pilings of the dock, il-luminated by a hanging string of yellow bulbs. I heard a shoe scrape on the stairway behind me and I turned.

It was the hunchback, just starting down to the deck. "I seen 'em, too," he said in a low voice.

"The kids in the car?" I said. "Yeah, what about it?"

"It's the old team," he whispered. "It's the old team still tryin' to make it." He was suddenly scuttling down the stairs to his duty with the ropes.

Clannish, inbred—but Ed Kinney had forgotten to tell me that I might run into some slightly loony ones, too.

Comfortable, warm, old-fashioned, and presumably by the side of the lake, Lakeside Cottages struck me as a good omen. I was the only guest, yet a neat path had been shov-eled from the lodge down to my small cabin (Number Nine) and a boy named Roger Nelson carried my bags. He turned the lights on and showed me where the radio was.

"Are you visiting up here?" he asked. "I wouldn't want to be nosey, but we almost never get an overnight guest in the winter."

"No. I'm a reporter. I came up a day early, but I'm really here to cover the big game tomorrow night."

"That's great," he said, smiling. "You from *Life?*"

"No, just from Green Bay, I'm afraid." He handed me my key.

"I'm one of the assistant basketball managers," he said. "Means I carry stuff around a lot—though you'd never guess it from the important-sounding title."

"I won't tell a single soul in Green Bay what you *really* do," I said. He started to leave. "Well, good luck against Fish Creek," I said.

He smiled and shook his head. "It's Ephraim," he said. "The game's against Ephraim. Fish Creek wasn't even in the running this year."

"Of course. How could I be so forgetful? Good luck against Ephraim," I said. He smiled again and closed the door behind him.

Sure, it was Ephraim Bay. We'd even had a feature story on Kevin O'Hara, their six-foot-six, high-scoring center. Why had I said Fish Creek? I lay on the bed with a couple of fingers of whiskey in the bathroom tumbler, blowing fancy smoke rings. Then it came back to me. Simple.

The kids crossing the ice in the old car had BEAT FISH CREEK painted on its side. The slogan was probably a leftover from the baseball or football season.

After a while I stirred myself and got the notebook from my jacket pocket. First I'd get something to eat, then I'd get in a little work on the background for the feature story. I found the page with my notes on the briefing Ed Kinney had given me. On the second page, with a star beside it, was the name "Edward Maier."

"Ed coach fr abt ten yrs. Now retired. One of best small-school coaches in state. Runner-up three, four years in row, then champion team around 1947. Small town wild abt basketball. Maybe 60 kids in the high school, 59 of 'em bb players. Tall Swedes. Local disaster sometime in 40's or 50's. School fire? Anyway, several children died, including team members. Quick check in our files draws blank, but ask Ed, who will know all abt it." There were several other entries, but I decided to try Maier first.

There were all of four pages in the phone book. Edward Maier's number was a quaint 32-B. Then I had to turn a crank on the phone to ring the operator. I was back in the 1920's. "Please give me 32-B," I said.

"There's somebody staying at Lakeside," I heard the operator say to somebody with her. "He's calling Ed Maier." Then I heard her say, "How should I know why he wants to talk to Ed?"

"Operator, honey," I said in my coziest voice. "My name is Charley Pope. I'm a sports reporter on *The Green Bay News*. I get a hundred and thirty dollars a week. I'm forty years old, six-foot-one, one hundred and eighty-five pounds, married, and the father of two. I'm here to cover the game tomorrow night. And now, operator, honey, please ring Ed Maier for me."

"Well, it's nice meeting you, Mr. Pope!" she said. "We don't get many visitors in the wintertime." I heard a whispered aside to her friend, "Newspaperman, and he sounds real nice. No, I *don't* know why he's calling Ed Maier."

When she finally did get the call through, there was an answer almost immediately at the other end. It sounded like a hiccup.

"Is this Mr. Ed Maier? I'm up here to cover . . ." and I went on through my introduction. There was silence for almost a minute.

I knew that Ed Maier was still conscious, though, because I could hear a deep and regular breathing over the line. "Listen, Mr. Maier," I finally said, "if it's more convenient I can come over to see you tomorrow. But I'd rather make a short call this evening, if it's okay."

More deep breathing. Then he spoke one word in a hoarse voice. *"Hurry!"* And he hung up.

Thumbtacked to the wall of my cottage was a postcard-sized map of the island. I studied it until I thought I'd worked out my route from Lakeside to Town Line Road, where Maier lived. It was now almost seven. I'd talk with the old boy for about an hour and try to get back to get some dinner around eight. I went out to my car.

The map was probably okay, but the snow and the scar-

26

city of signs tricked me, because the next one I saw read GUNNAUGSSON ROAD, which was a dirt road that didn't appear on the map at all. I wandered from that onto another road that turned out to be Detroit Harbor Road. This did appear on the map, running the length of the island south to north. My only trouble was that I didn't know which way was north. After a couple of miles of rough going through the snow a red neon savior gleamed out of the dark. God bless Gus' Bar. Eats, Beer, Mixed Drinks.

And there they both were, just as advertised. The one, massive old-fashioned dark wood; and the other, behind it—massive old-fashioned barkeep. A jukebox was sobbing at the top of its voice when I went in.

"Ed Maier?" said the bartender, shaking his head slowly, as if this were just too much. He mopped the bar for a while. "Ed Maier," he finally said reluctantly, "you mean *coach* Ed Maier?"

"Yes, I mean *coach* Ed Maier on Town Line Road. Can you tell me how to get there?"

"Guess I could," he said. He started to polish some glass beer steins. "What do you want with him?"

"I want to offer him a job in the movies," I said. "Now, where do I find him?"

"Well," said Gus reflectively, "when you go out the door, point yourself right. Go about twenty-five yards. Then go left on Town Line right down to the very end. That's where Coach lives."

As I was going out the door he said, "If you're a reporter on the Green Bay paper and you get a hundred and thirty dollars a week, how come you tell people you can get them in the movies?"

"How come you sell poisoned beer?" I asked and left.

But the directions were right, anyway. I found Maier's ramshackle little cottage in a winter-bare birch grove. There was a pile of firewood outside the front door, a little drift of smoke from the chimney, and a dim light inside the window. The door was opened even before I could get out of the car.

Ed Maier was one of those people who look about 30 from a distance of 20 yards. Blond hair combed straight back, very fair skin, athletic build, and no pot. At half the distance he had added ten years, maybe 15. He wore high

27

boots, heavy pants, and a plaid windbreaker. You began to see the creases in his face, the jowls, the round-shouldered middle age in his stance.

When you got right up there to shake hands, you saw, by the lamplight in the doorway, the undertaker's next. Or at least that was the way he struck me at the moment. The blue eyes were glazed. The face was a Rand McNally of varicose veins. The flesh looked like puff paste. Ed Maier seemed to be the victim of one of those diseases that age a man too rapidly.

He invited me in and offered me coffee. He had two cups ready and one of those old conical coffeepots steaming on one of the hot flagstones of the hearth. On the littered table there was a plate with some thick slices of bread and cheese. I made myself a sandwich and sat across from him in a rocker near the fire. I meant to ask him why he'd said "Hurry!" that way, but I didn't quite know how to put it.

He began, "Well, you can quote me as saying we've had a great season. No, sir, I won't be coy about that. The boys have marvelous spirit and we've been getting near onto seventy percent of the rebounds. Thank Red Hockstader for that. Six-four and a natural for All-State. Best center I've ever coached."

"But, Coach," I said gently, "I never heard of Red Hockstader. The Nicolet Island center is a kid named Kris Holmsund."

"Think I don't know that?" said the old man. "I thought you said you wanted to talk about the championship team. That was 1947."

I would have sworn that the brew in his coffee cup came more from Kentucky than from Brazil. He took a long swig.

"They really had her fixed up," he said. "The old American Legion Hall. Flags, bunting, more smorgasbord than you ever seen in your life. Couple barrels of beer. Band all in new uniforms. Vee for victory. Big sign read, WELCOME TO OUR CHAMPS. Broke my heart." He drifted off into silence. "They were all my boys. Just like sons."

I wasn't getting anywhere. We were drifting pretty aimlessly in the old man's memory, though we seemed to be skirting the edge of that disaster—school fire or whatever it was—Kinney had told me to check on. I made a guess and tried again.

"So they never showed up at the American Legion Hall for the victory celebration? Is that the way it was, Coach? Remind me just how it happened, will you?"

I poured myself some more coffee and made another cheese sandwich. The fire burned hot in the fireplace, but so many of the windowpanes were broken and patched with cardboard that I kept feeling an intermittent draft.

"My wife Julia was alive then. The whole thing broke her up terrible. And Sally run off to Milwaukee and married a bum. Drunken bum, I heard. Not that I've even thought of her for twenty years."

Now we were really lost in the fog. Might as well give it up for tonight, I thought—but I decided to try once more. "Coach, tell me how it all came about. What happened first that led up to . . . ?"

He nodded. "Well, you know," he said patiently, as if repeating an oft-told tale. "You know we won by four points in the overtime. And when we got back to Blackrock, the ferryboat was late. No sign of her. And all the boys crazy mad to get back to the celebration. And me half out of my head myself, I guess . . .

"Well, anyhow, I said wait. Red said no. *He* was going to drive it alone. I said he was a damn fool. He said it wasn't snowing. I said it was going to any minute and though the ice was thick enough, still there were probably weak spots in it here and there. So I took him out back of the smokehouse, where the others couldn't hear, and I talked Red out of it. Thought so. Then I went down the road to a house to use the telephone. When I came back the whole damn team had left. It was beginning to snow then . . ."

I suddenly understood the old tragedy of Nicolet Island. The champions were all dead, the triumphant team wiped out. But, of course, it was a lot more than that. Everybody on the island was related to one or more of the seven or eight boys on the team. But something was bothering me and I had to explode.

"Why in God's name, then, do the people of this place still let their kids toot around on the ice in old cars? You'd think they'd learn something from what happened. Why, just tonight, coming over, I saw another bunch in a car, chugging along across the strait."

As the old coach stared at me, the merciful potion from his coffee cup began to take hold. The lids seemed to fall over his eyes like the lids of dolls' eyes, pulled down by gravity. His head slowly sank to his forearm and he was silent.

"Coach?" I said experimentally. He didn't move. I debated whether to haul him off to his bed, but then I guessed that he probably spent a good many winter nights in the old easy chair in front of the dying fire—and the ancient phrase was a perfect literal description—in his cups.

I got into bed early and opened my book. I'd brought along Alan Moorehead's *The White Nile,* which I'd been saving to read and which now seemed to me a good, faraway kind of thing to dissipate all the nonsense I'd encountered that afternoon. Because now, in a quiet moment, it seemed to me that the whole business was nonsensical. And by the time I got sleepy enough to turn out the light, I'd succeeded. I was deep in Tanganyika with Livingstone.

I was shaving the next morning when I heard a knock at the cabin door. "Come in," I yelled, and Roger Nelson pushed open the door. Hearty good mornings on both sides. I was feeling refreshed and hungry. "How are the pancakes up there at the lodge?" I asked.

"Great," he said. "But you've got an invitation to breakfast—out. Mr. Ostenson sent me down to ask you."

"Him?" I said to the mirror. "On the ferry on the way over he took an intense dislike to my looks. Just about threw me in irons. What does he want now?"

"Oh, Axel," Roger said. "He was probably just in a bad mood because he was dying for a drink. Gets that way late in the afternoon. No, this is Nels Ostenson. He's the mayor here. Businessman. Rents out cottages and deals in real estate. He's a very nice guy, you'll see. I think he probably wants to make friends with the press. And you couldn't get better pancakes than they make at the Ostensons."

"Seduced!" I said. "Be out in a minute."

Roger showed me the way. The sun was so brilliant that it almost hurt; and under the bright sky, Nicolet Island looked as I'd hoped it would—the little street, snow-covered fields, sedate stone fences, and plain white farmhouses off in the distance. The snow squeaked under our boots.

"Did you ever meet Paul Hornung? What's Willie Davis like in person? Boy, and that Bart Starr! Did you interview him after that game with the Cowboys? How many counts does he take in the pocket when he sees his primary receiver is covered?" Roger kept asking me questions faster than I could answer them. We'd covered a fair amount of the Packer offensive game by the time we got to a frame office building with a sign reading, N. OSTENSON, BUILDERS, REAL ESTATE, PLUMBING & HEATING. Down the side of this, there was a cleared cement walk, between hedges, that led to a pleasant white clapboard house.

Nels Ostenson was a big gray-haired man with a Kris Kringle face and a ringing laugh. I liked him immediately. "By damn," he said, one hand on my shoulder, "my favorite author in person. I even read your tragedies—such as 'Colts Nose Out Packers Twenty-Four to Twenty.' But we won't talk about that. I'm sure everybody you meet talks Packers until you're sick of it."

He showed me into a pleasant room, where the sun shone through the front windows and bookcases lined the walls. A table with a white tablecloth was set up and almost as soon as we sat down, a teenage girl brought in some orange juice. ("Daughter Karen, Mr. Pope.")

And the pancakes were good—big and light and golden. After a decent pause to make a serious start on them he said, "I'm going to apologize all over the place, Charley. I think you had a bad introduction to our little town out here, and I'm sorry. Wish I'd known you were coming. First of all, Axel was nasty to you on the ferryboat, I understand. Well, you've got to know Axel to know why. He's a good boy, but he's kind of on edge these days—family trouble. Wife had an operation last summer and she's never really recovered. One kid just about in college and lots of money worries. So I think you ought to forgive him for blowing his stack. He didn't know who you were. I guess he got into one of his moods."

Nels said all this with a sort of grandfatherly grin and some wide waves of his fork. He had a snowy-white napkin tucked in his shirt collar, under his chin.

"I'd already forgotten. I shouldn't have gone poking around the pilothouse, anyway."

"Good! Good! Now that's settled," he said. "Too bad you had to run onto two of our worst pieces of hard luck just when you arrived. I'm sorry about Ed Maier. I should say straight off that poor Ed is in terrible shape. You know, one of the things about a little community like ours is that we probably make a big mistake by being too charitable. Now, some other place Ed would have been put in a home long ago. But folks around here just can't stand the idea of shutting a man up if he's harmless—even if it would be for his own good. Ed's been more or less off his rocker ever since his wife died.

"Trouble is, everybody who knew Ed in the old days loves him. Why, he was practically the local hero for nearly ten years. Nobody kinder than Ed; nobody better at handling the kids. And in a basketball-crazy place like this, somebody who puts out winning teams year after year just about owns the town. Sure, nowadays, he holes up in that shack of his, has the d.t.'s, is full of crazy persecution delusions— but still it seems like nobody has the heart to commit him. Probably my responsibility, but I'm just as weak-kneed as all the rest."

"I gathered something like that," I said. "He gave me a disconnected story about his daughter running away . . ."

"And about the team?" Nels asked. He paused for a minute, looking directly at me.

"Something about the old championship team he coached, yes."

Nels sighed. "It's his worst bugaboo. He had a real crackup back about Forty-seven, just after we won the championship. Pardon me if you've heard all this—but you have to understand something about that freak accident to understand what happened to him. You'll hear some crazy superstitious stories, but the truth is that we had one of those terrible, foolish accidents that winter and a lot of stupid rumors got started.

"What really happened is this. The team was coming

back one night from the championship game at Fish Creek. Bad weather, and Ed knew it was going to be worse. They got to Blackrock and the ferry was late coming over for them. We had a kid on the team at that time, Red Hockstader—great player but a big headstrong German kid. At Blackrock he talked the rest of the team into driving over the ice in his old car. You know, cross the strait and surprise everybody by sailing into the welcome party on their own wheels.

"Now, Ed did his damnedest to talk them out of it—and he thought he had. But he didn't figure on Red's being so stubborn. So when Ed went up the road for a few minutes, the kids set out. Ordinarily it might be quite possible to drive right across the strait, if you did it in daylight and watched out sharp for rotten spots in the ice. It's different at night.

"Well, the sad story is that they must have hit a rotten spot and the whole team went right down to the bottom of the strait. Not a trace." He stared out of the window for a minute. "Anything else people say is pure baloney."

I hesitated. Finally I said, "I believe you. But there is one thing that bothers me."

He put down his fork and untucked his napkin. "What's that?"

"Well, since I've been here I've heard some of these rumors and one of them is pretty weird. People say that once in a while somebody sees an old Ford out on the ice, trying to make it across to Nicolet Island. Wrapped in mist, chugging along. All that. The old team trying to get home."

Nels threw his napkin on the floor and stood up. "Those damn kids!" he said. "Those damn jokers. I'll have the law on them one of these days, even if I have to get Madison to send the state police up!" His face was red and he kicked at a doorstop as he walked up and down.

"Charley, I don't know what's got into this generation. You know, about sick jokes and black humor and all. I suppose most of that's harmless, but it does turn my stomach. Anyway, it's awful ghoulish when a practical joke is played on people who've really had members of their family killed or drowned, don't you think? So there's this bunch of smart-aleck kids in Blackrock who thought it was funny to buy an old car somewhere, paint it up with signs like the ones on

33

Hockstader's old jalopy, and give the ferry passengers a scare on dark nights by chugging out into the ice and letting themselves be seen."

"Do you know who they are?" I asked. "Can't you catch them?"

"I will some day," he said. "Just wait. I had the whole of Blackrock searched last time but they must have had the thing hidden pretty carefully. Not a soul in the vicinity lets on that he knows a thing. But we'll catch them!

"Cruelest thing is that old Ed really believes that car is out there. He swears that he hears it chugging along the shore by his house. Used to be he thought that only when he was drunk. Now he believes it all the time."

Before I left, Nels had calmed down a little and we talked about other subjects. Inevitably we got onto the Packers and I had to give him my personal impressions of Vince Lombardi.

Silence. Free Throw. The Nicolet Island guard leaned forward. Up on the toes, leaning more, then the calculated throw, a graceful arc, and the ball dropped through the basket, leaving in its wake a dancing net, a howling gym. Before the referee could place the ball back in action, the timekeeper sounded the buzzer. End of the third quarter. Score: Nicolet Island 51, Ephraim 51.

Ed Kinney thought the island's population to be approximately 200, and my educated crowd-estimate placed the local rooters at nearly that number. Most had arrived early, well before gametime, and had invaded the gray-wooden bleachers, leaving cramped space for the half-hundred Ephraim fans who had crossed over on the midafternoon ferry.

Captain Axel Ostenson was there. So was Nels. I scanned the faces. Roger, carrying a bucket, gave me a big wave. Only Ed Maier was missing.

I'd spent the day poking around the island, picking up bits of local lore and tramping over some snow-covered but attractive landscape. My ideas for a feature story with just a touch of the supernatural as a come-on had to be junked (OLD LEGEND OF A LOST TEAM STILL HAUNTS NICOLET ISLAND). Everybody had heard the tale, of course, and everybody had then said, "Poor Ed Maier," alcoholism was a terrible thing, and one of these days poor old Ed would probably have to be put away in an institution.

Only one thing stuck in the back of my mind and bothered me. When I'd seen Ed, he'd been garrulous and probably drunk. He'd rambled on about lots of things he seemed to want to get off his mind. But he'd never mentioned the "ghost-car" story . . .

The timekeeper's buzzer announced the fourth quarter. Both sides scored repeatedly, though the game remained close. Then, with two minutes remaining, the Ephraim center, six-foot-five and full of aggression, committed his fifth personal foul and was returned to the bench, giving the Nicolet Island five both home-court advantage and control of the boards. The game ended in thunderous glory. Nicolet Island 71, Ephraim Bay 68. Door County champions again.

At that exact moment the whole population of the island went slambang out of their Scandinavian heads with one great, hoarse, endless yell of victory. Now I know what the berserk Vikings must have sounded like. The siren on top of the volunteer firehouse began to blast the air. I made it down to the locker room holding my ears.

They were still yelling up there as I tried to interview a totally incoherent coach Ostberg and a bunch of soaking-wet lunatic kids. Never mind. I've been in this business a long time and I've got a whole notebook full of the clichés. "It was a team effort. I never could have done it without the whole team in there fighting all the way. A great bunch of boys," etc. I keep wishing somebody would say something different one day.

The American Legion Hall had just about all the red, white, and blue you could possibly put in without going blind. From the rafters was hung a huge sign—obviously put into place that afternoon—NICOLET ISLAND BASKETBALL TEAM, DOOR COUNTY CHAMPS. The island's German band, in splendid befrogged blue uniforms, boomed out victory marches. The ladies of the American Legion Auxiliary doled out mugs of—not the watery punch you might expect but a hot, spicy, and potent *glogg*. The smorgasbord was delicious. Every kid in town was dancing.

Scenes of great hilarity and joy in which I don't share and

large amounts of *glogg,* which I cherish but which affects me like a lullaby, sooner or later drive me homeward. I came out into the bitter cold of the parking lot to the strains—for the tenth time—of *Hail to the Victors Valiant* and hoped my car would start without any fuss.

It took a little effort, but at last the engine turned over. Suddenly I heard a noise, a sort of choking cough, from the back seat. I turned around. Huddled there, passed out apparently, was old Ed Maier. He'd come to hear the sound of victory, it seemed, but he just couldn't force himself to go inside. Lucky I'd come out early, or he'd probably have frozen to death.

So I drove him to his house. I hauled him out and dragged him into the house—he was stiff in more ways than one, but he was still breathing and seemed in no danger. I put him to bed on the studio couch in his front room and coaxed his fire into a blaze. Under the old Army blanket he breathed hoarsely. I guessed he was safe enough, but he'd have quite a headache in about 24 hours when he woke up.

I switched off the lamp and went to the door. Just as I got it halfway open, I heard Ed Maier's voice loud and clear in the darkness, *"Now hear the truth, by God."*

"Ed?" I said. "Are you all right? It's Charley Pope." I eased the door shut.

He seemed not to have heard me. He started to speak again in that clear, deliberate, unslurred voice, not like a drunk but like a man dictating a statement.

"Witness before God. Last night, before we went to Fish Creek, I made Sally tell me the story. Knocked up; at first I thought, well, hell, it does happen and this isn't the first shotgun match on the island. And then something funny about her and the way she was acting and crying and refusing to name the boy; and I guess I did slap her around a little, first time in her life since she was a small kid and had a spanking. But Julia's hysterical down there and I guess I'm strung tight because of the big game, and so I did hit her. And so she did tell, did tell, did tell. Horrible dirty thing; how could they do it? In Holmgren's barn, Sally and the whole team, the whole damn team, my boys, and I thought of them all as my boys, every one of them there with Sally, and she didn't care.

"And awful hard for me not to let on I knew. At Black-rock, by the smokehouse, Red didn't specially want to try the trip; they'd been joking about it and some said what a big sensation it'd be; but Red, no, he wasn't foolish. Was only after I gave him a big drink from my hip flask and called the whole bunch cowards. Cowards, cowards. 'You guys can beat Fish Creek, but you're scared to get out on the ice; I drove it myself a dozen times, once in a snow-storm. Cowards.'

"No, they weren't. When I got back, they'd gone . . ."

I waited for a long time. "Ed?" I asked. "You awake?" He was beginning to snore. He was out cold, as drunk as I'd ever seen a man, but the strange thing was that I believed every word of his story.

I woke the next morning to a semiblizzard. It wasn't a really serious, driving Wisconsin storm; it was more like a boy bliz-zard having a snowball fight. It howled as if laughing and threw snow on the town. Momentarily it would clear and there would be a faint haze of sunshine overhead; then it would rush in as if to smother us with a heavy blast of new snow. At those times it made a kind of snow twilight. It was like that when I drove up to the landing—so dark that the lights of the R. L. Ostenson were shining.

Axel met me as I came on board. He had been waiting especially for my arrival, and he shook my hand. "Please feel welcome to ride either in the pilothouse or in the lounge, Mr. Pope," he said. "But *please* don't stay out on the deck in this gusty weather. The deck is slippery and you could have a bad fall."

"I won't bother you, Axel," I said. "I appreciate your invi-tation, but I think I'll just hole up in the cabin and read my book this trip."

We smiled and he slapped me on the shoulder, then turned to go along the deck.

The hunchback drove my car aboard—that made only the third one. There seemed to be no more than half a dozen passengers this time. I settled down in an empty booth in the lounge and tried to translate my mind to the shores of Lake Victoria and the upper reaches of the White Nile.

37

Successfully, too. When I next looked up I realized that the engines were throbbing and that we had been under way for some minutes. I put down the book and walked over to look out the window.

The snow and wind were still playing their fitful games—nothing but whiteness all around us for one minute, then a sudden clear period when you could see the dark channel and maybe even 100 yards or so out across the expanse of ice. I stood there, lost in a kind of meditation, for some time.

Chugga-chugga-chugga. I couldn't believe it. I opened the door and went out onto the deck. Not near, not far, stubbornly paralleling our course somewhere out there on the ice.

I was suddenly furious. Nels was absolutely right. It was the most senseless, ghoulish, idiotic practical joke in the world. Those high school kids from Blackrock ought to be caught, have their car confiscated, be thrown in jail—even get a good whipping. Not only were they harassing the Nicolet Islanders in this stupid way but they were risking their own lives every time—look what had happened once before.

I went down to the car deck, full of this kind of resentment, hoping to get a glimpse of the old jalopy. Apparently nobody else had heard the sound, because I was all alone in the wind. I leaned over the rail and peered forward into the white confusion. The chugga-chugga seemed just a few yards away.

Then, suddenly, the breeze dropped, there was a clearing in the storm, and I saw it. I saw every detail. The old car was painted black, but the body had a lot of rust on it. One running board sagged. The left rear fender had crumpled. A light trail of snow streamed off the layer of white on top of the roof. The battered old license plate was, sure enough, WISCONSIN, 1947. But it wasn't any of this that made me jump off the ferryboat.

I still don't know quite how I did it. I remember taking hold of a rope and swinging over the side. It was probably lucky for me that no more than a yard or so of black channel showed between the boat's side and the ice shelf, and I swung across easily.

A puff of snowy wind came up again and the car was only

a dim form ahead of me. I ran. I seemed to hear some kind of shout from behind me, from the boat, but nothing was going to stop me now.

Ten yards, fifteen yards; I thought I'd never catch up. It was hard running, because the ice gave good footing one second and none at all the next.

When the snow suddenly cleared I saw that the old Ford had stopped. They were waiting for me, heads in stocking caps poked out of the windows, faces of the boys grinning with mischief. The driver's red hair poked out from beneath his cap. They loved my startled reaction.

Ed Maier's body lay at the end of a ten-foot rope that had been tied to the rear axle. The rope was under his armpits, not around his neck, but I knew that he was dead, anyway. His face was partly covered with ice dust, partly bloody scrapes, but I knew him. I do not think that there was the least bit of astonishment in his expression.

I didn't hear the ferryboat's engine stop. The first thing I knew was that the hunchback was scrambling across the ice, yelling at me. It was he who had seen me jump over-board.

When he came up to me, he found me standing all alone, staring into the snowfall that was now coming down thick and steady over the wide desolate ice expanse of the Porte des Morts.

Little seems to be known about Robert McNear, whose few stories are unusual and meticulously crafted. Such is the case with this tale of a ghostly spirit haunting—with good reason— an entire basketball team. He is the author of one mystery novel, Carpet of Death *(1976), which was published in Eng-land.*

A. J. thought his mother was senile, until he discovered he had left the best part of himself behind.

THREE

Little Jimmy
Lester del Rey

I've always thought that meeting a ghost would be a pretty comforting thing. By the time a man is past fifty and old enough to realize death, anything that will prove he doesn't come to a final, meaningless end should be a help. Even being doomed to haunt some place in solitude through all eternity doesn't have the creeping horror of just not being!

Of course, religion offers hope to some—but most of us don't have the faith of our forefathers. A ghost should be proof against the unimaginable finality of death.

That's the way I used to feel. Now, I don't know. If I could only explain little Jimmy. . . .

We heard him, all right. At Mother's death, the whole family heard him, right down to my sister Agnes, who's the most complete atheist I know. Even her youngest daughter, downstairs at the time, came running up to see who the other child was. It wasn't a case of collective hallucination, any more than it was something that can be explained by any natural laws we know.

The doctor heard it, too, and from the way he looked, I suppose he'd heard little Jimmy more than once before. He won't talk about it, though, and the others had never been around for a previous chance. I'm the only one who will admit to hearing little Jimmy more than that single time. I wish I didn't have to admit it, even to myself.

We were a big family, though the tradition for such families was already dying at the turn of the century. Despite the four girls who died before they had a chance to live, Mother and Dad wanted lots of children. Six of us boys and three

40

girls lived, and that justified it all to Mother. There would have been more, I guess, if Dad hadn't been killed by an angry bull while I was away saving the world for Democracy. Mother could have had other husbands, maybe—the big Iowa farm with its huge old house would have guaranteed that—but she was dead set against it. And we older kids drifted into city jobs, helping the others through college until they had jobs of their own. Eventually, Mother was left alone in the old house, while the town outgrew itself until the farm was sold for lots around it.

That left her with a small fortune, particularly after the second war. She didn't seem to need us, and she was getting "sot" in her ways and hard to get along with. So little by little, we began visiting her less and less. I was the nearest, working in Des Moines, but I had my own life, and she seemed happy and capable, even at well past seventy. We're a long-lived, tough clan.

I sent her birthday and holiday notes—or at least Liza sent them for me—and kept meaning to see her. But my oldest boy seemed to go to pieces after the second war. My daughter married a truck driver and had a set of twins before they found a decent apartment. My youngest boy was taken prisoner in Korea. I was promoted to president of the roofing company. And a new pro at the club was coaching me into breaking ninety most of the time.

Then Mother began writing letters—the first real ones in years. They were cheerful enough, filled with chit-chat about some neighbors, the new drapes on the windows, a recipe for lemon cream pie, and such. At first, I thought they were a fine sign. Then something in them began to bother me. It wasn't until the fifth one, though, that I could put my finger on anything definite.

In that, she wrote a few words about the new teacher at the old schoolhouse. I went over it twice before realizing that the school building had been torn down fifteen years before. When that registered, other things began connecting. The drapes were ones she had put up years before, and the recipe was her first one—the one that always tasted too sweet, before she changed it! There were other strange details.

They kept bothering me, and I finally put through a call.

Mother sounded fine, though a little worried for fear something had gone wrong with me. She talked for a couple of minutes, muttered something about lunch on the stove, and hung up quickly. It couldn't have been more normal. I got out my clubs and was halfway down the front steps before something drove me back to her letters.

Then I called Doctor Matthews. After half a minute identifying myself, I asked about Mother.

His voice assumed a professional tone at once. She was fine—remarkably good physical condition for a woman of her age. No, no reason I should come down at once. There wasn't a thing wrong with her.

He overdid it, and he couldn't quite conceal the worry in his voice. I suppose I'd been thinking of taking a few days off later to see her. But when he hung up, I put the clubs back in the closet and changed my clothes. Liza was out at some civic betterment club, and I left a note for her. She'd taken the convertible though, so I was in luck. The new Cadillac was just back from a tune-up and perfect for a stiff drive. There'd also be less chance of picking up a ticket if I beat the speed limit a little; most cops are less inclined to be tough on a man who's driving one of those cars. I made good time all the way.

Matthews was still at the same address, but his white hair gave me a shock. He frowned at me, lifting his eyes from my waistline to what hair I had left, then back to my face. Then he stuck out his hand slowly, stealing a quick glance at the Cadillac.

"I suppose they all call you A. J. now," he said. "Come on in, since you're here!"

He took me back through the reception room and into his office, his eyes going to the car outside again. From somewhere, he drew out a bottle of good Scotch. At my nod, he mixed it with water from a cooler. He settled back, studying me as he took his own seat. "A. J., heh?" he commented again, sounding a sour note here, somehow. "That sounds like success. Thought your mother mentioned something about your having some trouble a few years back?"

"Not financial," I told him. I'd thought only Liza remembered it. She must have written to Mother at the time, since I'd kept it out of the papers. And after I'd agreed to buy the

trucking line for our son-in-law, she'd finally completely for-
given me. It was none of Matthews' business—but out here,
I remembered, doctors considered everything their business. "Why, Doc?"

He studied me, let his eyes sweep over the car again, and
then tipped up the glass to finish the whisky. "Just curiosity.
No, damn it, I might as well be honest. You'll see her anyhow, now. She's an old woman, Andrew, and she has what
might be called a tidy fortune. When children who haven't
worried about her for years turn up, it might not be affection. And I'm not going to have anything happen to Martha
now!"

The hints in his remarks too closely matched my own
suspicions. I could feel myself tightening up, tensing with
annoyance and a touch of fear. I didn't want to ask the
question. I wanted to get mad at him for being an interfering
old meddler. But I had to know. "You mean—senile de-
mentia?"

"No," he answered quickly, with a slightly lifted eyebrow.
"No, Andrew, she isn't crazy! She's in fine physical shape,
and sane enough to take care of herself for the next fifteen
years she'll probably live. And she doesn't need any fancy
doctors and psychiatrists. Just remember that, and remember she's an old woman. Thirteen children in less than
twenty years! A widow before she was forty. Lonely all
these years, even if she is too independent to bother you
kids. An old woman's entitled to whatever kind of happiness
she can get! And don't forget that!"

He stopped, seeming surprised at himself. Then he stood
up and reached for his hat. "Come on, I'll ride out with
you."

He kept up a patter of local history as we drove down the
streets where corn had grown when I last saw this section.
There was a hospital where the woods had been, and the
old spring was covered by an apartment building. The big
house where we had been born stood out, sprawling in ugly
warmth among the facsimile piano-boxes they were calling
houses nowadays.

I wanted to turn back, but Matthews motioned me after
him up the walk. The front door was still unlocked, and he

went in, tilting his head toward the stairs. "Martha! Hey, Martha!"

"Jimmy's out back, Doc," a voice called down. It was Mother's voice, unchanged except for a puzzling lilt I'd never heard before, and I drew a quick breath of relief.

"Okay, Martha," Matthews called up. "I'll just see him, then, and call you up later. You won't want me around when you see who I brought you! It's Andrew!"

"How nice! Tell him to sit down and I'll be dressed in a minute!"

Doc shrugged. "I'll sit out in the garden a few minutes," he told me. "Then I'll catch a cab back. But remember— your mother deserves any happiness she can get. Don't you ruin it!"

He went through the back door, and I found the parlor and dropped onto the old sofa. Then I frowned. It had been stored in the attic in 1913, when Dad bought the new furniture. I stared through the soft dimness, making out all the old pieces. Even the rug was the way it had been when I was a child. I walked into the other rooms, finding them the same as they had been forty years before, except for the television set in the dining room and the completely modern kitchen, with a pot of soup bubbling on the back of the stove.

I was getting a thick feeling in my throat and the anxiety I'd had before when the sound of steps on the stairs brought my eyes up.

Mother came down, a trifle slowly, but without any sign of weakness. She didn't rest her hand on the banister. She might have been the woman to match the furnishings of the house, except for the wrinkles and the white hair. And the dress was new, but a perfect copy of one she'd worn when I was still a child!

She seemed not to hear my gasp. Her hand came out to catch mine, and she bent forward, kissing me on the cheek. "You look real good, Andrew. There, now, let's see. Umm-hmm. Liza's been feeding you right, I can see that. But I'll bet you could eat some real home-made soup and pie, eh? Come out in the kitchen. I'll fix it in a minute."

She wasn't only in fine physical shape—she was like a woman fifteen years younger than her age. And she'd even remembered to call me Andrew, instead of the various nick-names she'd used during my growing up. That wasn't se-nility! A senile woman would have turned back to the earliest one, as I remembered it—particularly since I'd had to work hard to get her to drop the childhood names. Yet the house. . . .

She bustled about the kitchen, dishing out some of the rich, hot soup. She hadn't been a good cook when I was a kid, but she'd grown steadily better, and this was super-lative. "I guess Doc must have pronounced Jimmy well," she said casually. "He's gone running off somewhere now. Well, after two weeks cooped up here with the measles, I can't blame him. I remember how you were when you had them. Notice how I had the house fixed up, Andrew?"

I nodded, puzzling over her words. "I noticed the old fur-niture. But this Jimmy. . . .?"

"Oh, you never met him, did you? Never mind, you will. How long you staying, Andrew?"

I tried to figure things out, cursing Matthews for not warn-ing me of this. Of course, I'd heard somehow that one of my various nephews had lost his wife. Was he the one who'd had the young boy? And hadn't he gone up to Alaska? No, that was Frank's son. And why would anyone hand over a youngster to Mother, anyhow? There were enough younger women in the family.

I caught her eyes on me, and pulled myself together. "I'll be leaving in a couple of hours, Mother. I just. . . ."

"It was real nice of you to drop over," she interrupted me, as she had always cut into our answers. "I've been meaning to see you and Liza soon, but fixing the house kept me kind of busy. Two men carried the furniture down, but I did the rest myself. Makes me feel younger somehow, having the old furniture here."

She dished out a quarter of a peach cobbler and put it in front of me, with a cup of steaming coffee. She took another quarter for herself and filled her big cup. I had a mental picture of Liza with her vitamins and diets. Who was senile?

"Jimmy's going to school now," she said. "He's got a crush on his teacher, too. More pie, Andrew? I'll have to save a piece for little Jimmy, but there are two left."

From outside, there was a sudden noise, and she jumped

up, to walk quickly toward the back door. Then she came into the kitchen again. "Just a neighbor kid taking a short cut. I wish they'd be a little nicer, though, and play with Jimmy. He gets lonesome sometimes. Like my kitchen, Andrew?"

"Nice," I said carefully, trying to keep track of the threads of conversation. "But it's kind of modern."

"That and the television set," she agreed cheerfully. "Some new things are nice. And some old ones. I've got a foam rubber mattress for my bed, but the rest of the room. . . . Andrew, you come up. I'll show you something I think's real elegant."

The house was clean, and no rooms were closed off. I wondered about that as we climbed the stairs. I hadn't seen a maid. But she sniffed in contempt when I mentioned it. "Of course I take care of it myself. That's a woman's job, ain't it? And then, little Jimmy helps some. He's getting to be mighty handy."

The bedroom was something to see. It reminded me of what I'd seen of the nineties in pictures and movies, complete with frills and fripperies. The years had faded the upholstery and wallpaper in the rest of the house. But here everything seemed bright and new.

"Had a young decorator fellow from Chicago fix it," she explained proudly. "Like what I always wanted when I was a young girl. Cost a fortune, but Jimmy told me I had to do it, because I wanted it." She chuckled fondly. "Sit down, Andrew. How are you and Liza making out? Still fighting over that young hussy she caught you with, or did she take my advice? Silly, letting you know she knew. Nothing makes a man more loving than a little guilt, I always found—especially if the woman gets real sweet about then."

We spent a solid hour discussing things, and it felt good. I told her how they were finally shipping my youngest back to us. I let her bawl me out for the way the oldest boy was using me and for what she called my snootiness about my son-in-law. But her idea of making him only junior partner in the trucking line at first wasn't bad. I should have thought of it myself. She also told me all the gossip about the family. Somehow, she'd kept track of things. I hadn't even known that Pete had died, though I had heard of the other two deaths. I'd meant to go to the funerals, but there'd been that big deal with Midcity Asphalt and then that trouble getting our man into Congress. Things like that had a habit of coming up at the wrong times.

When I finally stood up to go, I wasn't worried about any danger of a family scandal through Mother. If Matthews thought I'd be bothered about her switching back to the old furniture and having this room decorated period style—no matter what it cost—he was the senile one. I felt good, in fact. It had been better than a full round of golf, with me winning. I started to tell her I'd get back soon. I was even thinking of bringing Liza and the family out for our vacation, instead of taking the trip to Bermuda we'd talked about.

She got up to kiss me again. Then she caught herself. "Goodness! Here you're going, and you haven't met Jimmy yet. You sit down a minute, Andrew!"

She threw up the window quickly, letting in the scent of roses from the back. "*Jimmy!* Oh, *Jim-my!* It's getting late. Come on in. And wash your face before you come up. I want you to meet your Uncle Andrew."

She turned back, smiling a little apologetically. "He's my pet, Andrew. I always tried to be fair about my children, but I guess I like Jimmy sort of special!"

Downstairs, I could hear a door close faintly, and the muffled sounds of a boy's steps moving toward the kitchen. Mother sat beaming, happier than I'd seen her for years— since Dad died, in fact. Then the steps sounded on the stairs. I grinned myself, realizing that little Jimmy must be taking two steps at a time, using the banister to pull himself up. I'd always done that when I was a kid. I was musing on how alike boys are when the footsteps reached the landing and headed toward the room.

I started to look toward the door, but the transformation on Mother's face caught my attention. She suddenly looked almost young, and her eyes were shining, while her gaze was riveted on the door behind.

There was a faint sound of it opening and closing, and I started to turn. Something prickled up my backbone. Something was wrong! And then, as I turned completely, I recognized it. When a door opens, the air in the room stirs. We never notice it, unless it doesn't happen. Then the still-

47

ness tells us at once the door can't have really opened. This time, the air hadn't moved.

In front of me, the steps sounded, uncertainly, like those of a somewhat shy boy of six. But there was no one there! The thick carpet didn't even flatten as the soft sound of the steps came closer and stopped, just in front of me!

"This is Uncle Andrew, Jimmy," Mother announced happily. "Shake hands like a good boy, now. He came all the way from Des Moines to see you."

I put my hand out, dictated by some vague desire to please her, while I could feel cold sweat running down my arms and legs. I even moved my hand as if it were being shaken. Then I stumbled to the door, yanked it open, and started down the stairs.

Behind me, the boy's footsteps sounded uncertainly, following out to the landing. Then Mother's steps drowned them, as she came quickly down the stairs after me.

"Andrew, I think you're shy around boys! You're not fooling me. You're just running off because you don't know how to talk to little Jimmy!" She was grinning in amusement. Then she caught my hand again. "You come again real soon, Andrew."

I must have said the right things, somehow. She turned to go up the stairs, just as I heard the steps creak from above, where no one was standing! Then I stumbled out and into my car. I was lucky enough to find a few ounces of whisky in a bottle in the glove compartment. But the liquor didn't help much.

I avoided Matthews' place. I cut onto the main highway and opened the big engine all the way, not caring about cops. I wanted all the distance I could get between myself and the ghost steps of little Jimmy. Ghost? Not even that! Just steps and the weak sound of a door that didn't open. Jimmy wasn't even a ghost—he couldn't be.

I had to slow down as the first laughter tore out of my throat. I swung off the road and let it rip out of me, until the pain in my side finally cut it off.

Things were better after that. And when I started the Cadillac again, I was beginning to think. By the time I reached the outskirts of Des Moines, I had it licked.

It was hallucination, of course. Matthews had tried to

warn me that Mother was going through a form of dotage. She'd created a child for herself, going back to her youth for it. The school that wasn't there, the crush on the teacher, the measles—all were real things she was reliving through little Jimmy. But because she was so unlike other women in keeping firmly sane about everything except this one fantasy, she'd fooled me. She'd made me think she was completely rational. When she'd explained the return of the old furniture, she'd wiped out all my doubts, which had centered on that.

She'd made me take it for granted that Jimmy was real. And she had made me expect to hear steps when her own listening had prepared me for them. I'd been cued by her own faint reactions to her imagination—I must have seen some little gesture and followed her timing. It had been superbly real to her—and my senses had tricked me.

It wasn't impossible. It was the secret of many of the great stage illusions, aided by my own memories of the old house, and given life by the fact that she believed in the steps, as no stage trickster could believe.

I convinced myself of it almost completely. I had to do that. And finally I nearly dismissed the steps from my mind and concentrated on Mother. Matthews' words came back to me, and I nodded to myself. It was a harmless fantasy, and Mother was entitled to her pleasure. She was sane enough to care for herself, without any doubt, and physically far better than she had any right to be. With Matthews' interest in her, there was no reason for me to worry about anything.

By the time I pulled the car into the garage, I was making plans for setting up the trucking concern again, following Mother's advice about making myself the senior partner. It hadn't been a wasted day, after all.

Life went on, pretty much as usual. My younger boy was back home for a while. I'd looked forward to that, but somehow the Army had broken the old bonds between us. Even when I had time, there wasn't much we could talk about. I guess it was something of a relief when he left for some job in New York; anyhow, I was busy straightening out a brawl the older one got mixed up in. My daughter was expecting again, and her husband was showing a complete inability to coöperate with me. I didn't have much time to think about little Jimmy. Mercifully, Liza hadn't asked me about my trip; there was nothing to keep me from forgetting most of it.

I wrote Mother once in a while, now. Her letters grew longer, and sometimes Jimmy's name appeared, along with quite a bit of advice on the trucking business. Most of that was useless, naturally, but she knew more than I'd suspected about the ways of business. It gave me something to write back about.

I paid a fat fee to a psychiatrist for a while, but mostly he only confirmed what I'd already reasoned out. I wasn't interested in some of the other nonsense he tried to sell me, so I stopped going after a while.

And then I forgot the whole thing when the first tentative feeler from New Mode Roofing and Asphalt suggested a merger. I'd been planting the seed for the idea for months, but getting it set to put control in my hands was a tricky problem. I finally had to compromise by agreeing to move the headquarters to Akron, tearing up my roots overnight and resettling. Liza made a scene over that, and my daughter flatly refused to come. I had to agree to turn the trucking concern over to my son-in-law completely, just when it was beginning to show a profit. But the rift had been coming ever since he'd refused to fire my oldest boy from the job of driving one of the trailers.

Maybe it was just as well. The boy seemed to like it. We'd be in Akron, nobody would know about it, and he'd be better off than he was hanging around with some of the friends he'd had before. I meant to write Mother about that, since she'd suggested it once, and I suspected she'd had something to do with it. But the move took all my attention. After that, there was the problem of organizing the new firm.

I decided to see Mother, instead of writing to her. I wasn't going to be fooled again with the same hallucination. The new psychiatrist assured me of that, and advised the trip. I had already marked off the date on my calendar for the visit next month.

It didn't work out. Matthews called me at two o'clock in the morning with the news, after wasting two days tracing

me down through acquaintances. Nobody thought of looking me up in a business directory, of course.

Mother had pneumonia and the prognosis was unfavorable.

"At her age, these things are serious," he said. His voice
wasn't professional this time. "You'd better get here as
quickly as you can. She's been asking for you."

"I'll charter a plane at once," I told him. This would raise
the deuce with the voting of stock we'd scheduled, but I
couldn't stay away, obviously. I'd almost convinced myself
Mother would go on for another twenty years. Now. . . .
"How'd it happen?"

"The big storm last week. She went out in it with rubbers
and an umbrella to fetch little Jimmy from school! She got
sopping wet. When I reached her, she already had a fever.
I've been trying everything, but. . . ."

I hung up, sick. Little Jimmy! For a minute, I wanted him
to be real enough to strangle.

I pounded on Liza's door and got her to charter the plane
while I packed and roused out my secretary on the other
phone. Liza drove me to the airport where the plane was
warmed up and waiting. I turned to say good-by, but she
was dragging out a second bag from the back.

"I'm going," she announced flatly.

I started to argue, saw her expression, and gave up. A few
minutes later, we took off.

Most of the rest of the family was already there, hovering
around outside the newly decorated bedroom where
Mother lay under an oxygen tent; huddles of the family and
their children were in every other room on the second floor,
staring at the closed door and discussing things in the harsh
whispers people use for a scene of death.

Matthews motioned them back and came over to me at
once. "No hope, I'm afraid, Andrew," he said, and there
were tears in his eyes.

"Isn't there anything we can do?" Liza asked, her voice
dropping to the hoarse whisper of the others. "Anything at
all, Doctor?"

He shook his head. "I've already talked to the best men
in the country. We've tried everything. Even prayer."

From one side of the hall, Agnes sniffed loudly. Her militant atheism couldn't be downed by anything, it seemed. It didn't matter. There was death in the house, thick enough to smell. I had always hated the waste and futility of dying. Now it had a personal meaning, and it was worse. Behind that closed door, Mother lay dying, and nothing I could do would help.

"Can I go in?" I asked, against my wishes.

Matthews nodded. "It can't hurt now. And she wanted to see you."

I went in after him, with the eyes of the others thrusting at me. Matthews waved the nurse out and went over to the window; the choking sound from his throat was louder than the faint hiss of the oxygen. I hesitated, then drew near the bed.

Mother lay there, and her eyes were open. She turned them toward me, but there was no recognition in them. One of her thin hands was poking at the transparent tent over her. I looked toward Matthews, who nodded slowly. "It won't matter now."

He helped me move it aside. Her hand groped out, while the wheezing sound of her breathing grew louder. I tried to follow her pointing finger. But it was Matthews who picked up the small picture of a young boy, put it into her hands for her to clasp to her.

"Mother!" It ripped out of me, louder than I had intended. "Mother, it's Andy! I'm here!"

Her eyes turned again, and she moved her parched lips. "Andrew?" she asked weakly. Then a touch of a smile came briefly. She shook her head slightly. "Jimmy! Jimmy!"

The hands lifted the picture until she could see it. *"Jimmy!"* she repeated.

From below, there was the sound of a door closing weakly and steps moving across the lower floor. They took the stairs, two steps at a time, but quickly now, without need of the banister. They crossed the landing. The door remained closed, but there was the sound of a knob turning, a faint squeak of hinges, then another sound of a door closing. Young footsteps moved across the rug, invisible, a sound that seemed to make all other sounds fade to silence. The steps reached the bed and stopped.

Mother turned her eyes, and the smile quickened again.

One hand lifted. Then she dropped back and her breathing stopped.

The silence was broken by the sound of feet again—heavier, surer feet that seemed to be planted on the floor beside the bed. Two sets of footsteps sounded. One might have been those of a small boy. The others were the quick, sharp sounds that only a young woman can make as she hurries along with her first-born beside her. They moved across the room.

There was no hesitation at the door this time, nor any sound of opening or closing. The steps went on, across the landing and down the stairs. As Matthews and I followed into the hall, they seemed to pick up speed toward the back door. Now finally there was a soft, deliberate sound of a door closing, and then silence.

I jerked my gaze back, to see the eyes of all the others riveted on the back entrance, while emotions I had never seen washed over the slack faces. Agnes rose slowly, her eyes turned upwards. Her thin lips opened, hesitated, and closed into a tight line. She sat down like a stick woman folding, glancing about to see whether the others had noticed.

From below, her daughter came running up the stairs. "Mother! Mother, who was the little boy I heard?"

I didn't wait for the answer, nor the thick words with which Matthews confirmed the news of Mother's death. I was back beside the poor old body, taking the picture from the clasped hands.

Liza had followed me in, with the color just beginning to return to her face. "Ghosts," she said thickly. Then she shook her head, and her voice softened. "Mother and one of the babies, come back to get her. I always thought. . . ."

"No," I told her. "Not one of my sisters who died too young. Nothing that easy, Liza. Nothing that good. It was a boy. A boy who had measles when he was six, who took the stairs two at a time—a boy named Jimmy. . . ."

She stared at me doubtfully, then down at the picture I held—the picture of me when I was six. "But you—" she began. Then she turned away without finishing, while the others began straggling in.

We had to stay for the ceremony, of course, though I

guess Mother didn't need me at the funeral. She already had her Jimmy.

She'd wanted to name me James for her father, and Dad had insisted on Andrew for his. He'd won, and Andrew came first. But until I was ten, I'd always been called Jimmy by Mother. Jimmy, Andy, Andrew, A. J. A man's name was part of his soul, I remembered, in the old beliefs.

But it didn't make sense, no matter how I figured it out by myself. I tried to talk it over with Matthews, but he wouldn't comment. I made another effort with Liza when we were on the plane going back.

"I can believe in Mother's spirit," I finished. I'd been over it all so often in my own mind that I had accepted that finally. "But who was Jimmy? We all heard him—even Agnes's daughter heard him from downstairs. So he wasn't a delusion. But he can't be a ghost. A ghost is a returned spirit—the soul of a man who has died!"

"Well?" Liza asked coldly. I waited, but she went on staring out of the plane window, not saying another word.

I used to think meeting a ghost would offer reassurance to a man. Now I don't know. If I could only explain little Jimmy. . . .

One of the luminaries of the Golden Age of science fiction, Lester del Rey was born in Minnesota in 1915. A sharecropper's son, the Great Depression ended his higher education after two years at George Washington University (1932–33). His first story, "The Faithful" (1938), led to a remarkable career as a writer. In his grim novella, Nerves *(1942), he was the first to write of the possible consequences of a nuclear power accident. He is currently editor of the Del Rey Books line of Ballantine in New York.*

Ed enjoyed having friends that no one else could see, even if he didn't make them up.

FOUR

Floral Tribute

Robert Bloch

They always had fresh flowers on the table at Grandma's house. That's because Grandma lived right in back of the cemetery.

"Nothing like flowers to brighten up a room," Grandma used to say. "Ed, be a good boy and take a run over. Fetch me back something pretty. Seems to me there was doings yesterday afternoon near the big Weaver Vault—you know where I mean. Pick out some nice ones and, mind you, no lilies."

So Ed would scamper off, climbing the fence in the back yard and jumping down over the old Putnam grave and its leaning headstone. He'd race down the paths, taking short-cuts through bushes and behind statues. Ed knew every inch of the cemetery long before he was seven—he learned it playing hide-and-seek there with the gang after dark.

Ed liked the cemetery. It was better than the back yard, better than the rickety old house where Grandma and he lived; and by the time he was four, he played among the tombs every day. There were big trees and bushes everywhere; lots of nice green grass, and fascinating paths that wound off endlessly into a maze of mounds and white stones. Birds were forever singing or darting down over the flowers. It was pretty there, and quiet, and there was nobody to watch, or bother, or scold—as long as Ed remembered to stay out of the way of Old Sourpuss the caretaker. But Old Sourpuss lived in another house: a big stone one, over on the other end at the big cemetery entrance.

Grandma told Ed all about Old Sourpuss and warned

him against letting the caretaker catch him inside the grounds.

"He doesn't like to have little boys playing in there," she said. "Especially when there's a funeral going on. Way he acts, a body'd think he owned the place. Where's nobody's got a better right to use it as they see fit than we have, if the truth were known.

"So you go ahead and play there all you want, Ed, only don't let him see you. After all, a body's only young once, I always say."

Grandma was swell. Just plain swell. She even let him stay up late at night and play hide-and-seek with Susie and Joe, behind the headstones.

Of course, she didn't really care, because at night was when Grandma had her company over.

Almost nobody came to see Grandma in the daytime any more. There was just the ice-man and the grocery boy and sometimes the mailman—usually he just came about once a month with Grandma's pension check. Most days there was nobody in the house except Grandma and Ed.

But at night she had company. They never came before supper, but along about eight o'clock, when it got dark, they started drifting in. Sometimes a whole bunch. Most always, Mr. Willis was there, and Mrs. Cassidy, and Sam Gates. There were others, too, but Ed remembered these three the best.

Mr. Willis was a funny man. He was always grumbling and complaining about the cold, and quarreling with Grandma about what he called "my property."

"You have no idea how cold it gets," he used to say, sitting over in the corner next to the fireplace and rubbing his hands. "Day after day it seems to get colder and colder. Not that I'm complaining too much, mind you. It's nothing as bad as the rheumatism I used to have. But you'd think that they'd at least have given me a decent lining. After all the money I left them, to pick out a cheap pine job like that, with some kind of shiny cotton stuff that didn't even last through the first winter—"

Oh, he was a grumbler, that Mr. Willis. He had a long, pale old man's face that seemed to be all wrinkles and scowl. Ed never really got a good look at him, because right after supper when they went into the parlor, Grandma would turn out all the lights and just keep the fire going in the fireplace. "We got to cut down on bills," she used to tell Ed. "This little widow's mite of mine is hardly enough to keep body and soul together for one, let alone an orphan, too."

Ed was an orphan; he knew that, but it never bothered him. Nothing seemed to bother him the way things bothered people like old Mr. Willis.

"To think I'd come to this in the end," Mr. Willis would sigh. "Why, my family owned this place. Fifty years ago it was just a pasture—nothing but meadowland. You know that, Hannah."

Hannah was Grandma's name: Hannah Morse. And Grandpa's name had been Robert Morse. Grandpa had died a long time ago in a war and Grandma never even knew where he was buried. But first he had built this house for Grandma. That's what made Mr. Willis so mad, Ed guessed.

"When Robert built this house, I gave him the land," Mr. Willis complained. "That was fair and square. But when the city came in and took over—made me take a price for the whole shooting-match—there was nothing fair and square about that. Bunch of crooked lawyers, cheating a man out of his rightful property, with all their gib-gab about forced sales and condemning. Way I see it, I still got a moral right. A moral right. Not just to that itty-bitty little plot where they planted me, but to the whole shebang."

"What do you plan to do," Mrs. Cassidy would say, "Evict us?"

Then she would laugh, real soft, because all of Grandma's friends sounded soft no matter how happy or mad they got. Ed liked to watch Mrs. Cassidy laugh, because she was a big woman and she laughed all over.

Mrs. Cassidy wore a lovely black dress, always the same one, and she was all powdered and rouged and painted up. She talked to Grandma a lot about something called "perpetual care."

"I'll always be grateful for one thing," Ed remembered her saying. "And that's my perpetual care. The flowers are

57

so pretty—I picked out the design for the blanket myself. And they keep the trim so nice, even in winter. I wish you could see the scrollwork on the box, too: all that handcarving in mahogany. They certainly spared no expense, let me tell you, and I'm mighty grateful. Mighty grateful. Why, if I hadn't forbid it in the will, I'll bet they'd have put up a monument. As it is, I think the plain Vermont granite has a little more restraint—you know, dignity."

Ed didn't understand Mrs. Cassidy very well, and besides, it was more interesting to listen to Sam Gates. Sam was the only one who had paid much attention to Ed.

"Hi, sonny," he would say. "Come over and sit by me. Want to hear about the battles, sonny?"

Sam Gates was a young-looking man, always smiling. He'd sit there in front of the fire, with Ed sprawled out at his feet, and then there would be wonderful stories to hear. Like the time Sam Gates met Abe Lincoln—not President Lincoln, but just plain Abe, the lawyer from down in Springfield, Illinois. Then there was the story about something called the Bloody Corner, where the boys in blue really gave 'em the cold steel.

"Wisht I could have lasted out to see the finish," Sam Gates would sigh. "'Course by '64 wasn't one of us on either side didn't know how it would end. After Gettysburg we had 'em on the run. And maybe it's just as well I didn't have to go through all that messing around with Reconstruction, or whatever they called it. No, siree, sonny, I guess I was lucky in a way at that. Leastways, I never had to grow old, like Willis here. Never had to marry and settle down and raise a family and end up mumbling in the corner, trying to gum my porkchops. I'd have come to the same thing at the last, anyhow—isn't that so, friends?"

And Sam Gates would look around the room and wink. Sometimes Grandma got mad at him.

"Wish you wouldn't carry on that way," she said. "Watch your language, please. Little pitchers have big ears. Just because you're all sociable and come around on account of this house being more or less a part of the property—so to speak—that's no reason you got to go putting ideas in the head of a six-year-old. It ain't decent."

That was a sure sign Grandma was mad: when she said

"ain't." And at such times Ed usually got up and went out to play with Susie and Joe.

Thinking back, years later, Ed couldn't remember the first time he played with Susie and Joe. The moments they spent together were quite fresh in his memory, but other details escaped him: where they lived, who their parents were, why they only came around at night, calling under the kitchen window.

"Oh, Ed-*deeee!* C'mon out and play!"

Joe was a black-haired, quiet kid of about nine. Susie was Ed's age or even a little younger; she had curly, taffy-colored hair and always wore a ruffled dress which she was careful not to stain or dirty, no matter what games they played.

Ed had a crush on her.

They played hide-and-seek all over the cool, dark graveyard, night after night: calling faintly and giggling quietly at one another. Even now, Ed recalled how quiet the children were. He tried vainly to remember other games they played, like tag, where they'd touch each other. He was sure, somehow, that he had touched them, but no single instance came in recollection. Mainly he remembered Susie's face, her smile, and the way she called in her little-girl voice.

"Oh, Ed-*deeee!*"

Ed never told anyone what he remembered, afterwards. Because afterwards was when the trouble started. It began when the people from the school came and asked Grandma why he wasn't attending first grade.

They got to talking with her, and then they talked to Ed. There was a lot of confusion—he remembered Grandma crying, and a big man with a blue suit on came in and showed her a lot of papers.

Ed didn't like to think about these things, because they marked the end of everything. After the man came, there were no more evenings around the fireplace, no more games in the cemetery, no more glimpses of Joe or Susie.

The man made Grandma cry and talked about incompetence and neglect, and something called a sanity hearing, just because Ed had been dumb enough to tell him about playing in the graveyard, and about Grandma's friends.

"You mean to tell me you got this poor kid so mixed up that he thinks he sees them too?" the man had asked

Grandma. "That can't go on, Mrs. Morse—filling a child's head with morbid nonsense about the dead."

"They ain't dead!" snapped Grandma, and Ed had never seen her quite so mad, even though she'd been crying. "Not to me they ain't, and not to him, nor anyone who's friendly. I've lived in this house nigh all my life, ever since Robert was taken from me in that foreign war in the Philippines, and this is about the first time a stranger ever marched into it. What you and your kind would call a living stranger, that is. But the others—they come regular. Seeing as how we share the same property, so to speak. They ain't dead, Mister; they're just *neighborly,* is all. And to Ed and me they're a darn sight more real than your kind ever was!"

But the man didn't listen to Grandma, even though he stopped asking questions and began treating her nice and polite. Everybody was nice and polite from then on; the other men that came, and the lady who took Ed away on the train to the orphanage in the city.

That was the end. There were no fresh flowers every day at the orphanage, and while Ed met plenty of kids, he never saw anyone like Joe or Susie.

Not that everyone, kids and grownups alike, wasn't nice to him. They treated him just so, and Mrs. Ward, the Matron, told him that she wanted Ed to think of her as his own mother—that being the least she could do, after his harrowing experience.

Ed didn't know what she meant by "harrowing experience" and she wouldn't explain. She wouldn't tell him what had happened to Grandma, either, or why she never came to visit him. In fact, anytime he asked any questions about the past she had nothing to say except that it was best to try and forget all that had happened before he came to the orphanage.

Gradually, Ed forgot. In the score of years that followed, he forgot almost completely—that was why it was so hard to remember, now. And Ed wanted to remember, very badly.

During the two years in the hospital at Honolulu, Ed spent most of his time trying to remember. There was nothing else for him to do, lying flat on his back that way, and besides, he knew that if he ever got out of there he'd want to go back.

Just before he went into the service, after getting out of the orphanage, he'd received a letter from Grandma. It was one of the few letters Ed ever received in his lonely lifetime and at first the return address on the envelope and the name "Mrs. Hannah Morse" had meant nothing to him.

But the letter itself—just a few scrawled and spidery lines written on ruled notebook paper—brought a rush of confused memories.

Grandma had been away, in a "sanotarium," as she put it, but she was back home now and had found out all about the "put-up job they worked to get you into their clutches." And if Ed would like to come back home—

Ed wanted very desperately to come back home. But he was already in uniform and waiting orders when the letter came. He wrote, of course. He wrote all the while he was overseas, and sent her an allotment, besides.

Sometimes Grandma's answers reached him. She was waiting for his leave to come. She was reading the papers. Sam Gates said it was a horrible thing, this war.

Sam Gates—

Ed told himself that he was a grown man now, Sam Gates was a figment of the imagination. But Grandma kept writing about her figments: about Mr. Willis and Mrs. Cassidy, and even some "new friends" who came to the house.

"Lots of fresh flowers these days, Ed boy," Grandma wrote. "Scarcely a day goes by without them blowing taps over yonder. Of course a body isn't so spry any more—I'm pushing seventy-seven, you know, but I still get over for flowers same as always."

The letters stopped coming when Ed got hit. For a long while, everything stopped, for Ed. There was only the bed and the doctors and the nurses and the hypo every three hours and the pain. That was Ed's life—that, and trying to remember.

Once Ed nearly told a skull doctor about the whole deal, but he caught himself in time. It was nothing you could talk about and hope to be understood, and Ed had enough trouble without bucking for a Section Eight.

When he was able to, he wrote again. Nearly two years had passed and the war was long since over. So many things had happened that Ed didn't even dare to hope very much. For Hannah Morse would be "pushing eighty" by now, if—

He got an answer to his letter a few days before his medical discharge came through.

"Dear Ed." The same spidery scrawl, probably a sheet from the same ruled notebook. Nothing had changed. Grandma was still waiting and she'd just known that he hadn't given up. But there was a funny thing she wanted him to know about. Did he remember old Sourpuss, the caretaker? Well, old Sourpuss was hit by a truck last winter, and ever since then he'd taken to dropping in with the rest of them evenings, and now he was friendly as could be, nice as pie. They'd have so much to talk about when Ed came back—

So Ed came back.

After twenty years, after a new lifetime, Ed came back. There was a long month in Honolulu, waiting for sailing—a month filled with unreal people and events. There were nights in a barroom, there was a girl named Peggy and a nurse named Linda, and there was a hospital buddy of Ed's who talked about going into business with the dough they'd saved up.

But the barroom was never as real as the parlor back in Grandma's house, and Peggy and Linda weren't in the least like Susie, and Ed knew he would never go into business.

On the boat, everybody seemed to be talking about Russia and inflation and housing. Ed listened and nodded and tried to remember some of the phrases Sam Gates used to use when he told about Old Abe down in Springfield, Illinois.

Ed took a plane from Frisco, wiring ahead to Mrs. Hannah Morse. He got in at the airport in mid-afternoon, but he couldn't catch a bus for the last forty-mile ride until just before supper. He grabbed a bite to eat at the station and then jolted into town along about twilight.

A cab took him over to Grandma's.

Ed was trembling when he got out in front of the house

on the edge of the cemetery. He handed the driver a five and told him to keep the change. Then he stood there until the cab drove away, before he got up enough nerve to knock on the door.

He took a long, deep breath. Then the door opened and he was home. He knew he was home because nothing had changed. Nothing at all.

Grandma was still Grandma. She stood there in the doorway and she was little and wrinkled and beautiful. An old, old woman, peering up at him in the dimness of the firelight, and saying, "Ed, boy—I declare! It is you, isn't it? Land, what tricks a body's mind can play. I thought I'd still be seeing a little shaver. But come in, boy, come in. Wipe your feet first."

Ed wiped his feet on the mat, same as always, and walked into the parlor. The fire was going in the fireplace and Ed put on another log before he sat down.

"Hard to keep it up, boy," Grandma said. "Woman gets to my age." She sat down opposite him and smiled.

"You shouldn't be alone like this," Ed told her.

"Alone? But I'm not alone! Don't you remember Mr. Willis and all the others? They sure enough haven't forgotten you, I can tell you that. Hardly talk about another thing except when you were coming back. They'll be over, later."

"Will they?" Ed said softly, staring into the fire.

"Of course they will. You know that, Ed."

"Sure. Only I thought—"

Grandma smiled. "I understand, all right. You've been letting the other folks fool you, the ones who don't know. I met a lot of them up to the sanotarium; they kept me there for nigh ten years before I caught on to how to handle them. Talking about ghosts and spirits and delusions. Finally I just gave up and allowed they were right and in a little while they let me come home. Guess you went through the same thing, more or less, only right now you don't know what to believe."

"That's right, Grandma," Ed said. "I don't."

"Well, boy, you needn't worry about it. Or about your chest, either."

"My chest? How did you—"

"They sent a letter," Grandma answered. "Maybe it's

right, what they said, and maybe it's wrong. But it doesn't matter, either way. I know you aren't afraid. You wouldn't have come back if you were afraid, would you, Ed?"

"That's right, Grandma. I figured that even if time was short, I belonged here. Besides, I wanted to know, once and for all, if—"

He was silent, waiting for her to speak. But she merely nodded, face bowed and dim in the shadows. At last she replied.

"You'll find out soon enough." Her smile flashed up at him, and Ed caught himself remembering a dozen familiar gestures, mannerisms, intonations. Come what may, that was something nobody could take away from him—he was home.

"Land, I wonder what's keeping them?" Grandma said, rising abruptly and crossing over to the side window. "Seems to me they're pretty late."

"Are you sure they're coming?" Ed could have bitten his tongue off a moment after he uttered the question, but it was too late then.

Grandma turned stiffly. "I'm sure," she said. "But maybe I was wrong about you. Maybe you ain't sure."

"Don't be mad, Grandma—"

"I ain't mad! Oh, Ed, have they really fooled you after all? Did you go so far away that you can't even remember?"

"Of course I remember. I remember everything; even about Susie and Joe and the fresh flowers every day, but—"

"The flowers." Grandma looked at him. "Yes, you do remember, and I'm glad. You used to get fresh flowers for me every day, didn't you?"

She glanced at the table. An empty bowl rested on the center.

"Maybe that will help," she said. "If you'd go get some flowers. Now. Before they come."

"Now?"

"Please, Ed."

Without a word, he walked out into the kitchen and opened the back door. The moon was up, and there was enough light to guide him along the path to the fence. Beyond, the cemetery lay in silver splendor.

Ed didn't feel afraid, he didn't feel strange, he felt nothing at all. He boosted himself over the fence, ignoring the sharp, sudden pain below his ribs. He set his feet upon the gravel path between the headstones and he walked a little ways, letting memory guide him.

Flowers. Fresh flowers. Fresh flowers from fresh graves. It was all wrong, it was Section Eight for sure, but at the same time it was all right. It had to be.

He saw the mound over at the side of the hill, near the end of the fence. Potter's field, but there were flowers on one grave; the single bouquet rested against a wooden marker.

Ed stooped down, scenting the freshness, feeling the damp firmness of the cut stems as he lifted the cluster from the marker. The moon was bright.

The moon was bright, and he read the plain block letters.

HANNAH MORSE
1870–1949

Hannah Morse was Grandma. The flowers were fresh. The grave wasn't more than a day old—

Ed walked back along the path very slowly. He found it very hard to get back over the fence without dropping the bouquet, but he made it, pain and all. He opened the kitchen door and walked into the parlor where the fire had burned very low.

Grandma wasn't there. Ed put the flowers in the bowl anyway. Grandma wasn't there, and her friends weren't there, either. But Ed didn't worry any more.

She'd be back. And so would Mr. Willis and Mrs. Cassidy and Sam Gates, all of them. In a little while, Ed knew, he might even hear the faint, faraway voices under the kitchen window calling.

"Oh, Ed-*deeee!*"

He might not be able to go out tonight, the way his chest was acting up. But sooner or later, he'd go. Meanwhile, they would be coming, soon.

Ed smiled and leaned back in the chair before the fire, just making himself at home and waiting.

Born in Chicago, Illinois, in 1917, Robert Bloch sold his first professional short story to Weird Tales *in 1935, two months after high school graduation. He has been a professional writer ever since, with some twenty novels and nearly four hundred shorter works to his credit. Best known for his terror novel,* Psycho *(1959), he moved to Hollywood to concentrate on film and television scripts. His best-known shorter work is the eerie, much-reprinted classic of horror, "Yours Truly, Jack the Ripper." His latest novel,* Lori, *has just been published.*

John Jeremy could recover any body from the river, but he kept his methods secret. Twelve-year-old Peter was determined to find out why.

FIVE

Stillwater, 1896
Michael Cassutt

They are big families up here on the St. Croix. I myself am the second of eight, and ours was the smallest family of any on Chestnut Street. You might think we were all hard-breeding Papists passing as Lutherans, but I have since learned that it is due to the long winters. For fifty years I have been hearing that Science will take care of winters just like we took care of the river, with our steel high bridge and diesel-powered barges that go the size of a football field. But every damn November the snow falls again and in spring the river swells from bluff to bluff. The loggers can be heard cursing all the way from Superior. I alone know that this is because of what we done to John Jeremy.

I was just a boy then, short of twelve, that would be in 1896, and by mutual agreement of little use to anyone, not my father nor my brothers nor my departed mother. I knew my letters, to be sure, and could be trusted to appear at Church in a clean collar, but my primary achievement at that age was to be known as the best junior logroller in the county, a title I had won the previous Fourth of July, beating boys from as far away as Rice Lake and Taylors Falls. In truth, I tended to lollygag when sent to Kinnick's Store, never failing to take a detour down to the riverfront, where a Mississippi excursion boat like the *Verne Swain* or the *Kalitan*, up from St. Louis or New Orleans, would be pulled in. I had the habit of getting into snowball fights on my way to school and was notorious for one whole winter as the boy who almost put out Oscar Tolz's eye with a missile into which I had embedded a small pebble. (Oscar Tolz was a

God damned Swede and a bully to boot.) Often I would not get to school at all. This did not vex my father to any great degree, as he had only a year of schooling himself. It mightily vexed my elder brother, Dolph. I can still recall him appearing like an avenging angel wherever I went, it seemed, saying, "Peter, what in God's name are you doing there? Get away from there!" Dolph was all of fourteen at the time and ambitious, having been promised a job at the Hersey Bean Lumberyard when the Panic ended. He was also suspicious of my frivolous associates, particularly one named John Jeremy.

I now know that John Jeremy was the sort of man you meet on the river—bearded, unkempt, prone to sudden, mystifying exclamations and gestures. The better folk got no further with him, while curious boys found him somewhat more interesting, perhaps because of his profession. "I'm descended from the line of St. Peter himself," he told me once. "Do you know why?"

I drew the question because my given name is Peter. "Because you are a fisher of men," I told him.

Truth, in the form of hard liquor, was upon John Jeremy that day. He amended my phrase: "A fisher of dead men." John Jeremy fished for corpses.

He had been brought up from Chicago, they said, in 1885 by the Hersey family itself. Whether motivated by a series of personal losses or by some philanthropic spasm I do not know, having been otherwise occupied at the time. I found few who were able or willing to discuss the subject when at last I sprouted interest. I do know that a year did not pass then that the St. Croix did not take at least half a dozen people to its shallow bottom. This in a town of less than six hundred, though that figure was subject to constant change due to riverboats and loggers who, I think, made up a disproportionate amount of the tribute. You can not imagine the distress a drowning caused in those days. Now part of this was normal human grief (most of the victims were children), but much of it, I have come to believe, was a deep revulsion in the knowledge that the source of our drinking water, the heart of our livelihood—the river!—was fouled by the bloating, gassy corpse of someone we all knew. There was nothing rational about it, but the fear was real nonetheless: when the whistle at the courthouse blew, you ran for it, for either the town was on fire, or somebody was breathing river.

Out would go the rowboats, no matter what the weather or time of night, filled with farmers unused to water with their weights, poles, nets, and hopes. It was tedious, sad, and unrewarding work . . . except for a specialist like John Jeremy.

"You stay the hell away from that man," Dolph hissed at me one day. "I've seen you hanging around down there with him. He's the Devil himself."

Normally, a statement like this from Dolph would have served only to encourage further illicit association, but none was actually needed. I had come across John Jeremy for the first time that spring, idly fishing at a spot south of town near the lumberyard. It was not the best fishing hole, if you used worms or other unimaginative bait, for the St. Croix was low that year, as it had been for ten years, and the fish were fat with bugs easily caught in the shallows. I had picked up a marvelous invention known as the casting fly and had applied it that spring with great success. And I was only too happy to share the secret with a thin, pale, scruffy fellow who looked as if he had skipped meals of late. We introduced ourselves and proceeded to take a goodly number of crappies and sunfish during the afternoon. "That's quite a trick you got there," John Jeremy told me. "You make that up all by yourself?"

I confessed that I had read about it in a dime novel, though if Oscar Tolz had asked me, I would have lied. John Jeremy laughed, showing that his teeth were a match for the rest of his ragged appearance.

"Well, it works good enough. Almost makes me wish I'd learned how to read."

By this point, as I remember it, we had hiked up to the Afton Road and were headed back to Stillwater. As we walked, I was struck by John Jeremy's thinness and apparent ill health, and in a fit of Christian charity—I was just twelve—I offered him some of my catch, which was far larger than his.

John Jeremy regarded me for a moment. I think he was amused. "Aren't you a rascal, Peter Gollwitzer. Thank you, but no. In spite of the fact that it's been a long dry spell, I'm still able to feed myself, though it don't show. I'll grant you that. In fact, in exchange for your kindness"—his voice took on a conspiratorial tone—"I shall reward you with this." And into my hand he pressed a five-dollar gold piece. "For the secret of the fly, eh? Now run along home."

My father was unamused by my sudden wealth, especially when he learned the source. "That man is worse than a grave robber. He profits through the misfortune of others." It was then that I learned John Jeremy's true profession, and that he had been known to charge as much as *five hundred dollars* for a single "recovery," as it was called. "One time, I swear by the Lord," my father continued, "he *refused* to turn over a body he had recovered because the payment wasn't immediately forthcoming! A man like that is unfit for human company." I reserved judgment, clutching the eagle in my sweaty palm, happier than I would have been with a chestful of pirate treasure.

June is a month to be remembered for tornados, with the wind screaming and trees falling and the river churning. In this instance there was a riverboat, the *Sidney,* taking a side trip from St. Paul—and regretting it—putting into town just as one of those big blowers hit. One of her deckhands, a Negro, was knocked into the water. Of course, none of those people can swim, and in truth I doubt Jonah himself could have got out of those waters that day. The courthouse whistle blew, though it was hard to hear over the roar of the wind, and Dolph (who had been sent home from the yard) grabbed my arm and tugged me toward the docks.

The crowd there was bigger than you'd expect, given the weather—not only townspeople, but many from the *Sidney,* who were quite vocal in their concern about the unfortunate blackamoor. Into our midst came John Jeremy, black gunnysack—he referred to it as his "bag of tricks"—over his shoulder. People stepped aside, the way they do for the sheriff, letting him pass. He sought out the *Sidney*'s captain. I took it that they were haggling over the price, since the captain's voice presently rose above the storm: "I've never heard such an outrage in my life!" But an agreement was reached and soon, in the middle of the storm, we saw John

Jeremy put out in his skiff. It was almost dark by then and the corpse fisher, floating with the wind-whipped water with all the seeming determination of a falling leaf, disappeared from our sight.

The onlookers began to drift home then while the passengers from the *Sidney* headed up the street in search of a warm, dry tavern. Dolph and I and the younger ones—including Oscar Tolz—stayed behind. Because of my familiarity with the corpse fisher I was thought to have intimate and detailed knowledge of his techniques, which, they say, he refused to discuss. "I bet he uses loaves of bread," one boy said. "Like in Mark Twain."

"Don't be a dope," Oscar Tolz said. "Books are not real. My old man says he's got animals in that sack. Some kind of trained rats—maybe muskrats."

"Like hell," said a third. "I saw that sack and there was nothing alive in it. Muskrats would be squirming to beat the band."

"Maybe they're *drowned* muskrats," I offered, earning a cuff from Dolph. Normally, that would have been my signal to shut my mouth, as Dolph's sense of humor—never notable—was not presently on duty. But that evening, for some reason, I felt immune. I asked him, "Okay, Dolph, what do *you* think he uses?"

One thing Dolph always liked was a technical question. He immediately forgot that he was annoyed with me. "I think," he said after a moment, "that John Jeremy's got some sort of compass." Before anyone could laugh, he raised his hand. "Now just you remember this: all the strange machines people got nowadays. If they got a machine that can make pictures move and another one can say words, how hard can it be to make a compass that instead of finding north finds dead people?"

This sounded so eminently reasonable to all of us that we promptly clasped the idea to us with a fervor of which our parents—having seen us bored in Church—thought us incapable. The boy who knew Mark Twain's stories suggested that this compass must have been invented by Thomas Edison, and who was to dispute that? Oscar Tolz announced that John Jeremy—who was known to have traveled a bit—might have busted Tom Edison in the noggin and stolen the compass away, which was why he had it and no one else did. "Especially since Edison's been suffering from amnesia ever since," I said. I confess that we grew so riotous that we did not notice how late it had gotten and that John Jeremy's laden skiff was putting in to the dock. We took one good look at the hulking and lifeless cargo coming toward us and scurried away like mice. Later I felt ashamed, because of what John Jeremy must have wondered, and because there was no real reason for us to run. A body drowned, at most, three hours could not have transformed into one of those horrors we had all heard about. It was merely the body of a poor dead black man.

I learned that John Jeremy had earned one hundred dollars for his work that afternoon, plus a free dinner with the captain of the *Sidney*. Feelings in Stillwater ran quite hot against this for some days, since one hundred dollars was the amount Reverend Bickell earned in a year for saving souls.

Over the Fourth I successfully defended my junior logrolling title; that, combined with other distractions, prevented me from seeing John Jeremy until one afternoon in early August. He was balancing unsteadily on the end of the dock, obviously drunk, occasionally cupping his hand to his ear as if listening to some faroff voice, flapping his arms to right himself.

He did not strike me as a mean or dangerous drunk (such a drinker was my father, rest his soul), just unhappy. "Florida!" he announced abruptly. "Florida, Alabama, Mississippi, Missouri, Illinois, Michigan, Wisconsin, here." He counted the state on his hand. "And never welcome anywhere for long, Peter. Except Stillwater. Why do you suppose that is?"

"Maybe it is better here."

John Jeremy laughed loudly. "I wouldn't have thought to say that, but maybe it is, by God." He coughed. "Maybe it's because I've kept the river quiet . . . and folks appreciate it." He saw none-too-fleeting disdain on my face. "True! By God, when was the last time the St. Croix went over its banks? Tell me when! Eighteen eighty-four is when! One year before the disreputable John Jeremy showed his ugly face in the quiet town of Stillwater. Not one flood in that time, sir! I stand on my record." He almost fell on it, as he was seized with another wheezing cough.

"Then the city should honor you," I said helpfully. "You should be the mayor."

"Huh! You're too innocent, Peter. A corpse fisher for mayor. No, sir, the Christian folk will not have *that*. Better a brewer, or a usurer—or the undertaker!"

He had gotten quite loud, and much as I secretly enjoyed my friendship with him, I recognized truth in what he said.

"You wouldn't want to be mayor, anyway."

He shook his head, grinning. "No. After all, what mayor can do what *I* do, eh? Who speaks to the river like I do? No one." He paused and was quiet, then added, "No one else is strong enough to pay the price."

Though I was far from tired of this conversation, I knew, from extensive experience with my father, that John Jeremy would likely grow steadily less coherent. I tried to help him to his feet, quite an achievement given my stature at the time, and, as he lapsed into what seemed to be a sullen silence, guided him toward his shack.

I was rewarded with a look inside. In the dark, I confess, I expected a magic compass, or muskrat cages, but all that I beheld were the possessions of a drifter: a gunnysack, a pole, some weights, and a net. I left John Jeremy among them, passed out on his well-worn cot.

Four days later, on a Saturday afternoon, in the thick, muggy heat of August, the courthouse whistle blew. I was on my way home from Kinnick's, having run an errand for my father, and made a quick detour downtown. Oscar Tolz was already there, shouting, "Someone's drowned at the lumberyard!" I was halfway there before I remembered that Dolph was working.

The sawmill at the Hersey Bean Lumberyard sat on pilings well into the St. Croix, the better to deal with the river of wood that floated its way every spring and summer. It was a God dammed treacherous place, especially when huge timbers were being pulled in and swung to face the blades. Dolph had been knocked off because he had not ducked in time.

The water was churning that day beneath the mill in spite

of the lack of wind and current. I suspect it had to do with the peculiar set of the pilings and the movements of the big logs. At any rate, Dolph, a strong swimmer, had been hurled into an obstruction, possibly striking his head, so observers said. He had gone under the water then, not to be seen again.

The shoreline just to the south of the yard was rugged and overgrown. It was possible that Dolph, knocked senseless for a moment, had been carried that way where, revived, he could swim to safety, unbeknownst to the rest of us. Some men went to search there.

I was told there was nothing I could do, and to tell the truth, I was glad. My father arrived and without saying a word to me went off with the searchers. He had lost a wife and child already.

John Jeremy arrived. He had his gunnysack over his shoulder and an oar in his hand. Behind him two men hauled his skiff. I stood up to meet him, I'm ashamed to say, wiping tears on my pantaloons. I had the presence of mind to know that there was business to be conducted.

"This is all I have," I told him, holding out the five-dollar gold piece I had carried for weeks.

I saw real pain in his eyes. The breath itself seemed to seep out of him. "This will be on the house," he said finally. He patted me on the shoulder with a hand that was glazed and hard and went down to the river.

My father's friends took me away then and put some food in me and made me look after the other children. I fell asleep early that warm evening and, not surprisingly, woke while it was still dark, frightened and confused. Had they found him? I wanted to know, and with my father still not home, I had no one to ask.

Dressing, I sneaked out and walked down to the lumberyard. The air was hot and heavy even though dawn was not far off . . . so hot that even the bugs were quiet. I made my way to the dock and sat there, listening to the lazy slap of the water.

There was a slice of moon in the sky, and by its light it seemed that I could see a skiff slowly crossing back and forth, back and forth, between two prominent coves to the south. A breeze came up all of a sudden, a breeze that chilled but did not cool, hissing in the reeds like a faraway voice. I fell forward on my hands and shouted into the darkness: "Who's there?"

No one answered. Perhaps it was all a dream. I do know that eventually the sky reddened on the Wisconsin side and I was able to clearly see John Jeremy's distant skiff.

Hungry now and deadly sure of my own uselessness in the affair, I drifted home and got something to eat. It was very quiet in the house. My father was home, but tired, and he offered nothing. I went out to Church voluntarily, and prayed for once, alone.

Almost hourly during that Sunday I went down to the St. Croix. Each time, I was able to spot John Jeremy, infinitely patient in his search.

It finally occurred to me about mid-afternoon that I had to do something to help, even if it came to naught. Leaving the house again, I walked past the lumberyard toward the brushy shallows where John Jeremy was, hoping that in some way my sorry presence would encourage a merciful God to end this. I was frankly terrified of what I would see— a body drowned a goodly time and in August heat at that— yet anxious to confront it, to move *past* it and get on with other business.

Two hours of beating through the underbrush, occasionally stepping into the green scum at water's edge, exhausted me. I believe I sat down for a while and cried, and presently I felt better—better enough to continue.

It was almost sunset. The sun had crossed to the Minnesota side and dipped toward the trees on the higher western bluffs, casting eerie shadows in the coves. Perhaps that is why I did not see them until I was almost upon them.

There, in the shallow water, among the cattails and scum, was John Jeremy's skiff. In it was a huge white thing that once was my brother Dolph. The sight was every bit as horrific as I had imagined, and even across an expanse of water the smell rivaled the pits of Hell . . . but that alone, I can honestly say, did not make me scream. It was another thing that made me call out, an image I will carry to my grave, of John Jeremy pressing his ear to the greenish lips of my brother's corpse.

My scream startled him. "Peter!" he yelled. I was as incapable of locomotion as the cattails that separated us. John Jeremy raised himself and began to pole toward me. "Peter, wait for me."

I found my voice, weak though it was. "What are you doing to my brother?"

He beached his nightmare cargo and stumbled out of the skiff. He was frantic, pleading, out of breath. "Don't run. Peter, hear me out."

I managed to back up, putting some distance between us. "Stay away!"

"I told you, Peter, I talk to the river. I *listen* to it, too." He nodded toward Dolph's body. "They tell me where the next one will be found, Peter, so I can get them out, because the river doesn't want them for long—"

I clapped my hands over my ears and screamed again, backing away as fast as I could. The slope was against me, though, and I fell.

John Jeremy held out his hand. "I could teach you the secret, Peter. You have the gift. You could learn it easy."

For a long second, perhaps a heartbeat and a half, I stared at his grimy hand. But a gentle wave lapped at the skiff and the God-awful creaking broke his spell. I turned and scurried up the hill. Reaching the top, I remembered the gold piece in my pocket. I took it out and threw it at him.

At twelve your secrets do not keep. Eventually, some version of what I'd seen and told got around town, and it went hard with John Jeremy. Stillwater's version of tar-and-feathering was to gang up on a man, kick the hell out of him, and drag him as far south as he could be dragged, possessions be damned. I was not there. Sometimes, as I think back, I fool myself into believing that I was . . . that John Jeremy forgave me, like Christ forgave his tormentors. But that did not happen.

Eventually, we learned that John Jeremy's "secret" was actually a special three-pronged hook attached to a weight that could be trolled on a river bottom. Any fool could find a body, they said. Maybe so.

But the flood of '97 damned near killed Stillwater and things haven't improved since then. A day don't go by now that I don't think of John Jeremy's secret and wish I'd said yes. Especially when I go down to the river and hear the water rustling in the reeds, making that awful sound, the sound I keep telling myself is not the voices of the dead.

A new writer whose stories are few but carefully crafted, Michael Cassutt is a California native who works for a television network. His first published story, "The Streak" (1977), is about murder on a baseball diamond; his later tales, nearly all science fiction, have appeared in Omni *and* Isaac Asimov's Science Fiction.

Murlock's wife died from a fever. Or did she?

SIX

The Boarded Window

Ambrose Bierce

In 1830, only a few miles away from what is now the great city of Cincinnati, lay an immense and almost unbroken forest. The whole region was sparsely settled by people of the frontier—restless souls who no sooner had hewn fairly habitable homes out of the wilderness and attained to that degree of prosperity which today we should call indigence than, impelled by some mysterious impulse of their nature, they abandoned all and pushed farther westward, to encounter new perils and privations in the effort to regain the meagre comforts which they had voluntarily renounced. Many of them had already forsaken that region for the remoter settlements, but among those remaining was one who had been of those first arriving. He lived alone in a house of logs surrounded on all sides by the great forest, of whose gloom and silence he seemed a part, for no one had ever known him to smile nor speak a needless word. His simple wants were supplied by the sale or barter of skins of wild animals in the river town, for not a thing did he grow upon the land which, if needful, he might have claimed by right of undisturbed possession. There were evidences of "improvement"—a few acres of ground immediately about the house had once been cleared of its trees, the decayed stumps of which were half concealed by the new growth that had been suffered to repair the ravage wrought by the ax. Apparently the man's zeal for agriculture had burned with a failing flame, expiring in penitential ashes.

The little log house, with its chimney of sticks, its roof of warping clapboards weighted with traversing poles and its "chinking" of clay, had a single door and, directly opposite, a window. The latter, however, was boarded up—nobody could remember a time when it was not. And none knew why it was so closed; certainly not because of the occupant's dislike of light and air, for on those rare occasions when a hunter had passed that lonely spot the recluse had commonly been seen sunning himself on his doorstep if heaven had provided sunshine for his need. I fancy there are few persons living today who ever knew the secret of that window, but I am one, as you shall see.

The man's name was said to be Murlock. He was apparently seventy years old, actually about fifty. Something besides years had had a hand in his aging. His hair and long, full beard were white, his gray, lustreless eyes sunken, his face singularly seamed with wrinkles which appeared to belong to two intersecting systems. In figure he was tall and spare, with a stoop of the shoulders—a burden bearer. I never saw him; these particulars I learned from my grandfather, from whom also I got the man's story when I was a lad. He had known him when living nearby in that early day.

One day Murlock was found in his cabin, dead. It was not a time and place for coroners and newspapers, and I suppose it was agreed that he had died from natural causes or I should have been told and should remember. I know only that with what was probably a sense of the fitness of things the body was buried near the cabin, alongside the grave of his wife, who had preceded him by so many years that local tradition had retained hardly a hint of her existence. That closes the final chapter of this true story—excepting, indeed, the circumstance that many years afterward, in company with an equally intrepid spirit, I penetrated to the place and ventured near enough to the ruined cabin to throw a stone against it and ran away to avoid the ghost which every well-informed boy thereabout knew haunted the spot. But there is an earlier chapter—that supplied by my grandfather.

When Murlock built his cabin and began laying sturdily about with his ax to hew out a farm—the rifle, meanwhile, his means of support—he was young, strong, and full of hope. In that eastern country whence he came he had married, as was the fashion, a young woman in all ways worthy

79

of his honest devotion, who shared the dangers and privations of his lot with a willing spirit and light heart. There is no known record of her name; of her charms of mind and person tradition is silent and the doubter is at liberty to entertain his doubt; but God forbid that I should share it! Of their affection and happiness there is abundant assurance in every added day of the man's widowed life; for what but the magnetism of a blessed memory could have chained that venturesome spirit to a lot like that?

One day Murlock returned from gunning in a distant part of the forest to find his wife prostrate with fever, and delirious. There was no physician within miles, no neighbor; nor was she in a condition to be left, to summon help. So he set about the task of nursing her back to health, but at the end of the third day she fell into unconsciousness and so passed away, apparently, with never a gleam of returning reason.

From what we know of a nature like his we may venture to sketch in some of the details of the outline picture drawn by my grandfather. When convinced that she was dead, Murlock had sense enough to remember that the dead must be prepared for burial. In performance of this sacred duty he blundered now and again, did certain things incorrectly, and others which he did correctly were done over and over. His occasional failures to accomplish some simple and ordinary act filled him with astonishment, like that of a drunken man who wonders at the suspension of familiar natural laws. He was surprised, too, that he did not weep—surprised and a little ashamed; surely it is unkind not to weep for the dead. "Tomorrow," he said aloud, "I shall have to make the coffin and dig the grave; and then I shall miss her, when she is no longer in sight; but now—she is dead, of course, but it is all right—it *must* be all right, somehow. Things cannot be so bad as they seem."

He stood over the body in the fading light, adjusting the hair and putting the finishing touches to the simple toilet, doing all mechanically, with soulless care. And still through his consciousness ran an undersense of conviction that all was right—that he should have her again as before, and everything explained. He had had no experience in grief; his capacity had not been enlarged by use. His heart could not contain it all, nor his imagination rightly conceive it. He did not know he was so hard struck; *that* knowledge would come later, and never go. Grief is an artist of powers as various as the instruments upon which he plays his dirges for the dead, evoking from some the sharpest, shrillest notes, from others the low, grave chords that throb recurrent like the slow beating of a distant drum. Some natures it startles; some it stupefies. To one it comes like the stroke of an arrow, stinging all the sensibilities to a keener life; to another as the blow of a bludgeon, which in crushing benumbs. We may conceive Murlock to have been that way affected, for (and here we are upon surer ground than that of conjecture) no sooner had he finished his pious work than, sinking into a chair by the side of the table upon which the body lay, and noting how white the profile showed in the deepening gloom, he laid his arms upon the table's edge, and dropped his face into them, tearless yet and unutterably weary. At that moment came in through the open window a long, wailing sound like the cry of a lost child in the far deeps of the darkening wood! But the man did not move. Again, and nearer than before, sounded that unearthly cry upon his failing sense. Perhaps it was a wild beast; perhaps it was a dream. For Murlock was asleep.

Some hours later, as it afterward appeared, this unfaithful watcher awoke and lifting his head from his arms intently listened—he knew not why. There in the black darkness by the side of the dead, recalling all without a shock, he strained his eyes to see—he knew not what. His senses were all alert, his breath was suspended, his blood had stilled its tides as if to assist the silence. Who—what had waked him, and where was it?

Suddenly the table shook beneath his arms, and at the same moment he heard, or fancied that he heard, a light, soft step—another—sounds as of bare feet upon the floor!

He was terrified beyond the power to cry out or move. Perforce he waited—waited there in the darkness through seeming centuries of such dread as one may know, yet live to tell. He tried vainly to speak the dead woman's name, vainly to stretch forth his hand across the table to learn if she were there. His throat was powerless, his arms and hands were like lead. Then occurred something most frightful. Some heavy body seemed hurled against the table with an impetus that pushed it against his breast so sharply as nearly to overthrow him, and at the same instant he heard and felt the fall of something upon the floor with so violent a thump that the whole house was shaken by the impact. A scuffling ensued, and a confusion of sounds impossible to describe. Murlock had risen to his feet. Fear had by excess forfeited control of his faculties. He flung his hands upon the table. Nothing was there!

There is a point at which terror may turn to madness; and madness incites to action. With no definite intent, from no motive but the wayward impulse of a madman, Murlock sprang to the wall, with a little groping seized his loaded rifle, and without aim discharged it. By the flash which lit up the room with a vivid illumination, he saw an enormous panther dragging the dead woman toward the window, its teeth fixed in her throat! Then there were darkness blacker than before, and silence; and when he returned to consciousness the sun was high and the wood vocal with songs of birds.

The body lay near the window, where the beast had left it when frightened away by the flash and report of the rifle. The clothing was deranged, the long hair in disorder, the limbs lay anyhow. From the throat, dreadfully lacerated, had issued a pool of blood not yet entirely coagulated. The ribbon with which he had bound the wrists was broken; the hands were tightly clenched. Between the teeth was a fragment of the animal's ear.

A dark genius of American letters, Ambrose Bierce was born in Ohio in 1842 and served in the Union army during the Civil War. A bitter and fearless man known for his witty writing (in one book review he wrote, "The covers of this book are too far apart"), he had a long, successful journalism career in San Francisco. His life ended with an eerie touch of mystery: he disappeared somewhere in Mexico in 1914.

Tommy and Annette were worried about their grandmother. They tried to get help, but no one believed that the people in the mirror were real.

SEVEN

Listen, Children, Listen!

Wallace West

My grandmother was fey.

At least that's what the neighbors said. She could predict the weather by the way her heel itched ("eetched," she pronounced it in the old Elizabethan way); always knew when any of her brood was coming down from Indianapolis for a visit to our tumbledown farm, and averred she often heard the singing of angels, or more terrifying sounds, during funerals at the New Harmony Church over the hill.

To me and sister Annette, Maw was as old as the gullies that cut up our clay fields . . . Probably she was sixty at the time I first remember her . . . She carried her lean body proudly, though her back was bowed from hard work. She had a gift for mimicry and a merry smile marred by the fact that she had been "salivated" in her youth by taking too much calomel to fight off the "fever 'n'aiger."

This affliction of the gums gave her a snaggle-toothed, witch-like look. Some of her yellow fangs were quite loose and moved when she sang. But, to our eternal wonder, they never fell out.

Maw had the wreck of a fine alto voice and regaled us by the hour with bloody old hymns or ballads like "The Ship's Carpenter" ("And three times 'round went our gallant ship e'er she sank to the bottom of the sea"); "Sourwood Mountain"; an endless, garbled song about a girl who masqueraded as a soldier to join her sweetheart and die in the wars between "Tors and Highlanzer," and another about the flightiness of all Gypsy lovers.

These songs were peculiarly appropriate because the Brown Murder was a recent memory down in our country. Patriarch Brown and his blind wife had been slaughtered with a monkey wrench in an angular, hemlock-shrouded farmhouse not far from ours, by "persons unknown."

Repercussions of the trial had hardly died away. There was talk of another investigation and the "persons," well known to everyone but the law, prowled the countryside of nights. They frightened farmers out of their wits by flashing dark lanterns under their doors and shouting threats at any who might dare tell what they knew. Paw woke once and fired his squirrel rifle at what he thought was a lantern. But it was only a suddenly-flaming ember in the fireplace. The bullet knocked a newel post off my bed.

Paw had to drive to the county seat once a week for supplies. Under the circumstances, he always promised Maw to be back by sundown. And always he met some old cronies.

Paw would be delayed until night closed in. Then, as little Annette and I lay in our bed beside the fireplace, refusing to go to sleep because we knew that Paw would bring us presents, even though he had spent money needed for food to do so, Maw would open the door, hook her bare foot around it so it wouldn't close behind her, and listen, tense with a terror that never failed to communicate itself to us.

Outside the katydids might be quarrelling. Or the baying of Mr. Morningstar's foxhounds, ignominiously hunting coon, might drift through the fall or winter air. (In summer Paw usually managed to return before nightfall.) Or an owl's hoot might cause Annette and me to cling together in a shiver.

Finally, when we could bear the silence no longer we would start whimpering and Maw would twist her weatherbeaten head back through the crack in the door and whisper:

"Listen, children. Listen! I think I hear Josiah's wagon. They haven't got him this time."

Often the belated team turned down some side road. Then she would murmur, hardly louder than the katydids, as she resumed her vigil:

"Shhh! Listen, children. Listen!"

When the tension had set my whole body aching with

what folks who don't know call "growing pains," and when the half-opened door had made the room almost as chill as the night, we would hear the far-away, mournful creak of wheels on the gravel road; the jingle of trace chains; the rumble of a half-empty joltwagon bed.

"Thank you, dear, just God," Maw would breathe. Then she would follow her bare foot through the door and bustle about re-heating the supper coffee and fixing a snack.

We would hear the wagon rumble into the yard. Next Paw would cuss Old Nell for her contrariness as he un-hitched and led her to the stable. And at last a great gray-beard, arms laden with bundles, would stumble through the front door to be greeted by two elves in long underwear, dancing about him and screaming:

"Whatcha got for me, Paw? Whatcha got this time?"

Usually it was jawbreakers, or peppermint sticks. Once, when we sold the hogs, it was a marvelous steamboat for me that you wound up with a key and that sank the first time I tried it in the branch.

He always brought something pretty and useless for Maw, too. And she scolded and loved him for buying it. And then he'd go over to the creaky chair where Aunt Ellen rocked slowly, pat her plump shoulder and hold out a comb for her hair or a cheap ring or a handkerchief. And Aunt Ellen would look away from the mirror—for the first time that day, perhaps—take the thing in her plump white hand, and smile.

(I should have mentioned Aunt Ellen before, but I forgot. In fact, everybody forgot Aunt Ellen. She wanted it so. She had been deeply in love when she was a girl, they said. But her young man wanted to see the world before he settled down. So he set out for that strange, half-mythical land called Europe. And he never came back. . . .)

After she was sure he would not return Aunt Ellen stopped speaking to people. She took her seat and just looked into the mirror. The rockers of that chair were worn almost through from constant use.

The mirror fascinated Annette and me. It was big . . . big as our front door and placed against the wall directly across from the entrance so that if you didn't look closely you thought it *was* another door. And it had a great, deeply pol-

85

ished frame carved in an intricate pattern that hurt your eyes if you looked too long.

I know now that it was the only thing of real value in the draughty log cabin. Maw said it was a "hearloom," brought from Virginia by her parents, the Whites, who had been "quality" in the Old Dominion before they migrated after the war of 1812, were stampeded by land agents into "locating" in the wrong part of the state, and rapidly dissipated their means on an unproductive wilderness.

Maw had made up a song about that mirror. "The Whites, 'tis said, were privateers when England ruled the waves" was the way it started. And it went on to tell how the mirror was part of their loot when they sacked and scuttled some tall merchantman.

To corroborate this story we had another relic, a "treasure chest" of the same dark wood, iron-bound and strong, which was used as a hens' nest underneath the house. Annette and I crawled under the floor from time to time to see if we could find any treasure still in it. But all we ever found was eggs.

After Paw had taken off his overcoat and Maw had put his packages in the lean-to kitchen, he would sit before the fire, suck coffee through his salt-and-pepper beard and regale us with news from the outside—how Uncle Joe Cannon's control of Congress was about to be broken, what the Young Turks were up to, how T. R.'s trustbusting would boost farm prices and make us all rich again, and how They had found the rusted monkey wrench in Brown's well.

At last, tired and happy, with our mouths puckered from too many jawbreakers, we'd go to bed. And we'd wake to a humdrum world which included school, collecting wood, milking our cow, riding Old Nell when she would let us, and maybe going to an ice cream social at New Harmony, until it was time for Paw to make another epic trip to Martinsville.

But life was never completely humdrum when Paw was around. He knew every bird by its call, could lead us to the best raspberry patches and made popguns, slingshots, and fly killers out of elder bushes and bits of string. When he tired of such things, his tales about Napoleon and Hannibal crossing the Alps would hold us spellbound.

Openhanded to a fault, Paw had lost most of his farm

through the years by going on neighbors' worthless notes or lending them money and not having the heart to ask for its return. Yet he was the materialist of the family and never tired of poking fun at Maw's voices and premonitions.

Dressed in overalls, shaggy, massive, and not always clean, he looked like a poor white. Nevertheless he had a good education and once confessed to me, when Maw's back was turned, that, in his youth, he had made a tour of the state lecturing on atheism. And he had an endless fund of slightly bawdy, sacrilegious stories which made Maw click her teeth at him and mourn that he would never go to heaven when he died.

Years slip past like water when one is young and we hardly noticed, Annette and I, that the bend in Maw's back was more pronounced and that Paw stopped oftener for breath when he plowed our stubbly fields or sawed the endless cords of wood which still could not keep the living room warm when wintry winds swept down from some place that he called Medicine Hat. (Annette and I used to pretend we were on a ship as we walked across the rag carpet in the living room while it billowed upward as air blew under it through cracks in the floor.)

And then, one night after the usual period of listening, when Maw finally had heard the wagon creaking, closed the door, and put on the bitter coffee, we heard Old Nell jog into the yard and stop without the usual volley of sulphurous curses. For a while Maw noticed nothing wrong. Then she slowly faced the door, lips firmly drawn over those wabbly teeth.

Annette and I, all ready for our jump out of the warm bed onto the icy floor, watched her uncomprehendingly until we saw that Aunt Ellen had given over her unending vigil at the mirror and turned her head. Then we too knew that something was very strange.

Placing one foot before the other with obvious effort, Maw started toward the door. She reached it, opened it, closed it against her bare shank.

"Josiah!" we heard her scream as the foot disappeared.

With a sigh Aunt Ellen rose and waddled after her.

Maw—she was still strong as an ox and could swing an ax

like a man—backed through the door after a while, holding Paw under the armpits. Aunt Ellen carried his feet.

"The old fool!" Maw was whimpering. "I knew they'd get him. The old fool. I told him not to stay so late."

After the funeral—Annette and I boasted at school that the Brown murderers had done for Paw, although a stroke undoubtedly was responsible—the cabin never felt quite like home again. First a deluge of uncles, aunts, and cousins descended and insisted we sell the farm and move to town.

"Josiah would not have it so," Maw told them while Aunt Ellen nodded corroboration. So they compromised by having a hired hand in to do the plowing and heavier work.

At first nothing seemed vitally wrong except the absence of Paw's explosive laughter and endless stories, plus a growing dearth of popguns and slingshots. Then, one rainy day when I had been brooding over one of his dog-eared books—*Vanity Fair*, it was—I looked up, caught sight of Maw, her potato peeling forgotten, sitting tense beside the kitchen table, and knew what it was that had been bothering me. Maw was still listening . . . always listening now. Without her husband's quizzical common sense to balance her, she was slipping imperceptibly into the never-never land which had so often beckoned.

Not long after that discovery I awakened, chilled, as the Seth Thomas clock clinked midnight. The door was open a crack and I could glimpse, by the flickering embers, Maw's foot in its accustomed place.

"Maw," I called.

"Shhh! Listen! I think I hear a wagon."

"Maw," I screamed. "Maw!"

"What is it, honey?" She came inside, crossed the room and placed a horny hand on my forehead in one of her rare caresses.

"You'll catch cold," I mumbled, somehow ashamed.

"I was just listening to the katydids. They sound . . . fresh, like spring water," she lied.

"Don't listen any more."

"All right, honey, I'll go to bed. Don't worrit yourself."

But she did not keep her promise.

Several months later I came home from school ahead of

Annette, who was dusting erasers. I heard animated conversation inside. Thinking it was one of the neighbor women who dropped in occasionally to gossip, I rushed in, eager not to miss anything, then stopped, heart in mouth.

Aunt Ellen was out of the house on one of the chores she now condescended to put her white hands to and Maw was occupying the old rocker before the mirror. But what frightened me was the chatter in two distinct voices which still continued.

"Maw," I gulped. "Who . . . who you talking to?"

"Why, with Mrs. . . . Mrs. Jones here, of course," she laughed although her eyes refused to meet mine. "Mrs. Jones, this is my grandson I was telling you about. Take off your cap, son, and say . . ."

"But Maw," I whimpered. "There's no one there. It's just your reflection in the looking glass."

"Why . . . why so it is," she stammered, brushing a hand across her eyes. "I was just fooling." She jumped to her feet and started bustling about like her old indefatigable self. "Now run along and fill the wood box. Then wash your hands and help me peel these taters. I'm way late with supper, what with having to stop to talk . . . I mean I must have set down to rest and went to sleep."

Then began one of the strangest battles in the history of fairie—two children against a mirror, for, of course, I enlisted poor blue-eyed, flaxen-haired Annette. I tried to explain to Aunt Ellen too, but she merely smiled and patted me with one fat hand while her prominent eyes fluttered back to the mirror.

I wrote a scrawl to Uncle Bill, my favorite, and he left his hardware store the next weekend and came down from the city with a little, chin-whiskered doctor. Since psychiatry was unknown in those days, the physician looked at Maw's tongue, thumped her chest, asked her a few questions which she answered with sly humor, and pronounced her sound.

"I think it's you that's imagining things, boy," said Uncle Bill when he took me for a walk in the woods after one of Maw's wonderful chicken dinners. "We're all upset by Paw's going. Just don't worry about things."

"But Uncle Bill," I protested. "I heard what I saw."

"I know. I know." His lean face had a worried look, I noticed. "But you're a highstrung youngster . . . Write me often, though. And I'll come down every time I can. Say! Look!" I could almost hear him sigh with relief at an opportunity to change the subject. "There's a patch of violets already. Let's pick some and take them back to Maw and Ellen."

After that, of course, I had to carry on the fight with only Annette to help.

We tried everything: Went right home when we could have been playing with the other kids after school, got Maw to sing for us by the hour, read out loud to her, inveigled her into the spring woods to pick flowers and look for birds' nests. Oh, it was a brave battle put up by a twelve- and a ten-year-old against something alien and, somehow, far wiser than we.

At first Maw managed to banish her visions when she heard us come into the yard. Then we had to strive harder and harder to break the spell.

And one day we both became twins!

It happened when Annette and I came home that time when the teacher took sick. It was much earlier than usual and we caught Maw rocking happily before the mirror, gossiping.

"I'm so glad you brought your own children to visit me today, Mrs. Jones," Maw exclaimed the moment our reflections appeared in the glass behind her. "My Tommy and Annette don't have many playmates, we live so far from any neighbors. I'm sure they'll be much happier now."

"But Maw," Annette protested as we ducked out of range. "Those ain't real children. You're just looking at us in the looking glass."

But the damage had been done and for once in the few times of my life I saw grandmother grow really angry.

"I'll have none of your sass, Annette," she stormed, rising and straightening her back until it cracked. "Mrs. Jones, I don't know what has come over my younguns. Now, will you two say you're sorry, or must I whip you right before company?"

Shamefaced and shaken, we did apologize. And from

that hour Mrs. Jones and her brats became our constant companions.

At first we hated and resented them, then, childlike, accepted the inevitable and even made the best of it. Sometimes, so real did Maw make the delusion become, we almost believed in the shadows. On rainy weekends we found ourselves inventing games to play with them. Perhaps, in time, we might have gone to inhabit Maw's world of dreams.

But Maw's health was failing rapidly. We tried to ignore the fact as she did, though it soon became pitifully obvious that Paw's loss had broken the iron will which had sustained her through so many adversities. Aunt Ellen more and more ceded her place before the mirror as she helped Annette and me do the lighter chores and even some of the cooking. Bill Bailey came over every day now. (Maw never paraded her shadows when he was around, knowing that the farmer was not to be trusted with such dream stuff.) And the money which aunts and uncles contributed willingly or grudgingly, according to their natures, was more and more needed to fill the gaps in our finances.

"Tommy," Annette said to me one afternoon as we were plodding home from school along the muddy, dogwood-bordered road, "What happens to people when they die?"

"Aw, I don't know," I kicked a loose stone with my copper-toed shoe. "Maw says the angels come and get 'em."

"But the angels didn't come and get Dickie." (Dickie was a wry-necked, pin-feathered rooster that Paw had taught to come when he called, dig fishing worms for us and jump through a barrel hoop.) "I went to look at Dickie's grave the other day. A dog had dug him up. There were just feathers—and bones."

"Aw," I said. "Chickens don't have souls. But Maw says that when Mrs. Bailey died last year, she was there and she saw . . ."

"We're going to be awful lonesome," my sister sighed. "And you'll have to get up and make the fire every morning."

"What do you mean?" I challenged.

"Nothing. Let's run. I'm cold." And she was off in a flutter of long legs, gingham, and pale yellow braids.

After such a conversation I hardly dared enter the house. When I did go in, after fooling around in the barn as long as possible, I found Maw singing lustily about some man who had gone to the gallows with a white dove riding on his shoulder to prove him innocent of the murder of his sweetheart.

"Where's Mrs. Jones and her kids?" I asked, flabbergasted.

"They went home," said Maw. "I told them to. Can't spend all my time gassing with an ugly old woman like that when I've got housecleaning to do."

And until long after sunset she made the feathers fly from the old pillows, beat up the crackling, cornshuck mattresses, sprinkled and swept the floors and polished the meager kitchen utensils. Annette and I, feeling as if we had been released from jail, helped with a will. Aunt Ellen, reinstated in her rocking chair, frowned and sneezed by turns at the commotion and dust.

"There," said Maw at last as she hung the home-made broom behind the kitchen range and sank into a chair, looking suddenly more worn and old than I had ever seen her. "There. It's all swept and garnished for when the bridegroom cometh."

"The bridegroom?"

"I was just fooling again, son." She stared down at her big-veined hands. "Must be getting old, I guess. I just meant that I have a feeling your Uncle Bill will come tomorrow. And you know how fussy he is about everything being neat and clean." She rose with a sigh, half of weariness, half of content. "Come. You and Annette get undressed. I'll sing you to sleep like I used to when you were little."

> "You look just like my daughter, sir,
> Who from me ran away . . ."

Her cracked voice still had its hypnotic quality. I felt my eyelids drooping despite my certain knowledge that I should stay awake.

"Maw," I mumbled. "I wanna drink."

Her bare feet padded into the kitchen. I heard the rattle of tin cup against galvanized bucket. Then the spring water was fresh on my dry lips.

"Maw," I rambled on. "I don't wanna sleep. Tell me about when you were a little girl back in Virginia . . . and the big white house and the black people . . ."

"Not tonight, honey. You're all tuckered out," she crooned, stroking my forehead and picking up the thread of that interminable song:

> "I a-am not your daughter, sir,
> And neither do I know.
> I a-am from Highlanzer
> And they call me Jack Monroe . . ."

I woke with a start, those last lugubrious lines still ringing in my ears:

> "She dre-ew out her broadsword.
> She bid this world adieu.
> Saying 'Goodbye to Jack Highlanzer'
> And 'Goodbye to Jack Monroe.'"

Have you ever awakened in a strange place—a hotel room perhaps—tried to locate a familiar lamp, the dim outlines of your own bedchamber, the tick of a friendly clock? Or have you sought frantically for a door, with your hands sliding futilely along unbroken walls?

This was the same room in which I had gone to sleep. The fire was almost out. By my side Annette breathed deep and low. I could hear Aunt Ellen snoring not far away. Through the open door a full moon stretched its carpet almost to my bed. Yes, despite these comforting sights and sounds, everything about me seemed topsy turvy and wrong.

My heart leaped and my bare toes curled as I realized what it was. Our front door was in the south wall of the cabin. The moonshine was pouring in through a wide opening in the *north* wall . . . through the place where the mirror stood! And a cold, cold wind was pouring in with it.

"Maw," I whispered, sitting up.

Only the chorus of katydids answered.

But this was spring!

At the same moment I saw a bare foot and ankle etched in moonlight as it hooked around the age-darkened frame of the glass.

"Please, Maw." I still struggled between dream and waking. "You'll catch cold out there."

She came partially inside the "door," then, and smiled at me. And I noticed, with the lack of surprise which accompanies nightmares, that her teeth were white and firm in the moonglow.

"Shhh!" she admonished. "I think I hear a wagon."

"But Paw is . . ." I began, then stopped spellbound.

Far in the distance, across hills bathed in beauty, and above the fresh staccato mutter of katydids, I, too, heard the creak of wheels on a gravel road, the jingle of trace chains, and the rumble of a half-empty jolt-wagon bed.

I crouched, hardly breathing, until the wagon stopped at our gate. (We always kept it closed now.)

Rusty hinges squeaked, and the thump, thumpety, thump of the wagon resumed across the yard.

"It's Uncle Bill, ain't it, Maw?" I pleaded.

"Uncle Bill ain't due till tomorrow, honey." She shaded her eyes against the moonlight with one slim hand. "No. It's just Josiah."

"But it can't be," I sobbed. "He . . . the angels took him."

"Angels wouldn't touch him with a ten foot pole, thanks to dear, just God," she chuckled. "He'll have a whole raft of packages after all this while." She started forward. "I'll go help him pack them in."

"No, Maw! Don't leave. Wait for me," I screamed as I plunged out of bed.

I regained consciousness to find Aunt Ellen bathing my forehead with hot vinegar. Annette was whimpering somewhere. My face was badly cut . . . I still wear the scar . . . and the mirror was shattered in its frame.

"Maw!" I struggled to get up. "She . . ."

"I know," said Aunt Ellen in just the thread of a voice unused for years as her plump white hands pressed me back against the pillows. "I understand."

94

When Uncle Bill arrived next morning, there was a great to-do and the neighbors organized a search of the surrounding woods and the creek bottom. Of course they found nothing. I knew they wouldn't. Annette and Aunt Ellen knew they wouldn't. And I think Uncle Bill knew it too. The rest of them patted my head and said poor boy, he's been under an awful strain.

Several months later a woman's body was found in White River. People said it must be Maw and the aunts, uncles, nephews, nieces, and cousins had a funeral.

But Annette and I wouldn't go.

A lawyer and public relations man born in 1900, Wallace West was an early contributor to Amazing Stories, *the world's first science fiction magazine, with "The Last Man" (1929), in which a woman's movement has eliminated men. "Dust" (1967) tells of a future United States in which pollution drives the human race back into the sea. His stories—many were made into novels, such as* Lords of Atlantis *(1960)—have appeared in six volumes.*

Kate's family was running from an unspeakable horror, but only Kate realized why they weren't getting away.

EIGHT

Professor Kate
Margaret St. Clair

"The boy that directed us on this road, pa," Kate said, leaning forward to speak to the man in the front seat, "—do you think he was real?"

John Bender Senior turned and regarded her. "What you mean by that, Käter?" he asked sternly. He had to raise his voice to be heard over the rumble of the wagon wheels.

Kate's fingers moved nervously over the bosom of her shirtwaist. "Why that . . . that he might be one of them we left in the orchard, back on the farm. This road ain't like a road that goes anywhere."

Her father's lean face grew dark with anger. "Stop dot talk, Käter. Stop your mouth."

"*Ja*, stop it, daughter," Mrs. Bender said. Her blue eyes were hard in her large white face. "Is nonsense, unsinn. How could it be one of dem? Didn't we bind dem to stay before we left?"

Kate sighed and sank back in her seat. Her brother John, who was sitting beside her (he was only her half-brother, she was wont to say with a touch of defiance), slipped his arm around her waist. "You're tired, Kate," he said. "It ain't them dead ones I'm afraid of. I'm afraid of a posse coming after us."

"Oh, do you think there'll be one?" Kate answered vaguely. Once more her hands were moving on her dress.

"Dead sure. Colonel York suspicioned us about his brother. They traced him as far as our farm."

"He didn't come back for the seance, though," Kate replied.

"No. But we knew he'd be back later for sure, with more men. Things was getting hot. That's why we left."

Kate laughed suddenly, a bold, ringing laugh. "Why we left! Didn't we look out the bedroom window that morning and see the ground heaving below in the orchard? Didn't you hear her little voice crying 'Mama! Mama!' the way she did when we buried her? Why we left!"

"I didn't hear or see nothing, Kate. I only said that to . . . to agree with you."

Once more Kate laughed. "You didn't hear anything? Why, you turned as white as a sheet!"

"As a ghost," her brother corrected after a moment had passed. "Make it a ghost, while you're doing it."

They jounced on. Bender, hunched over the reins, clucked now and then at the team. Once John said out of a long silence, "This here ain't much of a road, for a fact." Kate looked at him sideways without saying anything.

The sun began to sink. The air, which had been warm with spring earlier in the day, grew colder. A light breeze ruffled the long grass of the prairie. Kate, shivering, let John embrace her without resistance.

Old man Bender turned round to face them. "Hope we find dose houses soon," he said uneasily. "That boy said we'd get to them before night."

Kate raised her head from John's shoulder and looked him full in the eyes. His gaze wavered. He coughed and turned back to the team.

They stopped at last. "Is too dark to drive more," old man Bender said, his voice loud in the sudden silence. "Ve got to sleep here." He looked around the vacant flatness of the prairie, frowning, and then began to unharness the team.

John jumped from the wagon and then turned to help Kate. She was stiff from the long sitting; she almost fell into his arms. Mrs. Bender, meantime, was getting sacks and crocks of provisions out from under the front seat.

"Have an apple, son," she said, holding one out to the young man.

"No. I can't say as I care for the fruit from them trees."

Mrs. Bender began to munch the apple herself. Kate had

taken advantage of the distraction to withdraw from John's embrace and wander off. He looked after her, his forehead wrinkled. Then he began to help his mother with the preparations for the evening meal.

Suddenly Kate screamed. It was a high sound, not very loud. John dropped the bread he was holding and ran toward her.

He found her sitting on her heels, her black bombazine skirt drawn tightly around her haunches. She was holding a long thigh bone in one hand.

"It scared me when I first saw it," she said, looking up at him brightly. "The skull, I mean. And look, over there in the grass, there's another one."

John followed her gesture. He kicked the grass apart. After a short time he found the second skeleton, gleaming whitely even in the dim light. He stooped over, hunting, and came up at last with something in his hand.

"It was an Indian," he announced to Kate. "This here's what killed him. An arrow." He showed it to her.

She seemed to lose interest. "Oh, an Indian. Must of been a long time ago." She cocked her head and listened intently. "John, I hear voices. Not like them on the farm, though. Maybe it's the Indians. Listen!" She held up a hand, warning him.

There was the rustle of the grass, the plaintive note of a mourning dove. "I don't hear nothing," he said. He pulled at his mustache.

"You woudn't 'fess up to it if you did," she said. She giggled. "I want to have a seance, John. 'Member how they called me Professor Kate in the Parsons paper that time I lectured there on spiritualism?" She rose to her feet and faced him. "Maybe a seance would quiet the voices. On the farm it used to. Professor Kate wants to have a seance."

He slapped her. His hand left a red mark on her face, but she made no sign of having felt it. "Stop it, Kate. You want to drive all of us crazy? Why stir them up? And anyhow, it ain't nothing. We'll sleep in the wagon tonight and tomorrow start early. It's only two Indians. Ain't you used to dead people?"

He took her by the hand and led her back to the wagon. Sighing, she stumbled after him. "Do you think we'll get to

Vinita tomorrow, John?" she asked. "I'm so tired of riding. Father said we could leave the wagon and take the train once we got to the Indian Territory."

"Sure thing, you bet," he answered, without looking at her. "Get up early, ride all day. It ain't far."

John woke early, while it was still dark. He found water and washed in a cupful of it. After a moment he heard Kate getting down from the wagon. She came up to him, yawning and shivering.

He poured water for her and she scrubbed her face with a handkerchief. She straightened her hair with her hands. "How did you sleep, John?" she asked, putting her head on one side. "Did you rest well?"

"Naw. Why ask? I had dreams."

"Like my dreams, I guess. This ain't a good place. Listen, paw and maw are getting up."

They breakfasted on slabs of bread and cold pork. Old man Bender harnessed up the team and turned the wagon around. "We make a fine quick start," he said. "De stars ain't set yet. Before sun-up, we be back on the right road."

The pursuers rose nearly as early as the Benders did. The Benders were moved by fear, the posse by hate. As Captain Sanders swung into the saddle, he said to the lieutenant, "Today or tomorrow, sure. We're getting close."

The lieutenant (he, like Sanders, had gained his rank in the Grand Army of the Republic less than ten years before) said flatly, "We're not going to take them back to the county for trial."

"No. You don't try rattlers. We found eleven bodies in the orchard. But what I remember most is the body of the little girl. She must have been still alive when they buried her." The sun rose. The day wore on. At noon the Benders stopped at a farmhouse for water and learned that they were on the right road. They might be able to make Vinita by dark. Kate, sighing with relief, did not resist when John drew her down under the wagon seat.

Afterward they chatted idly over plans, what they should do with the money they had taken from the travelers who had stopped at the Bender farmhouse. John wanted to start a restaurant in Denison, Kate wanted to keep on with the seances and the lecturing. She spoke of the good luck she'd had curing deafness and epileptic fits. Or the four of them might buy another farm. Why not? They had plenty of rhino, John said.

As the sun began to wester, Kate dozed. She leaned against John, her body swaying to the steady jogging. Once she said petulantly, "Vinita sure is a long way off."

At sundown the posse reached a crossroads. Sanders dismounted to check the wagon tracks. As he grasped the pommel again he was frowning. "They've turned," he told the men with him, gesturing to the right. "They're headed back."

"Why?" asked the lieutenant after a moment.

Sanders shrugged. "The devil knows. May be trying to throw us off the track."

It was quite dark when the wagon stopped, Vinita still unreached. Kate was drunk with sleepiness. John roused her and helped her out.

"Vinita?" she asked as she reached the ground.

"No, Kate. Not yet. First thing tomorrow, I guess."

She stood looking around her. The moon had not risen; it was difficult to see anything. Suddenly she gathered up her skirts and ran like a wild thing. After a moment they heard her screaming, "John! John! We've come back. This is the same place!"

When he got up to her she pointed at the skeleton. She picked up the arrow and handed it to him. "They've brought us back to the same place."

He let the point fall from his fingers. "What do you mean? Who has?"

"The Indians. They wouldn't let us get away. They brought us back. The dead—don't you see, John?—the dead stick together."

He stared at her in the darkness. Then he grasped her by the shoulder and began to pull her after him with desperate energy. "Hurry! Hurry! The wagon! We've got to get away!"

But as they neared the wagon they heard a thunder and a plunging, and then old man Bender's voice crying despairingly, "Whoa! Whoa! Damn you, come back!"

"The team's run off," Kate said simply. "I knew they wouldn't let us get away."

He began to wrench at the wagon sides, tearing off planking. "We'll make a fire, a big fire. They can't get past it. And paw will get out the guns."

"That's right," Kate said, cheering. "And we'll stay awake, all of us, Maybe if. . . ."

There were noises on the other side of the wagon as the night got older. Once old man Bender said, "What's dot whooping!" and Kate laughed.

The fire died down and was replenished with the wagon seats. Kate yawned, and then John and the others. He said, "We've got to stay awake."

About two in the morning Professor Kate realized abruptly that the others were sleeping. She ran from one to the other, shaking them, screaming their names. They wouldn't wake.

Morning came. John said, "Guess we must have gone to sleep, h'um, Kate?"

"I guess so. I remember dreaming. I'm awful tired."

John Bender yawned. "Well, anyway, we're all right. We was silly to worry. And look, the team's come back."

Old man Bender was silently harnessing the horses. When he was done, they climbed in the wagon. The front seat was still intact, but John and his sister had to sit on the floor. After they had driven for about a mile, Kate said, "Where are we going, paw?"

"To—I can't call the name to mind, daughter."

"Bin—Binecia," she answered, stumbling over the syllables. "I wish we'd hurry up and get there."

"Stop it, Kate," John said. "We will."

In the afternoon Kate said, "I wish we'd pass some houses." Later, when it was almost sunset, she turned to her brother. "Do you know what's going to happen, John?" she asked.

"What?" he replied. It was the first word he had spoken to her since early morning.

"It's going to get dark. And then we'll stop and we'll be back by the Indians. Back by the ashes of our fire. Back where we spent last night." She began to cry.

"No. You're crazy. We must be almost to Venita."

"Venita? We'll never get there. We'll just keep driving, driving, driving. Something's gone wrong with time."

"Be quiet, damn you. I hear horses, voices." He laid his hand over her mouth.

Old Man Bender had stopped the wagon. "Something ahead," he said softly. "You two go look."

They stole forward, tiptoeing. "I can't see good," Kate whispered.

"Hush. It's men with horses. They're bending over something. But I can't see what they're doing. There's a mist."

Kate had turned away. "Let's go back to the wagon," she whispered.

"Why? I want to know what they're doing."

"Oh, I know already."

"Then tell me."

"You know without telling. What they're bending over—"

"Is us. Is our bodies. No! No! I won't have it!"

She was wringing her hands and wailing. "Oh, but it is! Last night—last night the Indians didn't let us get away," said Professor Kate.

Born in Kansas in 1911, Margaret St. Clair is known for her stories of distant futures both adventurous and beautiful. The daughter of an attorney, she was educated at the University of California and worked as a horticulturalist from 1938 to 1941. Nearly all her work is in the field of fantasy, including Vulcan's Dolls *(1952) and* The Shadow People *(1976). She also writes under the pen name Idris Seabright.*

A ghost can be a warning of danger—or a prophecy of good fortune.

NINE

The Skeleton on Round Island

Mary Hartwell Catherwood

On the 15th day of March, 1897, Ignace Pelott died at Mackinac Island, aged ninety-three years.

The old quarter-breed, son of a half-breed Chippewa mother and French father, took with him into silence much wilderness lore of the Northwest. He was full of stories when warmed to recital, though at the beginning of a talk his gentle eyes dwelt on the listener with anxiety, and he tapped his forehead—"So many things gone from there!" His habit of saying "Oh God, yes," or "Oh God, no," was not in the least irreverent, but simply his mild way of using island English.

While water lapped the beach before his door and the sun smote sparkles on the strait, he told about this adventure across the ice, and his hearer has taken but few liberties with the recital.

I am to carry Mamselle Rosalin of Green Bay from Mackinac to Cheboygan that time, and it is the end of March, and the wind have turn from east to west in the morning. A man will go out with the wind in the east, to haul wood from Boblo, or cut a hole to fish, and by night he cannot get home—ice, it is rotten; it goes to pieces quick when the March wind turns.

I am not afraid for me—long, tall fellow then; eye that can see to Point aux Pins; I can lift more than any other man that goes in the boats to Green Bay or the Soo; can swim, run on snowshoes, go without eating two, three days, and draw my belt in. Sometimes the ice floes carry me miles, for they all go east down the lakes when they start, and I have landed the other side of Drummond. But when you have a woman with you—Oh God, yes, that is different.

The way of it is this: I have brought the mail from St. Ignace with my traino—you know the train-au-galise—the birch sledge with dogs. It is flat, and turn up at the front like a toboggan. And I have take the traino because it is not safe for a horse; the wind is in the west, and the strait bends and looks too sleek. Ice a couple of inches thick will bear up a man and dogs. But this old ice a foot thick, it is turning rotten. I have come from St. Ignace early in the afternoon, and the people crowd about to get their letters, and there is Mamselle Rosalin crying to go to Cheboygan, because her lady has arrive there sick, and has sent the letter a week ago. Her friends say:

"It is too late to go today, and the strait is dangerous."

She say: "I make a bundle and walk. I must go when my lady is sick and her husband the lieutenant is away, and she has need of me."

Mamselle's friends talk and she cry. She runs and makes a little bundle in the house and comes out ready to walk to Cheboygan. There is nobody can prevent her. Some island people are descend from noblesse of France. But none of them have travel like Mamselle Rosalin with the officer's wife to Indiana, to Chicago, to Detroit. She is like me, French.* The girls use to turn their heads to see me walk in to mass; but I never look grand as Mamselle Rosalin when she step out to that ice.

I have not a bit of sense; I forget maman and my brothers and sisters that depend on me. I run to Mamselle Rosalin, take off my cap, and bow from my head to my heel, like you do in the dance. I will take her to Cheboygan with my traino—Oh God, yes! And I laugh at the wet track the sledge make, and pat my dogs and tell them they are not tired. I wrap her up in the fur, and she thank me and tremble, and look me through with her big black eyes so that I am ready to go down in the strait.

The people on the shore hurrah, though some of them cry out to warn us.

*The old fellow would not own the Chippewa.

"The ice is cracked from Mission Point to the hook of Round Island, Ignace Pelott!"

"I know that," I say. "Good-day, messieurs!"

The crack from Mission Point—under what you call Robinson's Folly—to the hook of Round Island always comes first in a breaking up; and I hold my breath in my teeth as I skurry the dogs across it. The ice grinds, the water follows the sledge. But the sun is so far down in the southwest, I think "The wind will grow colder. The real thaw will not come before tomorrow."

I am to steer betwixt the east side of Round Island and Boblo. When we come into the shadow of Boblo we are chill with damp, far worse than the clear sharp air that blows from Canada. I lope beside the traino, and not take my eyes off the course to Cheboygan, except that I see the islands look blue, and darkness stretching before its time. The sweat drop off my face, yet I feel that wind through my wool clothes, and am glad of the shelter between Boblo and Round Island, for the strait outside will be the worst.

There is an Indian burying ground on open land above the beach on that side of Round Island. I look up when the thick woods are pass, for the sunset ought to show there. But what I see is a skeleton like it is sliding down hill from the graveyard to the beach. It does not move. The earth is wash from it, and it hangs staring at me.

I cannot tell how that make me feel! I laugh, for it is funny; but I am ashame, like my father is expose and Mamselle Rosalin can see him. If I do not cover him again I am disgrace. I think I will wait till some other day when I can get back from Cheboygan; for what will she say if I stop the traino when we have such a long journey, and it is so near night, and the strait almost ready to move? So I crack the whip, but something pull, pull! I cannot go on! I say to myself, "The ground is froze; how can I cover up that skeleton without any shovel, or even a hatchet to break the earth?"

But something pull, pull, so I am oblige to stop, and the dogs turn in without one word and drag the sledge up the beach of Round Island.

"What is the matter?" says Mamselle Rosalin. She is out of the sledge as soon as it stops.

I not know what to answer, but tell her I have to cut a stick

105

to mend my whip handle. I think I will cut a stick and rake some earth over the skeleton to cover it, and come another day with a shovel and dig a new grave. The dogs lie down and pant, and she looks through me with her big eyes like she beg me to hurry.

But there is no danger she will see the skeleton. We both look back to Mackinac. The island have its hump up against the north, and the village in its lap around the bay, and the Mission eastward near the cliff; but all seem to be moving! We run along the beach of Round Island, and then we see the channel between that and Boblo is moving too, and the ice is like wet loaf-sugar, grinding as it floats.

We hear some roars away off, like cannon when the Americans come to the island. My head swims. I cross myself and know why something pull, pull, to make me bring the traino to the beach, and I am oblige to that skeleton who slide down hill to warn me.

When we have seen Mackinac, we walk to the other side and look south and southeast towards Cheboygan. All is the same. The ice is moving out of the strait.

"We are strand on this island!" says Mamselle Rosalin. "Oh, what shall we do?"

I tell her it is better to be prisoners on Round Island than on a cake of ice in the strait, for I have tried the cake of ice and know.

"We will camp and build a fire in the cove opposite Mackinac," I say. "Maman and the children will see the light and feel sure we are safe."

"I have done wrong," says she. "If you lose your life on this journey, it is my fault."

Oh God, no! I tell her. She is not to blame for anything, and there is no danger. I have float many a time when the strait breaks up, and not save my hide so dry as it is now. We only have to stay on Round Island till we can get off.

"And how long will that be?" she ask.

I shrug my shoulders. There is no telling. Sometimes the strait clears very soon, sometimes not. Maybe two, three days.

Rosalin sit down on a stone.

I tell her we can make camp, and show signals to Mackinac, and when the ice permit, a boat will be sent.

She is crying, and I say her lady will be well. No use to go to Cheboygan anyhow, for it is a week since her lady sent for her. But she cry on, and I think she wish I leave her alone, so I say I will get wood. And I unharness the dogs, and run along the beach to cover that skeleton before dark. I look and cannot find him at all. Then I go up to the grave-yard and look down. There is no skeleton anywhere. I have seen his skull and his ribs and his arms and legs, all sliding down hill. But he is gone!

The dusk close in upon the islands, and I not know what to think—cross myself, two, three times; and wish we had land on Boblo instead of Round Island, though there are wild beasts on both.

But there is no time to be scare at skeletons that slide down and disappear, for Mamselle Rosalin must have her camp and her place to sleep. Every man use to the bateaux have always his tinderbox, his knife, his tobacco, but I have more than that; I have leave Mackinac so quick I forget to take out the storekeeper's bacon that line the bottom of the sledge, and Mamselle Rosalin sit on it in the furs! We have plenty meat, and I sing like a voyageur while I build the fire. Drift, so dry in summer you can light it with a coal from your pipe, lay on the beach, but is now winter-soaked, and I make a fireplace of logs, and cut pine branches to help it.

It is all thick woods on Round Island, so close it tear you to pieces if you try to break through; only four-footed things can crawl there. When the fire is blazing up I take my knife and cut a tunnel like a little room, and pile plenty evergreen branches. This is to shelter Mamselle Rosalin, for the night is so raw she shiver. Our tent is the sky, darkness, and clouds. But I am happy. I unload the sledge. The bacon is wet. On long sticks the slices sizzle and sing while I toast them, and the dogs come close and blink by the fire, and lick their chops. Rosalin laugh and I laugh, for it smell like a good kitchen; and we sit and eat nothing but toasted meat—better than lye corn and tallow that you have when you go out with the boats. Then I feed the dogs, and she walk with me to the water edge, and we drink with our hands.

It is my house, when we sit on the fur by the fire. I am so light I want my fiddle. I wish it last like a dream that Mamselle Rosalin and me keep house together on Round Island.

You not want to go to heaven when the one you think about all the time stays close by you.

But pretty soon I want to go to heaven quick. I think I jump in the lake if maman and the children had anybody but me. When I light my pipe she smile. Then her great big eyes look off towards Mackinac, and I turn and see the little far-away lights.

"They know we are on Round Island together," I say to cheer her, and she move to the edge of the fur. Then she say "Goodnight," and get up and go to her tunnel-house in the bushes, and I jump up too, and spread the fur there for her. And I not get back to the fire before she make a door of all the branches I have cut, and is hid like a squirrel. I feel I dance for joy because she is in my camp for me to guard. But what is that? It is a woman that cry out loud by herself! I understand now why she sit down so hopeless when we first land. I have not know much about women, but I understand how she feel. It is not her lady, or the dark, or the ice break up, or the cold. It is not Ignace Pelott. It is the name of being prison on Round Island with a man till the ice is out of the straits. She is so shame she want to die. I think I will kill myself. If Mamselle Rosalin cry out loud once more, I plunge in the lake—and then what become of maman and the children?

She is quieter; and I sit down and cannot smoke, and the dogs pity me. Old Sauvage lay his nose on my knee. I do not say a word to him, but I pat him, and we talk with our eyes, and the bright campfire shows each what the other is say.

"Old Sauvage," I tell him, "I am not good man like the priest. I have been out with the boats, and in Indian camps, and I not had in my life a chance to marry, because there are maman and the children. But you know, old Sauvage, how I have feel about Mamselle Rosalin, it is three years."

Old Sauvage hit his tail on the ground and answer he know.

"I have love her like a dog that not dare to lick her hand. And now she hate me because I am shut on Round Island with her while the ice goes out. I not good man, but it pretty tough to stand that."

Old Sauvage hit his tail on the ground and say, "That so."

I hear the water on the gravel like it sound when we find a place to drink; then it is plenty company, but now it is lonesome. The water say to people on Mackinac, "Rosalin and Ignace Pelott, they are on Round Island." What make you proud, maybe, when you turn it and look at it the other way, make you sick. But I cannot walk the broken ice, and if I could, she would be lef alone with the dogs. I think I will build another camp.

But soon there is a shaking in the bushes, and Sauvage and his sledgemates bristle and stand up and show their teeth. Out comes Mamselle Rosalin with a scream to the other side of the fire.

I have nothing except my knife, and I take a chunk of burning wood and go into her house. Maybe I see some green eyes. I have handle vildcat skin too much not to know that smell in the dark.

I take all the branches from Rosalin's house and pile them by the fire, and spread the fur robe on them. And I pull out red coals and put more logs on before I sit down away off between her and the spot where she hear that noise. If the graveyard was over us, I would expect to see that skeleton once more.

"What was it?" she whisper.

I tell her maybe a stray wolf.

"Wolves not eat people, mamselle, unless they hunt in a pack; and they run from fire. You know what M'sieu' Cable tell about wolves that chase him on the ice when he skate to Cheboygan? He come to great wide crack in ice, he so scare he jump it and skate right on! Then he look back, and see the wolves go in, head down, every wolf caught and drown in the crack. It is two days before he come home, and the east wind have blow to freeze that crack over—and there are all the wolf tails, stick up, froze stiff in a row! He bring them home with him—but los them on the way, though he show the knife that cut them off!"

"I have hear that," says Rosalin. "I think he lie."

"He say he take his oat on a book," I tell her, but we both laugh, and she is curl down so close to the fire her cheeks turn rosy. For a campfire will heat the air all around until the world is like a big dark room; and we are shelter from the wind. I am glad she is begin to enjoy herself. And all the time I have a hand on my knife, and the cold chills down my back where that hungry vildcat will set his claws if he jump on me; and I cannot turn around to face him because Rosalin thinks it is nothing but a cowardly wolf that sneak away. Old Sauvage is uneasy and come to me, his fangs all expose, but I drive him back and listen to the bushes behind me.

"Sing, M'sieu' Pelott," says Rosalin.

Oh God, yes! it is easy to sing with a vildcat watch you on one side and a woman on the other!

"But I not know anything except boat songs."

"Sing boat songs."

So I sing like a bateau full of voyageurs, and the dark echo, and that vildcat must be astonish. When you not care what become of you, and your head is light and your heart like a stone on the beach, you not mind vildcats, but sing and laugh.

I cast my eye behin sometimes, and feel my knife. It make me smile to think what kind of creature come to my house in the wilderness, and I say to myself: "Hear my cat purr! This is the only time I will ever have a home of my own, and the only time the woman I want sit beside my fire."

Then I ask Rosalin to sing to me, and she sing "Malbrouck," like her father learn it in Kebec. She watch me, and I know her eyes have more danger for me than the vildcat's. It ought to tear me to pieces if I forget maman and the children. It ought to be scare out the bushes to jump on a poor fool like me. But I not stop entertain it—Oh God, no! I say things that I never intend to say, like they are pull out of my mouth. When your heart has ache, sometimes it break up quick like the ice.

"There is Paul Pepin," I tell her. "He is a happy man; he not trouble himself with anybody at all. His father die; he let his mother take care of herself. He marry a wife, and get tired of her and turn her off with two children. The priest not able to scare him; he smoke and take his dram and enjoy life. If I was Paul Pepin I would not be torment."

"But you are not torment," says Rosalin. "Everybody speak well of you."

"Oh God, yes," I tell her; "But a man not live on the

breath of his neighbors. I am thirty years old, and I have take care of my mother and brothers and sisters since I am fifteen. I not made so I can leave them, like Paul Pepin. He marry when he please. I not able to marry at all. It is not far I can go from the island. I cannot get rich. My work must be always the same."

"But why you want to marry?" says Rosalin, as if that surprise her. And I tell her it is because I have seen Rosalin of Green Bay; and she laugh. Then I think it is time for the vildcat to jump. I am thirty years old, and have nothing but what I can make with the boats or my traino; the children are not grown; my mother depend on me; and I have propose to a woman, and she laugh at me!

But I not see, while we sing and talk, that the fire is burn lower, and old Sauvage has crept around the camp into the bushes.

That end all my courtship. I not use to it, and not have any business to court, anyhow. I drop my head on my breast, and it is like when I am little and the measle go in. Paul Pepin he take a woman by the chin and smack her on the lips. The women not laugh at him, he is so rough. I am as strong as he is, but I am afraid to hurt; I am oblige to take care of what need me. And I am tie to things I love—even the island—so that I cannot get away.

"I not want to marry," says Rosalin, and I see her shake her head at me. "I not think about it at all."

"Mamselle," I say to her, "you have not any inducement like I have, that torment you three years."

"How you know that?" she ask me. And then her face change from laughter, and she spring up from the blanket couch, and I think the camp go around and around me—all fur and eyes and claws and teeth—and I not know what I am doing, for the dogs are all over me—yell—yell—yell; and then I am stop stabbing, because the vildcat has let go of Sauvage, and Sauvage has let go of the vildcat, and I am looking at them and know they are both dead, and I cannot help him any more.

You are confuse by such things where there is noise, and howling creatures sit up and put their noses in the air, like they call their mate back out of the dark. I am sick for my old dog. Then I am proud he has kill it, and wipe my knife on its fur, but feel ashame that I have not check him driving it into camp. And then Rosalin throw her arms around my neck and kiss me.

It is many years I have tell Rosalin she did that. But a woman will deny what she know to be the trut. I have tell her the courtship had end, and she begin it again herself, and keep it up till the boats take us off Round Island. The ice not run out so quick any more now like it did then. My wife say it is a long time we waited, but when I look back it seem the shortest time I ever live—only two days.

Oh God, yes, it is three years before I marry the woman that not want to marry at all; then my brothers and sisters can take care of themselves, and she help me take care of maman.

It is when my boy Gabriel come home from the war to die that I see the skeleton on Round Island again. I am again sure it is wash out, and I go ashore to bury it, and it disappear. Nobody but me see it. Then before Rosalin die I am out on the ice-boat, and it give me warning. I know what it mean; but you cannot always escape misfortune. I cross myself when I see it; but I find good luck that first time I land; and maybe I find good luck every time, after I have land.

An early frontier novelist, Mary Hartwell Catherwood was born in Ohio in 1847 and educated at Female College in Granville, Ohio. She was a teacher in Illinois and New York before beginning her career as a writer. Her work is remembered because of its historical authenticity, which came from her interviews with French and English settlers of the colonial period. Her books included such colorfully titled novels as Craque-ó-Doom *(1881) and* The Days of Jeanne D'Arc *(1898). She died in 1902.*

Ed thought these Ozark hillbillies would be thrilled to have their farm be a film location and be pleased with the money. No one had told him how deep the old ways run.

TEN

One for the Crow
Mary Barrett

Ed chose the fast route, the new highway which was engineered to bypass Ozark and go directly into the hills. Had he taken the old road south from Springfield, he probably would have lived a longer and a happier life. He certainly would have enjoyed a more pleasant trip along a more scenic route than the one he elected.

About twenty miles out of town, on the old road, he would have come upon a scene with the misty charm of a French impressionist painting: from the hilltop, grapevines march down the slope in orderly rows; in the valley below, as if protected by the hills from change and blight, lies the clean, sleepy town of Ozark, Missouri.

From his vantage point on top of the hill, Ed would have seen the water tower rising white against the green hills beyond, and the iron-gray smokestack of the cheese factory. Had he then continued downhill, he soon would have come to an official sign: *Ozark, Pop. 800* and, on a nearby tree, a less formal but more enthusiastic announcement: *Welcome to Ozark, a good live town.*

Clattering across the Finley River bridge and passing an abandoned mill with its rusty wheel forever still, he would have arrived at the Ozark square where the red brick courthouse stands in the center.

There are always a few men sitting on shaded benches in front of the courthouse, chewing tobacco and occasionally exchanging a few words about the weather, the crops, chicken feed, pesticides. Any of these local experts could have warned Ed about the risks he was taking, but he might not have listened anyway, or heard what was said to him. He was that kind of guy. Besides, a warning of sudden death in such a setting would be difficult for anyone to believe, for the scene is deceiving. All appears to be peace and rural contentment; but primitive passions and strong hatreds are bred in the hills, and old ideas and old grudges die hard. Just five minutes' conversation with one of the fellows in front of the courthouse would have given him a warning, but to gain a little time, he missed his chance.

The powerful engine of his big rented car purred quietly under the hood as Ed looked out the window with distaste at the scrubby oaks and hickory trees struggling for life in the thin topsoil. He felt a city man's scorn for wasted space and a successful man's scorn for what he saw as failure.

"In this Godforsaken place," he said to himself, "the hillbillies will be glad for the chance at a little cash."

Ed had a reputation in Hollywood for always being on top of any job, and he was certainly going to be on top of this one with no trouble; *no trouble at all,* he thought.

He wheeled the car off the highway onto a likely-looking farm-to-market road. It was pitted from the winter freeze, and Ed was forced to slow down. A thin film of dust blanketed the weeds and wild strawberries growing on each side of the narrow road, but no matter. The air conditioned car was sealed against intrusion by the environment.

Ahead appeared the first sign of habitation—a dilapidated farmhouse with a much-patched roof. One window was covered with cardboard, like a patch over a missing eye. A thin streak of smoke drifted from the chimney. A white hen clucked dispiritedly in the front yard.

Ed turned the car off the road onto dry grass, stopped and stepped out, slamming the car door closed behind him. He looked around speculatively.

It was a clear, cloudless spring day, and after the steady hum of the car, the silence was startling. Far away, a meadowlark sang its pure notes.

Ed walked toward the house. "Hello," he called. "Anyone here? Anyone home?" There was no answer.

He rounded the corner of the house. There, bent low over the red earth, was a tall, bony man in faded blue overalls. His skin, tanned to leather, was bare to the sun over the bib of the overalls.

"What's the matter with you?" Ed demanded. "Didn't you hear me?"

The man didn't look up. He said shortly, but with no animus, "I heard you. Long ways off."

Ed came closer. "What are you planting there?"

The man at last stood up. He looked Ed in the eye and said, "Corn," the monosyllable discouraging conversation.

Ed tried to remember what he knew about corn. It was very little. He had seen some pictures, though, and they didn't look like this.

"I thought you planted corn in furrows," he said.

"Some do. Where there's not much rain. Plenty of rain here. Plant corn in hills. Four seeds to a hill."

"Why four?"

The man explained, matter-of-factly, "One for the cutworm, one for the crow, one for the dry rot, and one to grow."

"Oh," Ed said, unenlightened. "When will it come up?"

"Tassels out about July," the man answered. Then, clearly dubious, he asked, "You thinking to grow corn hereabouts?"

"Oh, no," Ed said hastily. "I'm just looking for local color."

The man looked around at the familiar greens and browns of his landscape, and then inquisitively back at Ed.

"The way people talk," Ed explained, "their customs, their folkways. Those things."

The farmer frowned; whether disapproving or puzzled, it was impossible to tell. "Reckon you better come inside, then, and talk to Ma. She knows all about folks' ways." Moving to the back door, he added, "I'm Luke Anderson. This is our place, Ma's and mine, since we lost our son."

Ed followed him through a squeaking screen door into the kitchen. It was cool and dark after the bright sun outside.

A woman with gray hair stood at a stained sink, shelling beans.

Luke said, without preamble, "This fellow wants to know about our ways."

The woman turned to them, her face expressionless. She wiped her hands on her cotton apron, slowly and deliberately. She inspected the visitor as she might have scrutinized a mule offered for sale. Like her husband, the woman was browned by the sun; and like him, she was economically lean, without an ounce of unnecessary flesh.

She pulled a straight wooden chair up to the kitchen table and put her hands on the oilcloth, palms down, as if preparing for a seance. Luke and Ed sat down too.

"Why do you want to know our ways?" she asked with guarded curiosity.

"We want to make a movie here in the hills," Ed said. "The setting has to look authentic. Real, you know." He was uncertain how much these ignorant people could understand. "We want to cast local people, in minor roles, of course. And we'll pay."

The woman was clearly not impressed. She looked at him sharply from startlingly light blue eyes. "They done made a movie once, nearby."

"I know," Ed said. It had been a disaster. Every possible thing had gone wrong—the entire cast sick, equipment breaking down and even disappearing, and the director actually dropping out of sight, never to be seen again. That had caused quite a stir in the press. It was, in fact, the only thing which saved the movie from being a box-office disaster. No one particularly mourned the loss of the director. He hadn't turned out any good work in years.

The woman said, "Those other movie folk built cabins and pretend barns from stuff they brought with them. Those things are still there. Maybe you could use them for your movie and not mess up a new part of the hills?"

Ed smiled indulgently. *These people are so naive.* "I'm afraid that won't do. That old set is much too artificial. We need virgin territory. Of course, we'll improve on it some. But the old site is ruined for our purposes."

The woman spoke quietly, "That's how it seems to us, too—spoilt. Spoilt for living. Spoilt for farming. Spoilt for looking at. You think to do that here, on this side of the hill? Spoil it?"

116

"Not at all," Ed said impatiently. *Don't these hicks understand anything?* "We'll bring new life to this place. Lots of tourists will come just to watch us shooting. There'll be new business, new money pouring in, lots of action."

A glance passed between husband and wife which Ed could not interpret.

The woman put both hands on the table and pushed herself to her feet. "Since you're here, you best stay on for dinner," she said.

The meal was quickly served. She put the plates on the oilcloth. Ed looked dubiously at the food. There were ham hocks, beans, and hot corn bread, with fresh warm milk. Ed managed to choke down enough not to offend. He thought wistfully of a cold martini and rare roast beef.

"I'll red up the dishes," the woman said. "You men go along to the front porch. We can set in the shade and talk awhile."

Ed followed Luke through the livingroom. The shades were down, and the room had the dimly-lit appearance of being underwater. The faded carpet was worn through to the floor in places. A sofa, tilting on three legs, was covered with an afghan. Ed thought with satisfaction, *We can use this. It certainly looks authentic.*

They stepped out onto the porch. The floorboards were warped, and for a moment the wavy effect made Ed dizzy. They sat down in straight wooden chairs, identical to those in the kitchen. The woman soon joined them.

They looked through the haze of the warm afternoon across the yard to a hill beyond. A wasp buzzed busily at his nest in a corner under the roof.

"That hill over there," Ed said. "We could use that in several scenes. It looks easy to climb."

The woman glanced at him. Her voice was soft but clear. "Some say that hill should be let be. Most folks won't go there for any reason."

"Oh?" Ed asked, intrigued.

"It's the Bald Knob," Luke said, as if that explained everything.

"Bald Knob?" Ed asked.

The woman explained, "A bald knob is nothing but a hill with no trees growing on top. This one's different, though."

"It's where the Bald Knobbers met," Luke said.

The woman leaned her head against the back of her chair and gazed off into the distance. "Was a time," she said, "when roads were bad and town too far away. We hadn't no pertection of the law. No one to see that cows wasn't stolen nor strangers didn't come, causing trouble." She paused and looked at Ed. If he found any significance for himself in the statement, however, he gave no indication.

She went on: "Some of the men hereabouts got together to make themselves the law officers. They had their meetings atop that bald knob there. Sometimes at night a person could see their bonfire. It was a good sight. Made a body feel safe to know someone was there, caring.

"Then real trouble set in. Some outsider come and set to build himself a fancy house on Bald Knob. He liked the view, he said. We never had much truck with outsiders. They never seem to catch our ways of thinking. This man was extra bad, building there on Bald Knob where our men had their meetings, and not understanding why that was wrong. He brought a curse to the hills and to all the folks hereabouts. We knowed 'twas him all right. No one else was new in these parts.

"There wasn't no rain for months on end. The cows went dry. The hens stopped laying. Folks was hungry, and we couldn't see no way out of our trouble. It was the outsider and the strangeness he brought to the hills. The hills don't tolerate no alien ways. Something had to change. So the Bald Knobbers came in the dark one night and killed him where he lay."

She paused to let the point strike home.

"Then the real lawmen came from Ozark. They heard of what was done, and they said our men had to be punished. The Bald Knobbers came to trial, and the jury said they had to be hanged. One of those was our son."

The tone of her voice hadn't altered in any degree with that statement, and Ed could almost imagine that he hadn't heard it correctly.

"The real lawmen had trouble, though, when it come to carrying out what they wanted to do. No one hereabouts would do the hanging. Those men were our own, and nobody would have it on his soul to kill their own folks. So the law sent off to Kansas City for a real hanging man."

Luke prompted, "Brought his own ropes."

"Yes. And built the gallows, one for each man, twelve in a row right there on the courthouse square. People come from miles around to watch.

"On the hanging morning, they brought the Bald Knobbers from the jailhouse—some men, and some just boys not yet to razor growed. Our son was one not yet a man."

The woman was silent for a moment, in tribute to the blindness of justice. "But then a strangeness come. Seemed like that hanging man just couldn't get his job done. There was something didn't want our folks to hang. Some say the rope he brought from Kansas City was green, and stretched. That's as may be. Maybe it was something else. Anyways, the trap would spring and a man would drop through, stretching that rope with his weight, and dangle there with his feet bouncing on the ground. You can't break no man's neck that way.

"When it was all over, they couldn't hang but two. At last, they just give up and let the others go. No one had the heart for any more. The Bald Knobbers were let go free and told to go away, somewheres else. They never been seen since."

She gazed at the top of the hill. "And yet, there's some folks say their spirits never left. Some say that at least one Bald Knobber never went away at all. Sometimes you can see a bonfire on Bald Knob at night. Some say the Bald Knobbers do pertect us yet. From strangers and the like."

Only the wasp, buzzing, made a sound in the still air.

Ed said, "That's quite a story. I'm going to climb that hill and see how things look on top."

Luke said quietly, "I wouldn't, if I was you."

The woman said, "Go, if you want." There was warning in her tone—and promise.

Across the still afternoon a mournful, cooing sound came from far away.

"Rain crow," Luke announced. "Means rain soon, for sure."

Ed looked up, unbelieving, at the clear sky, and smiled

complacently. "Well, I'd better go take a look at Bald Knob now, before the deluge."

He set out across the dry, brittle grass. In a few minutes Luke and the woman saw him start up the hill. Then he passed from sight among the oak trees.

The two stood up. "It'll be all right, Luke," the woman reassured, putting her hand on his arm. "He's there. I know he is. He'll take care of everything. Just like he done before, with that other movie man."

They went indoors.

Night came. Ed didn't return.

A watchful person might have thought that he saw a fire burning on top of Bald Knob as darkness set in.

Then the storm struck. Lightning flickered on the horizon. The first huge, spattering drops of rain fell, bringing the odor of moisture on dry land. A howling wind bent the trees. Then torrents of water poured from the sky. Lightning bolts flashed and thunder bounced from hill to hill.

Luke and the woman looked at one another wordlessly, and went to bed.

The morning sun shone on a world washed clean and shining. Luke and the woman set out up the hill. Ed's footprints were washed away. There was no sign that anyone had been there before them.

Luke found him just below the tree line. Above where Ed lay, the hilltop was bare. The big oak tree which lay on top of him had been split by a lightning bolt. Under it, Ed was crushed like a bug under a man's heel.

The woman spoke softly: "Get him out from there, Luke. We'll plant him in the hill, where we planted the other man."

Luke bent to the job.

"It was our son again," the woman said with pride. "He lured that man under the oak tree. Any hill man knows better than to go under a tree in a thunderstorm."

Luke intoned, "One for the cutworm, one for the crow. . . ."

A mystery writer who is a mystery herself, Mary Barrett published "The Silver Saltceller," the first of a half-dozen tales about women involved in crime, in Ellery Queen's Mystery

Magazine in 1970. "All our inquiries," the editor of Ellery Queen said, "about her background, hobbies, and writing aims have elicited no reply," leaving him to wonder if "Mary Barrett" is a penname. We, too, will respect her privacy.

Bart expected someone from the new boarding school to meet him at the train station. He didn't expect the school to be so unusual . . .

ELEVEN

School for the Unspeakable

Manly Wade Wellman

$\mathbb{B}$art Setwick dropped off the train at Carrington and stood for a moment on the station platform, an honest-faced, well-knit lad in tweeds. This little town and its famous school should be his home for the next eight months; but which way to the school? The sun had set, and he could barely see the shop signs across Carrington's modest main street. He hesitated, and a soft voice spoke at his very elbow:

"Are you for the school?"

Startled, Bart Setwick wheeled. In the gray twilight stood another youth, smiling thinly and waiting as if for an answer. The stranger was all of nineteen years old—that meant maturity to young Setwick, who was fifteen—and his pale face had shrewd lines to it. His tall, shambling body was clad in high-necked jersey and unfashionably tight trousers. Bart Setwick skimmed him with the quick, appraising eye of young America.

"I just got here," he replied. "My name's Setwick."

"Mine's Hoag." Out came a slender hand. Setwick took it and found it froggy-cold, with a suggestion of steel-wire muscles. "Glad to meet you. I came down on the chance someone would drop off the train. Let me give you a lift to the school."

Hoag turned away, felinely light for all his ungainliness, and led his new acquaintance around the corner of the little wooden railway station. Behind the structure, half hidden in its shadow, stood a shabby buggy with a lean bay horse in the shafts.

"Get in," invited Hoag, but Bart Setwick paused for a moment. His generation was not used to such vehicles. Hoag chuckled and said, "Oh, this is only a school wrinkle. We run to funny customs. Get in."

Setwick obeyed. "How about my trunk?"

"Leave it." The taller youth swung himself in beside Setwick and took the reins. "You'll not need it tonight."

He snapped his tongue and the bay horse stirred, drew them around and off down a bush-lined side road. Its hoofbeats were oddly muffled.

They turned a corner, another, and came into open country. The lights of Carrington, newly kindled against the night, hung behind like a constellation settled down to Earth. Setwick felt a hint of chill that did not seen to fit the September evening.

"How far is the school from town?" he asked.

"Four or five miles," Hoag replied in his hushed voice. "That was deliberate on the part of the founders—they wanted to make it hard for the students to get to town for larks. It forced us to dig up our own amusements." The pale face creased in a faint smile, as if this were a pleasantry. "There's just a few of the right sort on hand tonight. By the way, what did you get sent out for?"

Setwick frowned his mystification. "Why, to go to school. Dad sent me."

"But what for? Don't you know that this is a high-class prison prep? Half of us are lunkheads that need poking along, the other half are fellows who got in scandals somewhere else. Like me." Again Hoag smiled.

Setwick began to dislike his companion. They rolled a mile or so in silence before Hoag again asked a question:

"Do you go to church, Setwick?"

The new boy was afraid to appear priggish, and made a careless show with, "Not very often."

"Can you recite anything from the Bible?" Hoag's soft voice took on an anxious tinge.

"Not that I know of."

"Good," was the almost hearty response. "As I was say-

123

ing, there's only a few of us at the school tonight—only three, to be exact. And we don't like Bible-quoters."

Setwick laughed, trying to appear sage and cynical. "Isn't Satan reputed to quote the Bible to his own—"

"What do you know about Satan?" interrupted Hoag. He turned full on Setwick, studying him with intent, dark eyes. Then, as if answering his own question: "Little enough, I'll bet. Would you like to know about him?"

"Sure I would," replied Setwick, wondering what the joke would be.

"I'll teach you after a while," Hoag promised cryptically, and silence fell again.

Half a moon was well up as they came in sight of a dark jumble of buildings.

"Here we are," announced Hoag, and then, throwing back his head, he emitted a wild, wordless howl that made Setwick almost jump out of the buggy. "That's to let the others know we're coming," he explained. "Listen!"

Back came a seeming echo of the howl, shrill, faint and eery. The horse wavered in its muffled trot, and Hoag clucked it back into step. They turned in at a driveway well grown up in weeds, and two minutes more brought them up to the rear of the closest building. It was dim gray in the wash of moonbeams, with blank inky rectangles for windows. Nowhere was there a light, but as the buggy came to a halt Setwick saw a young head pop out of a window on the lower floor.

"Here already, Hoag?" came a high, reedy voice.

"Yes," answered the youth at the reins, "and I've brought a new man with me."

Thrilling a bit to hear himself called a man, Setwick alighted.

"His name's Setwick," went on Hoag. "Meet Andoff, Setwick. A great friend of mine."

Andoff flourished a hand in greeting and scrambled out over the windowsill. He was chubby and squat and even paler than Hoag, with a low forehead beneath lank, wet-looking hair, and black eyes set wide apart in a fat, stupid-looking face. His shabby jacket was too tight for him, and beneath worn knickers his legs and feet were bare. He might have been an overgrown thirteen or an undeveloped eighteen.

"Felcher ought to be along in half a second," he volunteered.

"Entertain Setwick while I put up the buggy," Hoag directed him.

Andoff nodded, and Hoag gathered the lines in his hands, but paused for a final word.

"No funny business yet, Andoff," he cautioned seriously. "Setwick, don't let this lard-bladder rag you or tell you wild stories until I come back."

Andoff laughed shrilly. "No, no wild stories," he promised. "You'll do the talking, Hoag."

The buggy trundled away, and Andoff swung his fat, grinning face to the new arrival.

"Here comes Felcher," he announced. "Felcher, meet Setwick."

Another boy had bobbed up, it seemed, from nowhere. Setwick had not seen him come around the corner of the building, or slip out of a door or window. He was probably as old as Hoag, or older, but so small as to be almost a dwarf, and frail to boot. His most notable characteristic was his hairiness. A great mop covered his head, bushed over his neck and ears, and hung unkemptly to his bright, deep-set eyes. His lips and cheeks were spread with a rank down, and a curly thatch peeped through the unbuttoned collar of his soiled white shirt. The hand he offered Setwick was almost simian in its shagginess and in the hardness of its palm. Too, it was cold and damp. Setwick remembered the same thing of Hoag's handclasp.

"We're the only ones here so far," Felcher remarked. His voice, surprisingly deep and strong for so small a creature, rang like a great bell.

"Isn't even the headmaster here?" inquired Setwick, and at that the other two began to laugh uproariously, Andoff's fife-squeal rendering an obbligato to Felcher's bell-boom. Hoag, returning, asked what the fun was.

"Setwick asks," groaned Felcher, "why the headmaster isn't here to welcome him."

More fife-laughter and bell-laughter.

125

"I doubt if Setwick would think the answer was funny," Hoag commented, and then chuckled softly himself.

Setwick, who had been well brought up, began to grow nettled.

"Tell me about it," he urged, in what he hoped was a bleak tone, "and I'll join your chorus of mirth."

Felcher and Andoff gazed at him with eyes strangely eager and yearning. Then they faced Hoag.

"Let's tell him," they both said at once, but Hoag shook his head.

"Not yet. One thing at a time. Let's have the song first."

They began to sing. The first verse of their offering was obscene, with no pretense of humor to redeem it. Setwick had never been squeamish, but he found himself definitely repelled. The second verse seemed less objectionable, but it hardly made sense:

> All they tried to teach here
> Now goes untaught.
> Ready, steady, each here,
> Knowledge we sought.
> What they called disaster
> Killed us not, O master!
> Rule us, we beseech here,
> Eye, hand and thought.

It was something like a hymn, Setwick decided; but before what altar would such hymns be sung? Hoag must have read that question in his mind.

"You mentioned Satan in the buggy on the way out," he recalled, his knowing face hanging like a mask in the half-dimness close to Setwick. "Well, that was a Satanist song."

"It was? Who made it?"

"I did," Hoag informed him. "How do you like it?"

Setwick made no answer. He tried to sense mockery in Hoag's voice, but could not find it. "What," he asked finally, "does all this Satanist singing have to do with the headmaster?"

"A lot," came back Felcher deeply, and "A lot," squealed Andoff.

Hoag gazed from one of his friends to the others, and for the first time he smiled broadly. It gave him a toothy look.

"I believe," he ventured quietly but weightily, "that we might as well let Setwick in on the secret of our little circle."

Here it would begin, the new boy decided—the school hazing of which he had heard and read so much. He had anticipated such things with something of excitement, even eagerness, but now he wanted none of them. He did not like his three companions, and he did not like the way they approached whatever it was they intended to do. He moved backward a pace or two, as if to retreat.

Swift as darting birds, Hoag and Andoff closed in at either elbow. Their chill hands clutched him and suddenly he felt light-headed and sick. Things that had been clear in the moonlight went hazy and distorted.

"Come on and sit down, Setwick," invited Hoag, as though from a great distance. His voice did not grow loud or harsh, but it embodied real menace. "Sit on that windowsill. Or would you like us to carry you?"

At the moment Setwick wanted only to be free of their touch, and so he walked unresistingly to the sill and scrambled up on it. Behind him was the blackness of an unknown chamber, and at his knees gathered the three who seemed so eager to tell him their private joke.

"The headmaster was a proper churchgoer," began Hoag, as though he were the spokesman for the group. "He didn't have any use for devils or devil worship. Went on record against them when he addressed us in chapel. That was what started us."

"Right," nodded Andoff, turning up his fat, larval face. "Anything he outlawed, we wanted to do. Isn't that logic?"

"Logic and reason," wound up Felcher. His hairy right hand twiddled on the sill near Setwick's thigh. In the moonlight it looked like a big, nervous spider.

Hoag resumed. "I don't know of any prohibition of his it was easier or more fun to break."

Setwick found that his mouth had gone dry. His tongue could barely moisten his lips. "You mean," he said, "that you began to worship devils?"

Hoag nodded happily, like a teacher at an apt pupil.

"One vacation I got a book on the cult. The three of us studied it, then began ceremonies. We learned the charms and spells, forward and backward—"

"They're twice as good backward," put in Felcher, and Andoff giggled.

"Have you any idea, Setwick," Hoag almost cooed, "what it was that appeared in our study the first time we burned wine and sulfur, with the proper words spoken over them?"

Setwick did not want to know. He clenched his teeth. "If you're trying to scare me," he managed to growl out, "it certainly isn't going to work."

All three laughed once more, and began to chatter out their protestations of good faith.

"I swear that we're telling the truth, Setwick," Hoag assured him. "Do you want to hear it, or don't you?"

Setwick had very little choice in the matter, and he realized it. "Oh, go ahead," he capitulated, wondering how it would do to crawl backward from the sill into the darkness of the room.

Hoag leaned toward him, with the air as of one confiding. "The headmaster caught us. Caught us red-handed."

"Book open, fire burning," chanted Felcher.

"He had something very fine to say about the vengeance of heaven," Hoag went on. "We got to laughing at him. He worked up a frenzy. Finally he tried to take heaven's vengeance into his own hands—tried to visit it on us, in a very primitive way. But it didn't work."

Andoff was laughing immoderately, his fat arms across his bent belly.

"He thought it worked," he supplemented between high gurgles, "but it didn't."

"Nobody could kill us," Felcher added. "Not after the oaths we'd taken, and the promises that had been made us."

"What promises?" demanded Setwick, who was struggling hard not to believe. "Who made you any promises?"

"Those we worshiped," Felcher told him. If he was simulating earnestness, it was a supreme bit of acting. Setwick, realizing this, was more daunted than he cared to show.

"When did all these things happen?" was his next question.

"When?" echoed Hoag. "Oh, years and years ago."

"Years and years ago," repeated Andoff.

"Long before you were born," Felcher assured him.

They were standing close together, their backs to the moon that shone in Setwick's face. He could not see their expressions clearly. But their three voices—Hoag's soft, Felcher's deep and vibrant, Andoff's high and squeaky—were absolutely serious.

"I know what you're arguing within yourself," Hoag announced somewhat smugly. "How can we, who talk about those many past years, seem so young? That calls for an explanation, I'll admit." He paused, as if choosing words. "Time—for us—stands still. It came to a halt on that very night, Setwick; the night our headmaster tried to put an end to our worship."

"And to us," smirked the gross-bodied Andoff, with his usual air of self-congratulation at capping one of Hoag's statements.

"The worship goes on," pronounced Felcher, in the same chanting manner that he had affected once before. "The worship goes on, and we go on, too."

"Which brings us to the point," Hoag came in briskly. "Do you want to throw in with us, Setwick?—make the fourth of this lively little party?"

"No, I don't," snapped Setwick vehemently.

They fell silent, and gave back a little—a trio of bizarre silhouettes against the pale moon glow. Setwick could see the flash of their staring eyes among the shadows of their faces. He knew that he was afraid, but hid his fear. Pluckily he dropped from the sill to the ground. Dew from the grass spattered his sock-clad ankles between oxfords and trouser-cuffs.

"I guess it's my turn to talk," he told them levelly. "I'll make it short. I don't like you, nor anything you've said. And I'm getting out of here."

"We won't let you," said Hoag, hushed but emphatic.

"We won't let you," murmured Andoff and Felcher together, as though they had rehearsed it a thousand times.

Setwick clenched his fists. His father had taught him to box. He took a quick, smooth stride toward Hoag and hit him hard in the face. Next moment all three had flung themselves upon him. They did not seem to strike or grapple or tug, but he went down under their assault. The shoulders of his tweed coat wallowed in sand, and he smelled crushed weeds. Hoag, on top of him, pinioned his arms with a knee on each bicep. Felcher and Andoff were stooping close.

Glaring up in helpless rage, Setwick knew once and for all that this was no schoolboy prank. Never did practical jokers gather around their victim with such staring, green-gleaming eyes, such drawn jowls, such quivering lips.

Hoag bared white fangs. His pointed tongue quested once over them.

"Knife!" he muttered, and Felcher fumbled in a pocket, then passed him something that sparkled in the moonlight.

Hoag's lean hand reached for it, then whipped back. Hoag had lifted his eyes to something beyond the huddle. He choked and whimpered inarticulately, sprang up from Setwick's laboring chest, and fell back in awkward haste. The others followed his shocked stare, then as suddenly cowered and retreated in turn.

"It's the master!" wailed Andoff.

"Yes," roared a gruff new voice. "Your old headmaster— and I've come back to master *you!*"

Rising upon one elbow, the prostrate Setwick saw what they had seen—a tall, thick-bodied figure in a long dark coat, topped with a square, distorted face and a tousle of white locks. Its eyes glittered with their own pale, hard light. As it advanced slowly and heavily it emitted a snigger of murderous joy. Even at first glance Setwick was aware that it cast no shadow.

"I am in time," mouthed the newcomer. "You were going to kill this poor boy."

Hoag had recovered and made a stand. "Kill him?" he quavered, seeming to fawn before the threatening presence. "No. We'd have given him life—"

"You call it life?" trumpeted the long-coated one. "You'd have sucked out his blood to teem your own dead veins, damned him to your filthy condition. But I'm here to prevent you!"

130

A finger pointed, huge and knuckly, and then came a torrent of language. To the nerve-stunned Setwick it sounded like a bit from the New Testament, or perhaps from the Book of Common Prayer. All at once he remembered Hoag's avowed dislike for such quotations.

His three erstwhile assailants reeled as if before a high wind that chilled or scorched. "No, no! Don't!" they begged wretchedly.

The square old face gaped open and spewed merciless laughter. The knuckly finger traced a cross in the air, and the trio wailed in chorus as though the sign had been drawn upon their flesh with a tongue of flame.

Hoag dropped to his knees. "Don't!" he sobbed.

"I have power," mocked their tormenter. "During years shut up I won it, and now I'll use it." Again a triumphant burst of mirth. "I know you're damned and can't be killed, but you can be tortured! I'll make you crawl like worms before I'm done with you!"

Setwick gained his shaky feet. The long coat and the blocky head leaned toward him.

"Run, you!" dinned a rough roar in his ears. "Get out of here—and thank God for the chance!"

Setwick ran, staggering. He blundered through the weeds of the driveway, gained the road beyond. In the distance gleamed the lights of Carrington. As he turned his face toward them and quickened his pace he began to weep, chokingly, hysterically, exhaustingly.

He did not stop running until he reached the platform in front of the station. A clock across the street struck ten, in a deep voice not unlike Felcher's. Setwick breathed deeply, fished out his handkerchief and mopped his face. His hand was quivering like a grass stalk in a breeze.

"Beg pardon!" came a cheery hail. "You must be Setwick."

As once before on this same platform, he whirled around with startled speed. Within touch of him stood a broad-shouldered man of thirty or so, with horn-rimmed spectacles. He wore a neat Norfolk jacket and flannels. A short briar pipe was clamped in a good-humored mouth.

"I'm Collins, one of the masters at the school," he introduced himself. "If you're Setwick, you've had us worried.

131

We expected you on that seven o'clock train, you know. I dropped down to see if I couldn't trace you."

Setwick found a little of his lost wind. "But I've—been to the school," he mumbled protestingly. His hand, still trembling, gestured vaguely along the way he had come.

Collins threw back his head and laughed, then apologized.

"Sorry," he said. "It's no joke if you really had all that walk for nothing. Why, that old place is deserted—used to be a catch-all for incorrigible rich boys. They closed it about fifty years ago, when the headmaster went mad and killed three of his pupils. As a matter of coincidence, the master himself died just this afternoon, in the state hospital for the insane."

A major writer of the supernatural, Manly Wade Wellman was born in Portugese West Africa, where his father was a medical missionary, in 1903. Brought to the United States at the age of six, he was educated at Wichita University and Columbia University and worked as a reporter until 1930, when he quit to become a full-time professional writer. In two decades more than 300,000 of his words were published in Weird Tales. *In 1946 his story, "A Star for a Warrior," won first prize in the first* Ellery Queen's Mystery Magazine *Annual Contest (William Faulkner came in second); the prize money permitted him to move to North Carolina, where he lived the rest of his life. Wellman published many full-length works, including two large collections of supernatural stories:* Worse Things Waiting *(1973) and* Lonesome Vigils *(1982). He died in 1986.*

*Although Ralph had never enjoyed much luck with women, it had never both-
ered him until Carlotta Stone showed him just how wrong he could be.*

TWELVE

Different Kinds of
Dead

Ed Gorman

Around eight that night, snow started drifting on the narrow Nebraska highway Ralph Sheridan was traveling. Already he could feel the rear end of the new Buick begin
sliding around on the freezing surface of the asphalt, and
could see that he would soon have to pull over and scrape
the windshield. Snow was forming into gnarly bumps on
the safety glass.

The small-town radio station he was listening to confirmed his worst suspicions: the weather bureau was predict-
ing a genuine March blizzard, with eight to ten inches of
snow and drifts up to several feet.

Sheridan sighed. A thirty-seven-year-old bachelor who
made his living as a traveling computer salesman—he
worked especially hard at getting farmers to buy his
wares—he spent most of the year on the road, putting up in
the small shabby plains motels that from a distance always
reminded him of doghouses. A brother in Cleveland was all
the family he had left, everybody else was dead. The only
other people he stayed in touch with were the men he'd
been in Viet Nam with. There had been women, of course,
but somehow it never worked out—this one wasn't his
type, that one laughed too loudly, this one didn't have the
same interests as he. And while his friends bloomed with
mates and children, there was for Sheridan just the road,
beers in bars with other salesmen, and nights alone in motel
rooms with paper strips across the toilet seats.

The Buick pitched suddenly toward the ditch. An experienced driver and a calm man, Sheridan avoided the common mistake of slamming on the brakes. Instead, he took the steering wheel in both hands and guided the hurtling car along the edge of the ditch. While he had only a foot of earth keeping him from plunging into the gully on his right, he let the car find its own traction. Soon enough, the car was gently heading back onto the asphalt.

It was there, just when the headlights focused on the highway again, that he saw the woman.

At first, he tried sensibly enough to deny she was even there. His first impression was that she was an illusion, a mirage of some sort created by the whirling, whipping snow and the vast black night.

But no, there really was a beautiful, red-haired woman standing in the center of the highway. She wore a trench coat and black high-heeled shoes. She might have been one of the women on the covers of the private eye paperbacks he'd read back in the sixties.

This time, he did slam on the brakes; otherwise, he would have run over her. He came to a skidding stop less than three feet from her.

His first reaction was gratitude. He dropped his head to the wheel and let out a long sigh. His whole body trembled. She could easily have been dead by now.

He was just raising his head when harsh wind and snow and cold blew into the car. The door on the passenger side had opened.

She got inside, saying nothing, closing the door when she was seated comfortably.

Sheridan looked over at her. Close up, she was even more beautiful. In the yellow glow of the dashboard, her features were so exquisite they had the refined loveliness of sculpture. Her tumbling, radiant hair only enhanced her face.

She turned to him finally and said, in a low, somewhat breathy voice, "You'd better not sit here in the middle of the highway long. It won't be safe."

He drove again. On either side of the highway he could make out little squares of light—the yellow windows of farmhouses lost in the furious gloom of the blizzard. The car heater warmed them nicely. The radio played some sexy jazz that somehow made the prairie and the snow and the weather alert go away.

All he could think of was those private eye novels he'd read as a teenager. This was what always happened to the Hammer himself, ending up with a woman like this.

"Do you mind?" she asked.

Before he had time to answer, she already had the long white cigarette between her full red lips and was lighting it. Then she tossed her head back and French inhaled. He hadn't seen anybody do that in years.

"Your car get ditched somewhere" he asked finally, realizing that these were his first words to her.

"Yes," she said, "somewhere."

"So you were walking to the nearest town?"

"Something like that."

"You were walking in the wrong direction." He paused. "And you're traveling alone?"

She glanced over at him again with her dark, lovely gaze. "Yes. Alone." Her voice was as smoky as her cigarette.

He drove some more, careful to keep both hands on the wheel, slowing down whenever the rear of the car started to slide.

He wasn't paying much attention to the music at this point—they were going up a particularly sleek and dangerous hill—but then the announcer's voice came on and said, "Looks like the police have really got their hands full tonight. Not only with the blizzard, but now with a murder. Local banker John T. Sloane was found murdered in his downtown apartment twenty minutes ago. Police report an eyewitness say he heard two gunshots and then saw a beautiful woman leaving Sloane's apartment. The eyewitness reportedly said that the woman strongly resembled Sloane's wife, Carlotta. But police note that that's impossible, given the fact that Carlotta died mysteriously last year in a boating accident. The eyewitness insists that the resemblance between the redheaded woman leaving Sloane's apartment tonight and the late Mrs. Sloane is uncanny. Now back to our musical program for the evening."

A bosso nova came on.

Beautiful. Redheaded. Stranded alone. Looking furtive.

He started glancing at her, and she said, "I'll spare you the trouble. It's me. Carlotta Stone."

"You?" But the announcer said—"

She turned to him and smiled. "That I'm dead? Well, so I am."

Not until then did Sheridan realize how far out in the boonies he was. Or how lacerating the storm had become. Or how helpless he felt inside a car with a woman who claimed to be dead.

"Why don't you just relax?"

"Please don't patronize me, Mr. Sheridan."

"I'm not patroniz— Say, how did you know my name?"

"I know a lot of things."

But I didn't tell you my name and there's no way you could read my registration from there and—"

She French inhaled—then exhaled—and said, "As I said, Mr. Sheridan, I know a lot of things." She shook her head. "I don't know how I got like this."

"Like what?"

"Dead."

"Oh."

"You still don't believe me, do you?"

He sighed. "We've got about eight miles to go. Then we'll be in Porterville. I'll let you out at the Greyhound depot there. Then you can go about your business and I can go about mine."

She touched his temple with long, lovely fingers. "That's why you're such a lonely man, Mr. Sheridan. You never take any chances. You never let yourself get involved with anybody."

He smiled thinly, "Especially with dead people."

"Maybe you're the one who's dead, Mr. Sheridan. Night after night alone in cheap little hotel rooms, listening to the country western music through the wall, and occasionally hearing people make love. No woman. No children. No real friends. It's not a very good life, is it, Mr. Sheridan?"

He said nothing. Drove.

"We're both dead, Mr. Sheridan. You know that?"

He still said nothing. Drove.

After a time, she said, "Do you want to know how tonight happened, Mr. Sheridan?"

"No."

"I made you mad, didn't I, Mr. Sheridan, when I reminded you of how lonely you are?"

"I don't see where it's any of your business."

Now it was her turn to be quiet. She stared out at the
lashing snow. Then she said. "The last thing I could remember before tonight was John T. holding me under
water till I drowned off the side of our boat. By the way,
that's what all his friends called him. John T." She lit one
cigarette off another. "Then earlier tonight I felt myself rise
through darkness and suddenly I realized was taking form. I
was rising from the grave and taking form. And there was
just one place I wanted to go. The apartment he kept in
town for his so-called business meetings. So I went there
tonight and killed him."

"You won't die."

"I beg your pardon?"

"They won't execute you for doing it. You just tell them
the same story you told me, and you'll get off with second
degree. Maybe even not guilty by reason of insanity."

She laughed. "Maybe if you weren't so busy watching the
road, you'd notice what's happening to me, Mr. Sheridan."

She was disappearing. Right there in his car. Where her
left arm had been was now just a smoldering red-tipped
cigarette that seemed to be held up on invisible wires. A part
of her face was starting to disappear, too.

"About a quarter mile down the highway, let me out if
you would."

He laughed. "What's there? A graveyard?"

"As a matter of fact, yes."

By now her legs had started disappearing.

"You don't seem to believe it, Mr. Sheridan, but I'm actually trying to help you. Trying to tell you to go out and live
while you're still alive. I wasted my life on my husband,
sitting around at home while he ran around with other
women, hoping against hope that someday he'd be faithful
and we'd have a good life together. It never happened, Mr.
Sheridan. I wasted my whole life."

"Sounds like you paid him back tonight. Two gunshots,
the radio said."

Her remaining hand raised the cigarette to what was left

137

of her mouth. She inhaled deeply. When she exhaled the smoke was a lovely gray color. "I was hoping there would be some satisfaction in it. There isn't. I'm as lonely as I ever was."

He wondered if that was a small, dry sob he heard in her voice.

"Right here," she said.

He had been cautiously braking the last minute and a half. He brought the car comfortably over to the side of the road. He put on his emergency flashers in case anybody was behind him.

Up on the hill to his right, he saw it. A graveyard. The tombstones looked like small children huddled against the whipping snow.

"After I killed him, I just started walking," she said. "Walking. Not even knowing where I was going. Then you came along." She stabbed the cigarette out in the ashtray. "Do something about your life, Mr. Sheridan. Don't waste it the way I have."

She got out of the car and leaned back in. "Goodbye, Mr. Sheridan."

He sat there, watching her disappear deep into the gully, then reappear on the other side and start walking up the slope of the hill.

By the time she was halfway there, she had nearly vanished altogether.

Then, moments later, she was gone utterly.

At the police station, he knew better than to tell the cops about the ghost business. He simply told them he'd seen a woman fitting the same description out on the highway about twenty minutes ago.

Grateful for his stopping in, four cops piled into two different cars and they set out under blood red flashers into the furious white night.

Mr. Sheridan found a motel—his usual one in this particular burg—and took his usual room. He stripped, as always, to his boxer shorts and t-shirt and got snug in bed beneath the covers and watched a rerun of an old sitcom.

He should have been laughing—at least all the people on the laugh track seemed to be having a good time—but instead he did something he rarely did. He began crying. Oh, not big wailing tears, but hard tiny silver ones. Then he shut off both TV and the lights and lay in the solitary darkness thinking of what she'd said to him.

No woman. No children. No love.

Only much later, when the wind near dawn died and the snow near light subsided, only then did Sheridan sleep, his tears dried out but feeling colder than he ever had.

Lonely cold. Dead cold.

Winner of the 1988 Shamus Award for Best Short Story, Ed Gorman has been called "one of the most important crime-fiction writers to emerge in the last decade. Born in 1943, Gorman was an advertising executive for twenty years before turning to writing. His first book, Rough Cut, *(about murder in an ad agency), was issued in 1985. Since then he has issued seven mysteries, three western novels, and four anthologies. Gorman is also co-editor of the trade journal* Mystery Scene *(with Robert Randisi) and a Private Eye Writers of America's new vice-president. His murder-at-sea mystery,* Several Deaths Later, *was recently published.*

Sometimes the myths of teenagers are all too real.

THIRTEEN

Deadlights

Charles Wagner

On U.S. 24 between Glasco and Beloit in Kansas, driving at night can be hazardous. Not all the headlights that follow you on that lonely, seventeen-mile stretch of road have cars connected to them.

Perhaps I should explain. Go back a few years.

It was late, around midnight. Bob, Dean, and I were heading back home to Beloit in Bob's Dodge Challenger. It was a fast car, so we usually took it. Dean's car wasn't exactly slow, but he kept messing it up and it was in the garage now with a carburetor problem and wouldn't be ready till morning.

I never teased Dean much about his Mustang because it was better than what I had, which was nothing. Like his car, Dean himself often had problems.

At the time, Dean's primary problem was with Lori, his girlfriend of the last few months. Dean was talking really big about what a bitch she was but Bob and I knew that if he punted her, he could be in for a long dry spell.

That night, she had punted him.

Dean sat in back on the way home, pouting. Usually I sat in back, being the shortest of us, but tonight Dean wanted to sulk, so Bob—all 6′ 3″ of him—encouraged Dean to sit in the back and let me ride up front.

The whole business of Glasco was a little silly. Bob's cousin Valery lived there and we figured she was an 'in' to all the Glasco girls. Of course, Glasco was half the size of Beloit so "all the Glasco girls" didn't really come to a lot.

We usually did all right, though. Especially Bob, because of his height and looks. Tonight, however, Dean's fight with Lori had dominated affairs.

We were quiet. A Led Zeppelin tape dangled from the eight-track but we were tired of it, and not feeling particularly rowdy, so we left it off. The only sounds were the rush of air and Bob's engine. It was warm so we had both front windows open. Wheat fields and milo cane went by in the dark flanking U.S. 24.

We had set a personal record after school that Friday: Running Le Mans-style to the car and driving like hell, we made it to Glasco in eleven minutes from the sound of the school bell. Our best time in four years of Glasco runs. It being April of our senior year (75 was our year and the number in our class), few opportunities remained to equal or surpass it.

Late that night, the legal limit was all the faster we felt like going.

"Shit!"

Dean was grumbling in the back seat, but Bob and I didn't pay any attention to him as he was probably still upset about Lori.

"Oh shit."

This time he sounded more worried than anything else.

I looked at Bob and he sighed audibly. "What is it, Dean?" Neither of us even glanced back at him.

"He's back."

"Who's back?" I asked.

"The lights."

"You mean there's a car behind us?" Bob said, trying to coax information out of him.

"No car—just headlights." Dean's voice was quiet with resolve.

Bob and I sneered at each other. I looked back.

There were a pair of headlights—bright beams—far, far behind us on 24. A month ago, Dean had told us a story about being followed by headlights that had no car making them. It was a story a couple of others around town had mumbled, most of those, drunk kids trying to explain away why they were out late by switching the subject to ghostly headlights. Like a lot of things Dean said, we took it with a grain of salt. (Dean is a good guy but he has that tendency to exaggerate.)

I squinted hard and saw only headlights, which was normal for that distance in the dark. Kansas is pretty flat and you can usually see for miles in open country.

"Okay, there's headlights back there," I reported.

I shrugged at Bob and he gave a mild head-shake. Dean was hunched into the Naugahyde, peering over the seat at the lights, as if they could detect him at that distance.

The headlights began to gain on us.

Bob pushed in the Led Zeppelin tape. "Communication Breakdown" poured out of the speakers. I flinched and lowered the volume on the tape deck.

"Look," Dean said. He was frozen in position, staring out the back window.

The headlights were really coming on now. Still on bright beam, they glanced off the rear view mirror into Bob's eyes.

"I wish he'd dim those things," Bob muttered.

"He never does," Dean placidly said.

"Is the driver a he?" I asked.

Dean shrugged. "There isn't any driver that you can see. I just say that."

By now, the headlights had drawn very near, making the cabin of Bob's Challenger almost as bright as day. Dean seemed to be trying to merge with the car seat. Bob motioned outside the window with his hand, waving the car past, but the lights stayed glued to our fender. I couldn't see any car, but then, the light was awfully bright.

The car, or whatever it was, didn't pass us. I began making half-peace-sign gestures at the lights with my hand. Bob maintained his speed, muttering "asshole" under his breath. "—communication breakdown, it's always the saaammmeeee—" rattled the speakers.

"Another minute. . . ." Dean said.

My eyes adjusted to the glare a little bit and I still couldn't see a car. The old highway 41 turnoff drew near.

"About now. . . ." Dean said, his voice softly patient.

The headlights eased off our tail, slowing to a near halt. They made the turn onto old 41. I tried to see what kind of car was behind them, but my eyes were adjusted to light too much to permit me to see anything other than the headlights swerving and Dean looking at me for some kind of confirmation.

"Well?" he asked.

"I'm not sure," was all I could say.

"I was busy driving," Bob said, pulling the tape out and sounding as apologetic as he could.

When we dropped Dean off at his house, he was still pissed at us.

Bob came over to my place that Saturday for a game of horse. We always played horse or one-on-one, but I preferred horse since I was short and had never won at the other. We were shooting the ball well that day with our shirts off and hanging from the trellis that marked the court's east boundary. Winter-pale, we were hoping to start our tans. The score was "ho" to "ho."

Dean's car swung into the drive and pulled up to the west side of the court. Dean stepped out with flourish, the perennial Banner Drive-Inn glass of coke in his hand. (I swear, the guy drank more pop than a Little League team.) We expected him to whip off his shirt and join the game.

Instead, he sauntered coolly over to the trellis and sucked on his Coke. "Guess what I heard," he said, staring into the cup.

I held the ball to my hip and waited.

"Well?" Bob said.

Dean pulled off the lid and stirred the ice with his straw. "Sumthin about those headlights. . . ."

"Yeah," I said. "Whad'ya hear?"

Dean cocked the cup to his mouth and tapped some ice in. "Some guy got killed in a wreck twenty years ago," he said, his words slurpy with ice, "out by the old 41 turnoff. My dad told me about it."

I won't repeat Dean's version of the tale. Since that Saturday, I've studied the incident and what follows is my version of what the papers reported:

There was a guy named Bill Phillips. His friends had called him "Tank" because he was built like a fire-plug, was strong, and had played fullback in school. He was a mechanic and a 1953 BHS grad. He had been driving back from Glasco in a big hurry and apparently tried to turn on to old 41. He was going too fast and rolled his Merc. His neck was broken. That was in May of 1955.

That was all the papers told me, but I did some talking

around and learned more. It was Bob's aunt—Valery's mom—that gave me most of the real story behind that odd wreck.

She said that Tank had been dating her best friend, Becky Hunter. Both girls lived in Glasco, so Tank did a lot of commuting between Beloit and Glasco, much as we did. Tank had been dating Becky for four years and he was working up to a proposal that Becky probably would've rejected, or so Bob's aunt believed.

She said Becky liked Tank all right, but she really wanted to go on to college and get a degree. Usually when a girl leaves Glasco—or Beloit, for that matter—for college, she meets a lot of new people. Most never come back, except for visits. And Tank was the kind of guy who wanted to settle down in Beloit.

Well anyway, Tank never got a chance to propose. He went to Glasco that May evening to see Becky but Bob's aunt told him she had already gone out. Hopping mad, Tank tore off in his Merc, hoping, probably, to overtake Becky and her date. Since Glasco didn't have a movie house, he figured they'd head for Beloit.

When Bob's aunt reached this part, it was pretty obvious to guess the rest. Driving hard at night, Tank undoubtedly wanted to get to Beloit before the show let out so he could catch the new guy and Becky before they got to their car. But when he got near the old 41 turnoff, another thought probably occurred to him.

Even in 1955, 41 was a vintage strip of road. Made in the 20's, it was a narrow piece of old, cracked concrete that ran north-south for thirty miles. It wasn't very well traveled but its shallow ditches made for excellent parking.

The thought that maybe, just maybe, Becky and this new guy were parking on old 41 got to Tank so hard, he didn't know which way to go. So he ended up going nowhere.

If you believe in ghosts, it's not hard to imagine Tank's ghost tearing up U.S. 24 looking for Becky. He'd keep his brights on so he could peer inside cars to see if Becky was there. Then he'd complete the turn onto old 41.

That's a pretty stupid notion.

Not many folks claim to have seen ghostly headlights on 24, and if they were for real, there wasn't much they could do to a person. Besides, Becky Hunter Collins moved to New York back in 1960 and Bob's aunt assured me that it wasn't fear of headlights that made the move attractive to her.

But in 1975, the newspaper story was all Bob, Dean, and I knew about the whole affair. Bob and I remained convinced that Dean was exaggerating about the "mysterious" headlights, but we were intrigued nonetheless.

That Saturday evening the three of us cruised Mill Street in Bob's Dodge before making the inevitable trip to Glasco. We had dates, except for Dean, but the prospect of encountering the lights again was stronger than any dim hope of sex.

We reached Glasco at sundown. Val joined us to keep Dean company.

The night was uneventful. We parked in a cemetery, hoping for some necking, but the girls weren't very scare-prone and easily avoided our attempts at "comfort." Disgusted, we took them home and left Glasco, but not before several hours had passed and four six-packs were downed.

On the way back, I was in my customary place in the back seat. Bachman Turner Overdrive was singing at us to "stay awake all night" over the eight-track and the windows were down. Lounging drunkenly, I glanced out the back.

There were headlights to our rear.

I watched for half a mile until the headlights became a red pickup that took the first farm turnoff. I sat back and watched Beloit twinkle in the west.

"—stay awake, stay awake—" the tape deck throbbed.

Sitting in the back reminded me of the times I sat in the back of Dad's big Chrysler when we were coming back from trips to Topeka to see my uncle. I'd stretch out in the back but wouldn't sleep.

I never sleep in cars.

Peering out the window, I'd gaze as far as I could see over the land. On the horizon, sometimes, thunderheads would stand, lit like pink cauliflower by lightning.

Other times, it would appear that there were large, vague objects trundling along—like nebulous tumbleweeds or something—trying to keep pace with our car. They would move just outside the edge of sight, rolling and lurching

145

along, but finally fall far behind. Others would be there to take up the chase until we got near town and the lights drove them away.

I knew they were illusions, like water on the road on a sunny day, but it was neat to imagine them chasing us.

Fortunately, we never had a flat or engine trouble.

Over the years, things didn't change all that much. When I got my restricted license, I began dreaming of a car of my own . . . but I remained stuck in back seats.

While reminiscing, I looked out the Challenger's side window into the darkness. I saw nothing strange—a farm light and a thunderhead far in the north. Lightning flashed inside the cloud. The color was blue like brains.

Light flashed suddenly in the compartment. I looked back to see two headlights on hi-beam coming over a low rise a mile back. They were gaining on us—fast.

Bachman/Turner switched songs. "Let it Ride" blared over the speakers.

I closed my eyes, trying to keep the pupils opened wide, and looked again.

There was no car visible behind the lights. Brightness became glare inside our car.

"Bob, Dean—he's here." Dean looked back as Bob stayed fixed to the road.

"Shit, it's him," Dean said. The headlights came right behind us like the night before. "—wouldja let it ride?" the tape deck asked.

"I don't see a car, fellas," I dutifully reported.

"Fuck him!" Bob growled, stomping on the pedal. The Challenger roared and hit 70.

The headlights didn't fade an inch.

"I can't hear an engine on that thing!" I shouted, not really sure that I could've heard anything at all outside the car.

The headlights stayed mutely on our tail at 85 mph.

"C'mon, Bob!" Dean pleaded. "Why bother?"

"It's been a shit-night and I wanna lose this ghost!"

"What!?" I yelled as we went over 90. "—would you say good-bye, wouldja let it ride—" Randy Bachman shrieked over the speakers.

"May as well try!!" Bob shouted, letting it all out on the floorboards. The car roared up to 100 mph.

The headlights didn't waver. It was high-noon bright inside the Challenger.

The 41 turnoff loomed ahead.

"I'll take the turn and he'll follow!" Bob yelled.

"No!!" Dean wailed. He reached for the wheel. Bob turned to slap his hand away. "—ride, ride, ride, let it ride—" chanted the tape deck. I grabbed an arm rest and dropped to the floor.

We skipped off the road and jumped the ditch at 90 mph. The Challenger bucked hard into the cultivated earth and the tires blew out. Dirty milo-cane churned into the car as I buffeted fetally on the floor, my arm cracking against the back seat as we ground to a dead halt in the milo field. Our headlights faintly lit the dead, brown stalks all around us. The tape had broken and FM hiss played softly in the car.

In the front seat, Bob and Dean remained, their heads imbedded in the dashboard.

Painfully, I turned my head and looked out, back through the swath we had made, and saw the headlights in the road. They had stopped, as if to allow their invisible driver to view the accident, and then started moving slowly forward. I watched them pass by, but they didn't turn on to old highway 41.

They just switched off.

There isn't much more to tell.

It's been four years since the wreck, and since then, I've gotten my college diploma and a car of my own. In a few weeks, I'll be moving to Wichita to start a new job, but for now it feels good sitting comfy in Beloit.

I reckon while I'm here visiting the folks, I'll stop by Bob and Dean's graves and leave them some flowers. That might make them feel a little better.

Lately, the talk around town is that the headlights that follow you from Glasco are back. The few that have seen them say they're different: four beams now, instead of two. Like the hi-beams of a Dodge. I know the rumor is true because I've seen the headlights myself.

Come to think of it, I'd *better* put flowers on my friends' graves.

Last night, coming into town, they tried to run me off the road.

Kansas-born Charles Wagner received a degree in electrical engineering from the University of Kansas in 1979, only to discover he didn't like engineering. "Deadlights" is his first published story and is the product of a writing class taught by horror writer Dennis Etchison at UCLA in 1982.

When Jens Jevins confessed to the murder of his wife, no one wanted to believe him—not even his wife.

FOURTEEN

The Bridal Pond
Zona Gale

The Judge had just said, "Case dismissed," and a sharp situation concerning cheese had thus become negligible when, before the next case on the calendar could be called, Jens Jevins came forward and said loudly:

"I wish to confess to the murder of my wife."

Now the courtroom was still, the fierce heat forgotten and the people stupefied, for Jens Jevins was the richest farmer in the township. No one tried to silence him.

He faced now the Judge and now the people, his face and neck the color of chicken skin, his tossed hair like a raveled fabric, his long right arm making always the same gesture. His clothes were good, and someone had pressed them.

"I planned to kill Agna for a long time. There was a time when for a week I slept with a pistol under my pillow, hoping for the strength to shoot her in her sleep. When I could tell by her breathing that it was time, I'd get up on my elbow and look at her, but I never had the courage to use the pistol—no, though I sat up in bed sometimes for half an hour with my finger on the trigger. Something would delay me—our dog would bark, or the kitchen clock would strike, or I would imagine my father shaking his head at me; and once she woke and asked me whether I had locked the porch door.

"Most of that week the room was as bright as morning, because the moon shone in, but as it rose later and hung higher, the room grew dark. And it seemed wrong to shoot Agna in the dark. Then I thought of a better plan."

The courtroom was held as a ball of glass, in which black figures hang in arrested motion. The silence was not vacant, but rich and winy, like a rest in music. It was the rest in the tread of a giant, one step, one step, and men crushed and powerless. The Judge, the bailiff, the spectators were crushed and powerless, all with staring eyes, and their short breath came through the mouth. Jens and Agna Jevins, they were known to all, and he so prosperous; and she a small complaining woman, who took prizes, with whom all must have talked on bright mornings, after she had lain asleep, close to death.

"At the south of our lot," Jens Jevins continued, conversationally, quite quietly, as if he were talking to some surveyors, "there is a long slope and then a pond, where in my father's time they took out clay to make bricks. This place is not fenced; it's separated from the highway by a few alders—some of you know," he said, with an air of surprise, remembering the spectators as living beings who had experienced his highway and the sight of his pond.

"I would go down there sometimes on spring evenings when the boys were catching frogs, and last week I went down, and they were catching frogs. And it was the night the Alexander boy fell in—well over his head he went, for the pond is above seven feet deep there, and sixteen farther out. I was standing near, so I was able to seize on him—I mention this because pulling him out put in my head the idea of what to do to Agna.

"So the next night I waited till late and I said to her that we might walk down and watch the boys catch frogs. She was glad to go and mentioned that I didn't often invite her to take evening walks any more, and we went down the slope. But I hadn't waited long enough; the boys were still there. She and I stood on the rim of the pond, and I edged her toward the place where the Alexander boy went in, and saw how easy it would be to send her down and keep her from climbing out. Only the boys were still there.

"It was dusk and the cars from town came down the highway and took the turn beyond our alders, and it looked as if they were all coming straight on to us, till they swung the corner. She says, 'What if one didn't see the turn and came crashing on to us?' and she shivered and said her shoulders were chilly, though the night was warm, and she wanted to go back to the house.

"So we went back and I read the evening paper aloud, about a young couple who had got married that day at Sun Prairie and had had a great doings. She said she wished we were starting over, and I said, 'I don't,' and went to bed.

"But in the night I woke up and thought of what she'd said. What if we were starting over? And what if I'd murdered her early, say, on the honeymoon? I saw that I couldn't have done it then. I wondered how I could do it now."

Now the Judge found his voice, and leaned down as if he were ill or drunken and said from his throat, "Why did you want to do it?"

Jens Jevins looked astonished. "I didn't *want* to do it," he said, "but there were thirty-seven years of it already and there might be twenty more."

Having answered, he continued:

"I began to see that what wasn't tragedy now would have been tragedy then. I thought of us driving though the country, if we'd been in the days of machines, like the Sun Prairie couple, Agna and me, you understand—and her young again. Her in the same blue dress, in the seat beside me. Me in a new suit, and shoes with the new not off the soles. Us talking and laughing, our valises stowed in the back. Going along the road. Along the road that swung round by our place and turned the corner by the alder trees. Dark it might be, or maybe a fog would have come down.

"We'd be talking and laughing, and the road strange, and I'd miss the turn, and the car'd come skimming between the alders, and across the base of the slope, and making for the clay hole. Spite of all I could do, on it'd come, heading for the clay hole. In the dark or maybe in the fog. And we wouldn't know we'd left the road till I'd see a light from somewhere lapping on the pond, and then it'd be too late. Straight in and down—in and down. Nothing I could do. Agna in her blue dress. On the day of our wedding.

"But now it was thirty years and past, and twenty more to come. I woke her up. I says, 'I can't sleep. It's warm. Let's go down and walk out somewheres.' She laughed and grumbled some, but she went with me. She was always one to go with me. We put on little and went down the slope to the pond. It was deep dark—the light of a star was deep in the water. We heard the frogs and smelled the first wild grape.

"I took her to the place where the Alexander boy had slipped in and where it was hard for anybody to climb out. I waited a minute. Another car was coming along the road. 'When it turns the corner,' I thought, 'when it turns!' Its lights shone straight and strong, they blinded us, they came on and on, toward us. Agna says, 'It's coming, it's coming! . . .'

"For the lights made no turn at the corner. The lights shot out from the alders. I could hear the talking and laughing in the car. In less than a flash of time the car shook the ground around us, and went crashing down and down into the deep of the water. But first the lights of the water, or of the dashboard, or of the sky, or of heaven struck full on their faces that were still laughing. Well, there on that seat I tell you I saw me in my wedding suit that was new, and beside me Agna, that was young again.

"There was a cry from Agna that was young and from me where I stood—and I saw what I'd done—reached back into the past and killed her that it was tragedy to kill. It was so that it had found me out. God had done it to me—just that way. I see it so. . . . All night I've walked in the woods, waiting for the time to tell. Now you know—now you know."

Jens Jevins stood head down, abruptly distracted, listless. The hundred voices in the room burst their silence. And after the first words, crude and broken, the women were saying, "Walked all night in the woods? But somebody has just pressed his clothes for him!"

Now the sound of running feet and the cries of men reached the room, and as these increased none knew whether to run down in the street or to stay in the courtroom, where Jens Jevins might say something more. But now a great gasping voice cried from the stair: "Car gone into Jevins' clay hole!" . . . and immediately the room was emptied of all but those who must stay, and Jevins, who seemed not to have heard.

As one man, and he breathing his horror, the town of Tarnham ran down the highway, and did not take the turn but kept straight on and flowed over the green and spangled slope and surrounded the Jevins' pond. Some highway men, placing signs, had seen the corner of a top protruding from the water.

And now policemen and firemen were lifting from the water, slowly and with sickening lurchings and saggings, a black coupé, new by the signs, and within it, the seated figures of man and woman. And all about them, on sides and back of the car, were gay ribbon streamers, white and pink, and the lettering said: *Yes, we're just married.* And such signs were also pasted in paper, and from them was dangling a water-soaked old shoe. A young chap, he was, with his hands still on the wheel and the emergency brake set, and a rose on his coat lapel; and his young bride, in her neat gown of blue, had her hands folded in her lap, over a little silver bag.

Now the Sheriff came, leading Jens Jevins, and pushed through the crowd, and the people moved respectfully, for the tale of the courtroom had not yet gone about. The Sheriff and Jens Jevins went to the two figures, taken from the car and covered on the grass, and Jens said in a loud voice, "There we are!" And now he shouted in agony, "Agna, Agna! Jens!" and cast himself on the ground beside the two still figures.

The people were stupefied, not knowing what to feel, with the men and women from the courtroom murmuring his story. Jens Jevins—and he so prosperous and known to them all. They had seen him yesterday, buying and selling. Could his wife have been in the car, too—the complaining woman, who took prizes?

No, for here she came walking down the slope from the house, wondering at the crowd gathered about their pond. She looked questioning, in her neat black dress and her striped scarf, and they made way for her; and a neighbor who had been in the courtroom cried, "Mrs. Jevins, Mrs. Jevins! The car that you saw last night go into the water had a bride and groom!"

But Agna Jevins said, "What car! I saw no car go into the water."

"What! You were not out here in the night and saw this car. . . ."

"I?" cried Agna Jevins. "I was in bed the whole night, and Jens too. What car?"

They told her. She covered her eyes and said, "God forgive me, I heard a cry and thought of saying so to Jens, but he was sleeping soundly."

Jens and the Sheriff moved toward her, and when he came up to her Jens began speaking softly, "All our friends, Agna, thinking of us through the night. And who could have imagined that we were spending the whole night so, side by side; and with the sunrise, we still so near to each other, saying nothing. Who could have told us in our early youth: 'You will rest on that night in a bed of ooze, and none shall know or care that you lie passionless and forgotten'? Who could have known that our wedding day and our death night would be one, because of a pond beyond alders, pleasant and secure? We have died with our dream and our happiness upon us, neither trouble nor weariness has touched us, nor the slow rust of unending days. I have no need to send you to your death, for we have died in the safety of our youth and not in the deep of days already dead. . . ."

They led him to his house. Weeping, Mrs. Jevins said, "It must have come on him all of a rush. For I pressed his clothes and got his breakfast and he went out of the house. And nothing had changed."

The legend grew that Jens Jevins had had a vision of that happening of the night, and that it had sent him off his head.

Born in Wisconsin in 1874, Zona Gale was educated at the University of Wisconsin, where she received Bachelor and Master degrees. After working as a reporter on a Milwaukee newspaper for two years, she was on the staff of the New York World *until 1904, when she sold her first short story and returned to Wisconsin to focus on writing fiction. The Broadway dramatization of her novel of small town Wisconsin life,* Miss Lulu Bett, *won her a Pulitzer Prize in 1920. She died in 1938.*

The world of the white man comes to a halt as every Indian moves toward South Dakota. What does this have to do with the disappearance of a New York street hustler?

FIFTEEN

A Wounded Knee Fairy Tale

Craig Strete

He was hustle-looking, hustle-hungry. Sitting there in the doorway of the cut-rate record shop, watching the Sunday afternoon in New York scene. Eyes scanning the freaks and the lunch hour ladies, the alarm-clock, time-card-punching cowboys. Sunday afternoon and Johnny on the record store steps looking for a new boy. He could always tell the new ones, almost smell them. He just sat there, looking for a home in every face.

This boy coming down the street. Some kind of Indian costume. God! Authentic-looking, maybe even real deer-skin and wood-and-bone chokers, the whole trip. In New York City, and looking out of place in this authentic suit right down to the moccasins. That whole thing there, he added that up. It had a smell to it of money. Those kinds of costumes are strictly heavy paper over the counter. This boy coming down the street.

Johnny looked at the boy's face and knew he had a mark. A freak, a face-painted freak on Sunday afternoon in New York. The boy was out-of-town action, hick town, he looked out of place. Strictly a stranger, lost, bewildered, looking like he just got off the boat and everything is new to him.

When that boy went by, Johnny moved out behind him, stalking him like a cat. He kept close, planning, figuring angles, figuring how to take him before the other hustlers moved in. When the boy stopped to look at his reflection in a store window, Johnny moved up and touched him on the shoulder, touched him softly, caressingly.

"You're going to need a guide. Someone to show you the city. Show you the sights. Huh, boy? You're new, boy, you're new here and you need someone to take care of you." Johnny grinned, mixing threat and invitation in his voice. The marks liked Johnny. He had full, soft lips, he talked his hustles nice. He wore old clothes but they were always clean and he had that little-boy look. The little-boy look, the curly hair, the clean, hairless face, the soft neuter movements that made the marks go for him.

"I show you real nice. You're going to like how I show you." Johnny said it right, said it dirty.

But that face-painted freak, that costumed crazy, he was like a million miles away. He just stared at his reflection in the window. Then he spoke, a language of lilting polysyllables, strange inflections. He seemed to speak as much to himself, as much to his reflection, as to the hustler.

"Hell!" muttered Johnny. "I shoulda known you'd be a damn foreigner." The hustler smiled again and gave it another try. "Habla Español?"

Behind the boy, Valdez was coming along, coming up behind the boy. Valdez with that empty walk when he's empty, hungry for himself, hungry for that next best mark. Johnny saw him coming, saw that high-pressure hype with the big chest and overmuscled arms, and his face went black with rage. Valdez came up quick, nose out like a fish nibbling bait.

Johnny grabbed the boy, spun him around, tried to pull him away. There was a hiss like animal fat burning in a cook fire and the space where Johnny stood was empty. There was a stench, an odor of scorched hair. Valdez had frozen in place, one arm extended, reaching for Johnny's new boy.

The strange boy turned and looked at Valdez, turned and looked. Valdez was paralyzed. The strange boy's face was changing color, going from brown to blood red, and then he was gone. So gone. It was a goddamn trip. He was there and then nothing. It was like a light bulb going out. Sunday afternoon in New York and there was this freak in this damn Indian costume, and two hustlers had tried to take him and one had disappeared like out of some goddamn fairy tale and the other hustler had watched them both disappear. Man, it could only happen in New York City on a Sunday afternoon.

It wasn't a question of security. It didn't matter if you cut your teeth on the hammer and sickle or on the stars and stripes. It was a gathering of frightened children, a hodgepodge of military and government personnel. There was a full crew of university eggheads, linguists, chiropodists, Russian spies, anyone who might know something, anyone willing to go. Quacks, religious fanatics, candy-ass liberals going to cheer, librarians, intelligence agents from everywhere, militiamen, army men, sailors in white suits, marines shaved bald like smart monkeys, Indian experts with long knives and CARE packages from the state liquor stores, Indian experts with degrees in Pawnee sex practices, phony Indians with hairy knuckles and raised eyebrow ridges, mouth breathers. Ambassadors and diplomats, senators and state governors, painted ladies and the criminally insane, an indistinct group, in inseparable aggregation, all moving together, all running like thunder-frightened cattle.

It began when someone reported that all the tribes were gathering, some FBI informer in a position to know, a reformed Indian with his pants down, waiting for government aid. Some sort of big powwow. Not unusual, not unheard of. That's what the informer said, several tribes had gathered together before, had had their little powwows. But this was different. Before the information could get out on the difference, the reformed Indian fell asleep with a knife in his back.

It *was* different. Suddenly, with no reason given, leaving possessions and homes abandoned, all the tribes began marching toward Wounded Knee. Cars, boats, airplanes, every imaginable type of vehicle was full of Indians moving toward Wounded Knee. A ceremony at the place where the hoop of the nations was broken. A civil disorder. Like Kent State, like Vietnam, like Korea, one civil disorder pretty much like any other. They could handle it. They told everyone they could handle it.

But on the morning of the day the tribes began moving,

at 10:45 Eastern Standard time, the lights went out in New York, the dynamos at Niagara froze solid. At Oak Ridge, the powerful atomic reactors fell silent. In Russia, the great bear in night was plunged into a deeper night and confusion. The clocks of the world stopped at 10:45. All over the world, there was the non-sound of things stopping, of machines falling silent.

At 11:30 Eastern Standard time, the only movement, the only sounds made by machines were made by vehicles moving toward Wounded Knee. Cars full of Indians speeding down the highways long after they had run out of gas. A twin engine plane with two Mohawk families, gliding silently westward over Chicago, both engines feathered, pulled at a speed that strained the wings, pulled forward with both engines silenced while the pilot shouted into a dead headset.

It was a selective madness. Nothing worked that had moving metal parts. Guns, cars, bicycles, garbage disposals, electric garage door openers, all the metal parts frozen solid, fused together, worthless. Only Indians moved freely, their cars worked, their planes, everything they touched, worked. Only Indians had guns that worked. It was stranger than New York City on a Sunday afternoon. Only Indians had guns that worked. And they moved toward Wounded Knee over the bodies of the obstacle course between them and Wounded Knee.

Ten days it took them to gather, ten days for the South American peoples to float up the rivers, to come out of the jungles and hidden places where white men had never been. Ten days to reach the ports and catch the airplanes and boats that waited for them there. Waited there to take them to Wounded Knee.

And the other people of the world, they went crazy. Aliens? An invasion from another planet? A warning from God?

The grasshopper people, government people, military replicas of people, they all danced to the same questions. They came running, crawling on knees suspiciously like helpless fists. Moving like old age toward Wounded Knee. They walked and rode horses. The more important of them rode in hastily built wooden carriages that broke down frequently. In growing numbers, they marched, moved, and

crawled. In their path they found only emptiness and still-
ness, as if a storm had passed leaving the air cleaned and
purified. Like hungry junkies with needle intensity, with one
goal, one vein, they too moved on Wounded Knee.

The group mind, the briefcase mentality, the committee
of single-minded purpose found him. They found him
dancing with the Rosebud Sioux. They found him dancing
with the Ojibway, the Cherokees, the Seminoles, the
Kiowas, all the tribes of creation spread out over the land
like the buffalo. Marching and dancing, moving in the wind
lke the leaves of corn, moving in one vast hoop that
stretched across the flat land like one all-encircling snake.
They found him dancing with the bird people, dancing with
the animal people. They found him dancing with the fox
people, the bear people, the wind river people. All around
like soft blankets, the spirits of the dead circled the dancers,
circled above, moving through the scattered bodies of their
children, moving in the shadow and light.

They saw him and he was unlike any man that had ever
walked their earth. His face was fire, his shoulders were
feathered with black eagle wings, and when he laughed it
was thunder and when he smiled it was lightning.

One of the generals, too long accustomed to a desk, too
long gone from the world of men, moved forward among
the watchers, pushed his way through the rapidly forming
committees and study groups. He elbowed his way past the
religious bleat, the organic cheering section, he broke
through and marched forcefully toward the dancers.

As he moved toward the path of the great circle, the dancers began falling silently to the ground. The women, the
children, the old ones, the fierce young men, the proud
young women, they all fell back to rest. To rest.

They rested, surrounded by whites held at bay by guns
that worked, guarded by tall warriors at the edge of the
hoop, fierce-eyed men with rifles. The bodies of those who
had come too close kept the others away. Every so often, a
liberal believing all men were brothers would add his body
to the piles of the dead.

The general was undeterred. The old general walked past
the guard who kept the gun pointed at his chest. For some

reason, no one made a move to shoot him. The old general walked up to one of the old men.

"How!" the general said, and he put his hand up, open-palmed, like a demented John Wayne. "On behalf of your President, I—"

There was a hiss like animal fat burning in the cook fire and the general and the rest of his sentence were gone.

And the white people moved back as if a spring had snapped within them. And they fled in one flowing wave. The one who fell from the sun stood at the top of the great Hoop of the Nations, and as one they rose up, all the peoples of the creation, they rose up. They danced, the old and the young and the sick and the lame, all whole now, all one.

And they danced in clouds of ghosts, whirling around and around, and as they passed beneath the winged man, there was the sound of a thousand things moving in darkness and light, shaking, a thousand things moving and breaking in the time of the going away. And gently, like the stroke of soft-feathered birds, the eyes of the man of thunder and lightning fell upon the people, his eyes touched them and they moved quietly like dying angels, floating like memories to the sun.

Faster and faster, the drums, the drums that went faster and faded and faster and faded and then stopped, each note like a monument, each note rising into the air like a flight of birds. And then they were gone. Gone. The Hoop, the spirits of the dead, the dancers, the drums of the people, all fallen into the sun.

And the being who fell from the sun stood alone. Alone. He spread his wings and let the sun spin above him. And the spin of the sun filled his wings and he left the earth. He left the earth.

Behind him on the plain, in the silence, in the dust, a general and a New York City hustler materialized, embraced in each other's arms. Embraced in each other's arms on sterile ground in a world that would never grow up.

Sterile children in a world that would never grow up.

Born in Indiana in 1950, Craig Strete was educated at Wright State University and the University of California at Irvine. The writer of scripts for numerous television shows under various pseudonyms, he won the Fourteenth Annual Georgia Book Award of the University of Georgia. His work has been translated into Dutch, French, and German.

The price of some sins outlasts the sinners.

SIXTEEN

Shaggy Vengeance
Robert Adams

"It was back in the late 1880s," Professor Bauer began, "that the last sizable herd of Northern Plains Bison was located along the banks of Blutig Creek, where it twisted its course through what came to be called *das Schlachthaustal.*"

Peggy, my wife, seated on the couch beside me with her legs tucked under her like the graceful feline she often resembled in movement, shivered suddenly and pressed closer to my side. A gust of the storm blowing down from Canada chose that moment to strike our cozy, if rented, house with a force that rattled doors and windows and shot tiny darts of icy air in an erratic pattern through the room, like a volley of phantom arrows from the bows of long-dead Indian warriors.

"Can't we talk about something else?" she asked. "If this keeps up, I won't get a wink of sleep, and I have to teach tomorrow, too, if you'll remember."

I was in the second semester of my first year at Buffalo Mountain Agricultural College back then, and Peggy was teaching second grade at Lost Herd Elementary School. While she was earning a bit less than she had back east, I was earning enough more to make up the difference and, moreover, I was doing what I wanted to do—teaching college-level English to kids who really had a desire to learn something. And after two years of attempting to teach high school English to roomsful of dead-end kids whose only interests were discussing the finer points of constructing zip-guns, smoking reefers in the boys' room, and carving their initials into anything within reach—mineral, vegetable or

162

animal—with the switchblade knives, which items were *de rigueur* for school dress in their primitive, savage subculture.

Each time I had forced myself to enter East Yorkville High, I had felt less like a teacher than like Clyde Beatty, with chair and whip and blank pistol, endeavoring to put wild, killer animals through the prescribed paces. Now, I was happy. I often found myself whistling something light and jolly as I drove my battered eleven-year-old Rambler the six or so miles from the outskirts of Lost Herd along the new and almost arrow-straight road to the college six miles away, even on mornings I had to follow the snowplow to get there.

Peggy, bless her, was content anywhere there were lots and lots of children, but she also was city-born-and-bred and she missed the appurtenances of big-city life—museums, theaters, ballet, symphony. But she loved me and did not complain . . . often or much.

There were comparatively few men involved in elementary or even in secondary education in those days, but such few as there were at Lost Herd School—from the courtly-mannered, stylish Principal Frederick Räbel to the strapping, likeable assistant athletic director, Rudi Keilermann—moved in a worshipful attendance upon my petite, vivacious, blonde wife. Since this sort of thing had been happening to Peggy for most of her twenty-six years, she took it all in stride, easily negotiating the tightly constricted and hazard-strewn path that such open masculine adulation set for her.

She got the same reaction from the fathers of most of her pupils, too. But, as she was really good at her chosen work—the kids liked her and she could get through to them—her relations with the other female teachers and the mothers were close and unstrained.

She had never learned to drive and, on those rare mornings when it was feasible, she pedaled her bike the eight blocks down Büffel Street to the school, but most of the time she rode in on the rickety bus on its return from the northwestern farms with its load of kids.

There were four of these ancient, rattletrap conveyances in Lost Herd—well, six actually, but the other two were no longer in working order and were being used as parts reservoirs at the behest of the tightfisted school board, its members worthy descendants of the more-than-thrifty, Germanic peasants who had settled this area eighty or so years back. I shuddered every time I saw my sweet, little Peggy climb aboard one of the automotive nightmares and watched it chug off, usually emitting backfires as loud as the reports of a 20mm Bofors and invariably trailing an opaque cloud of coal-black smoke.

My little Rambler coupe *looked* every bit as bad as a typical Lost Herd school bus, but I maintained it in its optimum condition, driving into Lost Herd at least one night in every couple of weeks to Wolff Knipsengeldt's service station, where that worthy would allow me to use his tools and lift, sell me whatever I needed at cost and even order parts he did not stock. The price of this largesse being that I give ear to his endless, often bloodcurdling anecdotes of his days as a driver for Dutch Schultz in the Chicago area of the twenties. The townsfolk had heard these tales reiterated for years and would no longer sit still for them, so the rare newcomers or the transients were Wolff's only audience.

Professor Olaf Bauer, a jovial little gnome of a man, was easily twice my age and, with his round, rosy cheeks, thick moustache and drooping meerschaum hunter's pipe, more resembled one of those jolly figures found on "Souvenir of München" *bierkrugen* than he did a professor of agrology and agronomy. Through his father, he was a grandson of one of the founders of Lost Herd. He had leapt at the chance to return when the state had decided to build one of the strategically located branch colleges hereabouts, acted as sort of an unofficial liaison between the college and the town, and had become my fast friend within weeks of my arrival.

Olaf was a widower and seldom saw his children, who were scattered about the county with families of their own now, so he took to dropping in on Peggy and me on a semi-regular, twice-weekly basis, always bringing several long, green or brown bottles of wine to accompany the dinner. He and Peggy got along fabulously, chattering happily away in German (her maiden name was von Annweiler) or, haltingly, in the Norwegian he had absorbed with his Norse mother's milk and was, at Peggy's request, teaching her.

That particular night, with the dishes stacked in the kitchen, our bellies full of hearty, Germanic fare cooked by Peggy in her superlative manner, three bottles of an imcomparable Wehlener Sonnenuhr Moselle and vanilla ice cream, we had congregated before the coal grate in the small living room of our frame house, Olaf and I with our pipes and all three of us with scalding black coffee and snifters of brandy.

Mausi, the huge, rangy, grey tomcat, was apparently a fixture of the house, since he was resident on the premises when Peggy and I arrived. He had remained because he earned his keep, waging constant, no-quarter war against the horde of field mice and voles which seemed to prefer a heated house to a frozen, and usually snow-covered, prairie for their winter habitat. Mausi was also an infallible prophet of coming blizzards or deep snows. Any night he refused to go out we always could expect bad weather by morning, no matter what some glib meteorologist might declare on the radio.

As I faced him across Mausi's hearth rug, I remarked, "Olaf, how did the town ever get the name, Lost Herd. This certainly isn't ranching country and I didn't think the old trail-herds ever got this far north."

Olaf had raised his bushy eyebrows a notch. "You drive from here to the college every day, Frank; haven't you ever stopped and read that state marker-sign just beyond the first bridge where the road curves around the base of Buffalo Mountain?"

When I admitted I had not, he began the tale.

"In those days there were very few Indians hereabouts. Those who later were brought back here and settled on the Buffalo Mountain Reservation were then still living under guard in the south, Oklahoma Territory, I think. But one very old Indian lived on the mountain and sometimes came into the town, which then was called 'Freiheitburgh,' to trade a few skins and furs for tobacco, dried beans, and the odd bit of hardware.

"My own *Grossvater* Bauer often saw him and was several times in Messerschmidt's store when the old Indian came in. *Grossvater* used to say that he looked as old as the mountain itself, that Indian, with snow-white hair and teeth worn almost to the gums, hands like bony claws covered with dark parchment and beady, black eyes sunk deep into the sockets.

"Those few who could speak his language said that he called the mountain on which he lived 'The Mother of Buffalo' and claimed that the mountain had given birth to the ancestors of the buffalo, long ago, before even the Indians came here.

"*Grossvater* knew the old man's Indian name and used to tell it to me, but I confess I've forgotten it, now. The translation from whatever tongue it was into English by way of *Grossvater*'s Plattdeutsch would be something on the order of 'Guardian-Priest of the Mother of Buffalo.'

"The folks from Freiheitburgh and round about had known of the small herd in the little valley or *Tal* as long as they had been settled here, but the valley's creek was subject to annual floodings of meltwater from the mountain and was too narrow, anyway, for farming, so the bison were left alone except when one or two men rode over and shot the occasional animal for meat. But not just the meat, either, for they were frugal folks and, like the Indians, they used every part of a carcass.

"Another reason they kept close about the bison herd was that they wanted no part of professional buffalo hunters, not around their town and farms and womenfolk.

"Buffalo hunters have often been glamorized, but there was nothing glamorous about the real article. They were a class made up of the utter dregs of frontier society—brutal, vicious, filthy men. They seldom washed, wore clothes until they rotted off, and carried with them everywhere the stench of blood and death.

"Indians killed them on sight, peaceable towns that wanted to stay that way hired mankillers to keep the buffalo hunters and similar riffraff out; only the Army tolerated these pariahs, and then only because their extermination of the bison was helping the Army by eliminating the natural larder of the Plains Tribes.

"Well, all through the seventies and early eighties while the bison fell in their millions under the big-bore rifles of the hunters, who took only the hides and sometimes the tongues, leaving billions of tons of meat to rot, the small herd thrived in its little valley, showing little proclivity to stray far from the mountain, and not threatening crops enough to warrant exterminating it.

"By the late eighties, the buffalo hunters' grisly time was over; they had done their chosen work too well and too completely. The Plains Bison was considered extinct by the scholars of that time, and the species very narrowly missed that classification.

"Such few hunters as were still in the field spent more time gathering wagonloads of buffalo bones and carting them to the railheads than they did shooting their rifles.

"Therefore, when a big-mouthed railroad employee who had been served a fresh bison steak in the town of Freiheit-burgh mentioned the fact, the hunters converged on this area like buzzards to a dead horse."

"But," I interjected, "hadn't any of them passed through here earlier? I thought they scoured the territories after the larger herds were slaughtered."

Olaf shrugged and took a sip of his brandy. "I suppose those who passed nearby thought that, as the land was mostly farms, the bison had all been killed off by the farmers. But when they heard the truth, dozens came—by rail, by horse, by wagon and Red River cart. They didn't waste much time in the town, but headed straight for Buffalo Mountain.

"None of the folks hereabouts liked thinking of what was going to happen to the bison, but they were hard-working, peace-loving people and they didn't consider the shooting of a few score wild beasts sufficient reason to rile the hair-trigger tempers of a group of fifty or sixty rough, cruel men. The town marshall, Horst Zeuge, gave notice that he and his three regular deputies would protect the town, but that anybody who went out to the hunters' camp was on his own.

"The first night after most of the hunters arrived, they set up camp, brought whiskey and started a drinking bout that ended in a pitched battle between three or four different groups of them. The next morning, the survivors were too hung over to do any shooting so they just scouted out the herd. They boozed the second night, too, and somehow the wagon containing most of the ammunition for the big rifles caught fire and burned to the axles.

"Three of the leaders took what money hadn't been spent on whiskey into town and bought out Messerschmidt's small stock of heavy caliber ammunition, placing orders for more as soon as the railroad could get it up to Freiheitburgh.

"*Grossvater* said that from noon until it was too dark to see, all the town could hear the booming cracks of the big rifles. There were not many shots though the next day, for most of the ammunition was by then gone and the hunters had no more money to buy the lead and powder and primers they would have needed to make more cartridges.

"When the three hunter leaders finally came into town on the day the train was due with their ordered ammunition, they brought two wagons piled high with scraped, green hides and a cart with two barrels of fresh tongues. Old Messerschmidt got all three loads, giving the hunters what value they didn't get in ammunition in whiskey.

"*Grossvater* was then one of the town marshall's regular deputies and he berated Messerschmidt for selling more whiskey to the hunters, but the old merchant said that if they should get drunk and kill a few more of each other, why then that would be that many fewer for the federal marshall the town had sent for after the first shootout to handle.

"After the hunters had left for their camp with the new stocks of ammunition, one of the earliest settlers, who could speak the Indian language, came to the marshall's office, and with him was the old Indian. Through the translator, Guardian-Priest of the Mother of Buffalo implored Marshall Zeuge to stop the strangers from killing more bison, but Zeuge gave the same answer he had given to the white folks. Then he advised the old man to go up on his mountain and stay there until the territorial marshall came and brought things back to normal.

"*Grossvater* was there that afternoon, and he said that Guardian-Priest just stood and stared at the marshall and the rest of them for two or three minutes; then he started to speak . . . *in good German.*

" 'The Mother of Buffalo has been good to you who have come from a far land, as she was good to those who lived in this land before you, as she was good to the ones who pre-

ceded them. Her children's bodies have given you suste-
nance, warm hides, horn and bone and sinew for your
tools, chips for your fires. Nor have the Mother's children
gone forth from their valley to eat or despoil your maize or
the strange grasses you grow for the tiny seeds.

"'Yet now you see strangers come to kill all The Mother's
children, not for food and tools, but only for hides and the
evil joy of killing for the sake of killing. The Mother has given
of her children to help you in your times of need. In this, her
time of need, you turn away your faces from her.

"'I am a very old man. I have done and will do all that
one old man can do to protect The Mother's children, while
you many and far younger men will do nothing.

"'But be warned: The Mother will neither forget nor forgive your perfidy. As her children are dying in their little
valley, so too will the get of your loins die there, one day.
Skinless and tongueless and dead will your children lie in
that valley, even as The Mother's children now lie there.'"

Olaf had emptied his pipe of ashes and now he began to
stuff it afresh with the dark mixture from his old, cracked
pouch.

Peggy gulped half her brandy and shivered. "I thought
you weren't going to tell ghost stories tonight, Olaf? You lied
to me."

The old man eyed her from beneath his shaggy brows. "I
lied to you, *liebchen*? I did not lie to you. I have told nothing
but the truth as it was told to me, and my *Grossvater* was
known all his life as a truthful man, not given to exaggera-
tion or embroidery."

Peggy shivered yet again. "But that curse, Olaf, that poor
Indian's curse, I'm all gooseflesh from it."

Olaf chuckled. "Now, *liebchen*, you know how and why
voodoo works against primitives and not, usually, against
civilized people. It is necessary to believe in curses, to be
superstitious. You are clearly superstitious.

"So, too, were my ancestors, but only in a European vari-
ety of superstition, so the old Indian's curse had no effect
upon them, as it certainly would have upon other Indians."

Peggy shook her tiny head, gripping the snifter so tightly
that her knuckles shone white and I was sure that any minute the stem would snap off or the globe break.

"No, Olaf, the curse was not directed at them, but at their children and grandchildren, at all those children who descended from them."

Olaf finished stuffing his huge pipe, struck a match and went through the meticulous routine of lighting it before he answered.

"Well, if so, the curse has had no effect to date, not one that I know of anyway."

I still wanted to hear the conclusion of the story, so I said, "Did they kill the rest of the herd the next day?"

He shook his head. "No, what with the whiskey, they had another drinking bout and, instead of shooting the next day, they moved their camp further from town, into the valley itself, which was a fatal mistake, as it turned out. With the marshall's warning and all, nobody rode out there until the territorial marshall came in on the train with a platoon of the Tenth Cavalry. He and Zeuge and *Grossvater* rode out with the soldiers, but there were no hunters to arrest.

"Somehow or other, they'd managed to stampede the herd, what was left of it. The bison had apparently run right over the camp in the middle of the night, since most of the bodies found were still rolled in their blankets. That camp was a gruesome sight, *Grossvater* averred.

"The only survivor was found a couple of days later by a farmer. He wasn't quite right in the head and didn't live long, but the story he told was that the first night in the new camp, they had caught an old Indian skulking about. The hunters hated Indians as much as Indians hated them. They skinned him alive before they finally killed him.

"That night the bison came. As I said, the one survivor was mentally unbalanced by it all. He repeatedly swore that the herd that struck the camp was led by an Indian on a pony, but of course no one believed him.

"But the strangest thing of all is that no one ever saw the herd after that, to this very day. Soldiers and settlers rode up and down that valley and all over the mountain, but never found even a fresh buffalo chip. The federal marshall, who had been a plainsman in his youth, was of the opinion that the herd, after it overran the camp, kept going north and passed on into Canada. *Grossvater* agreed with him.

"During the First World War, when things and people

were suspect if German, it was decided to change the name of Freiheitburgh and the name finally decided upon was Lost Herd. It is as simple as that, my good, young friends."

Peggy, with her prescience, must have known of the horror that was coming, for she awakened me that night and many another for several weeks with her nightmare-spawned screams. I must confess that I, too, felt a little prickle up the back of my neck each time I drove past Buffalo Mountain, after that, or crossed the fine, new concrete bridge over Blutig Creek, but being a sane, well-educated man, I rationalized it to the point at which it no longer bothered me on a conscious level.

In early March we had a week of unseasonal warmth, followed by a howling storm and freezing rain that left everything for miles coated with ice, including the nice, new road. That was the night on which two of our college boys were coming back from a weekend visit to their families on farms just the other side of Lost Herd.

Hansi Zeuge was known to be a good, careful driver and his almost-new Triumph sportscar was equipped with chains and said to have been in perfect mechanical condition. Nonetheless, a country road crew found the Triumph smashed into the rail of Blutig Creek bridge around dawn of a Monday morning. The two bodies were found atop the ice of the creek below. Hansi and Wilhelm Hüter were buried in sealed caskets, not unusual in bad smashups.

The next accident was less than a month later and at almost the same spot. There were four fatalities in the second mishap, three of them locals, one a boy from downstate. Strangely, in the wake of the second accident, a bevy of law-enforcement types descended on Lost Herd, poked and pried about the town and the area, and questioned a number of residents.

The resident MD at the college, Herman Blaurig, had done his residency in New York and welcomed my occasional visits to his clinic. His cousin was county coroner and as we sat in his office one afternoon sipping tea laced with dark rum, "Frank," he said, "have you wondered why the state cops have been nosing around here?"

I nodded. "Sure, Doc, everybody has."

He glanced about the room with a conspiratorial eye, then lowered his voice. "Now don't go spreading this around. We don't want to scare folks, Frank, but they was some damn peculiar things about the four kids that was killed week before last. And the two boys before them, for that matter.

"My cousin, Doc Egon, is the main reason the cops is here. The first two, the Zeuge boy and Willi Hüter, was thrown clear through the convertible top, prob'ly parts of them went through the windshield, too, and they must've slid some way on the ice and they likely laid down there for some hours, so Egon figgered what all was done to them could be explained by the accident itself or by animals getting at the bodies, 'fore they was found.

"But in this last one, Frank, it was a four-door seedan. The driver seems to of lost control right where the road starts to curve 'round the mountain. The car skidded, flipped end over end a couple of times and wound up burning in the creek. All four kids was flung out while it was still moving. Some drummer seen the fire and all and barrel-assed into town and the sheriff and rescue squad and fire company and all got there no more'n a hour after it happened.

"And that's where the funny part starts. All four of them kids was thrown into snowbanks on the sides of the road. The clothes of three of them was torn off in pieces, even their boots, the skin had been torn or abraded off all three of them and some critter had torn out their tongues. Aside from the tongues being gone, their faces and heads hadn't been touched."

As he added hot tea and dollops of rum to our cups, I asked, "You said three, what happened to the fourth one?"

He sucked at his prominent incisors for a moment, then shook his head. "Nothing, Frank, not one dang thing! It was that Garrity boy from downstate. His neck was broke clean and he had some more broken bones and accompanying contusions, but he was fully dressed. His nose had been mashed flat, his front teeth were broken off and his face generally torn up some, but he still had his tongue."

The doctor blew hard on his tea, then sipped it noisily. "Egon figgers that any animals would've got to three of them kids would've got to the othern, too. So he figgers warn't a four-legged critter, that's why he called in the state on it.

"Now, Frank, don't you go tellin' all this here to your pretty little wife and scare her half to death. But you be dang sure you lock up tight at night until they catch this lunatic."

I didn't tell Peggy any of it. Maybe I should've; she thinks so . . . now. Maybe, if I had, none of the worst part would have happened. But Hell, you can "if" and "maybe" yourself into a straitjacket and a soft room. I didn't tell her because I love her and I knew she was sensitive as all Hell and I didn't want to upset her.

Grimfaced, well-armed men tramped and drove and rode horses all over the area, working outward from Buffalo Mountain in wide spirals, but they never found much of anything. Some hoofprints in the snow down by the creek that some said were bison, but were felt to be simply strayed cattle from one of the small-scale, local dairy-beef operations.

I did buy a pistol—an elderly Colt Peacemaker with a four-inch barrel, which I loaded with five of the huge cartridges and hid in the glove compartment of the car, so as not to alarm Peggy, who was terrified of firearms of any description.

Spring came in without any more deaths and the community settled down into its usual pursuits. Olaf began to drive over for the twice-weekly dinners again; I recommenced my evenings at Wolff Knipsengeldt's automotive infirmary.

At the college, the faculty and students returned from spring break to stare in wonder at the five bison which had, after knocking down some yards of fencing, joined the dairy herd in its pasture. They all were young, healthy animals— two heifers and three immature bulls. The Canadian Government was known to maintain a herd of bison in the province just north of us, and the initial supposition was that these were strays from that herd.

When I told Peggy about the bison she was thrilled and, two nights later at the first of our dinners since the break, she and Olaf cooked up the idea for a couple of bus loads of the children from Lost Herd Elementary coming out to see these first bison to reappear in these parts since the 1880s.

I had misgivings about the whole affair, principally because I feared that if those decrepit buses tried to maintain any speed in excess of twenty-five miles per hour for some six whole miles, they would rapidly disintegrate right there on the highway, held together as all four were with rust, peeling paint, rubberbands, masking tape, and prayer.

The outing was cleared with the school board and set for a Thursday afternoon. It was decided that the second and third grades would go: Peggy's class and the one taught by a Miss Irunn Gustafsson who was also a school bus driver. The forty-odd children were to go in two buses—apparently the board members had no more faith in their four automotive abortions than did I.

On the Wednesday evening before that hellish day, I had driven in to Wolff Knipsengeldt's, immediately after dinner. He had sent word that that day's mail had finally brought a part we had ordered from the closest Nash-Rambler dealer, far downstate. When, at length, the old mechanic and I had finished the installation, washed up a bit and were sharing a couple of bottles of cold beer, while relaxing in the tilt-back front seats of my car, Wolff lolled his grizzled head back and reached up to ring his scarred knuckles on the horizontal section of the two-inch steel rollbar—sometime in its checkered past, my little car had apparently been used as a stock-car or a dragster, of which period the rollbar welded to the frame was the only souvenir, aside from an extremely heavy suspension.

After another pull at his beer bottle, Wolff said, "Frankly, tinny as they makes cars today, you'uz shore smart to leave this-here bar on. Ef this-here little sweetie-pie ever comes to roll 'r flip, that-there bar'll save your life, likely.

"You mark my words, Franky, the day's gonna come, and not too long a-comin' neither, whin the friggin' in-surance comp'nies or evun the Guv'mint's gonna make the folks builds cars—Ford and Chrysler and Gen'rul Motors and all—put in stuff like rollbars and steerin' wheels won't bust up your ribs, and rubber or suthin to pad the dashboards and a whole lotta stuff like thet, just like they made 'em all put in safety glass in windshields, a while back.

"Hell, prob'ly won't be long 'fore near ever car you see'll have seat belts, too. Standard!"

This was a new one on me. "Seat belts, Wolff? Such as airplanes use? That kind? What earthly good would they be in a car?"

Without answering me, he set his half-full bottle on the floorboards and got out of the car. I assumed he was going around to the john, but I was wrong. Presently, he returned bearing a paper-wrapped parcel. Sitting back down and holding his bottle tightly between his bony knees, he delved under the wrappings and extracted two pieces of black webbing each about two inches wide and obviously of some length, though folded upon themselves several laps and secured with thick rubber bands; each dangled metal fittings from the ends, and the centers of each mounted a thick, square piece of chrome a bit wider than the webbing and bearing some automotive hallmark I could not make out in the dim interior of the Rambler.

Wolff handed one of the things to me and said, "These-here is seat belts, Franky. Old man Zeuge got me to order 'em for to go on poor little Hansi's TR. An' you know, Hansi an' Willi seen my light—I'z workin' late on ol' Miz Heidi Wagner's '47 Hudson—an' they drove in here to get gas, thet same night they'z kilt. I tol' him then I'd done got these-here in an' I could put 'em on right then, wouldn' a took more'n twenny, thirty minits, but them poor *Burschen,* they dint wanta take the time, then. Chances are, if they hadn't been in sich a all-fired hurry," he sighed, belched, and sniffed strongly, then hawked and spit out the window.

But his story had told me what I wanted to know. I could see the value of the strips of webbing. If the two boys had been belted into the sportscar, the impact would not have hurled their bodies through roof or windshield and twenty long feet down onto a hard-frozen creek. They still might have been injured, but they, most likely, would still be alive, at least.

Knowing Wolff's frugality—though he'd do almost anything for someone he considered a friend, the wag throughout Lost Herd was to the effect that he was capable of extracting blood from turnips and of squeezing a silver dollar until the eagle defecated—I asked, "These things must be damned expensive, Wolff, anything that goes on a sportscar is. Why haven't you sent them back for a refund?"

"Englische Dummköpfe!" he exclaimed, with feeling. "I tried to, Franky. You know I don't write letters too good, but I tol' thet sweet Miss Gustafsson whatall I wanted to say, one day an' she writ the purties' letter you ever did see an' done it with a typewriter, t'boot. She tol' the dealer I got these-here belts from in Ch'cago all 'bout them *Jungen* a getting kilt an' all, but it dint do no damn good.

"Them bastids, they sint 'em back to me, *postage due,* along of this-here snotty letter, said I'd bought the fuckers an' now they'uz mine! So they just been layin back in the office closit with a bunch of old Hupmobile and Maxwell parts was in there whin I bought this-here place."

To shorten a long story, when I drove back home that night, the Triumph seat belts had been installed in my car. I knew that Peggy would not like the extra expense, but I thought the added safety feature might win over her cautious nature. May God bless and keep old Wolff Knipsengeldt, wherever he may be today, for those seat belts saved our lives, Peggy's and mine.

Wednesday had been rainy and Wednesday night had been cold and drizzly with a brisk wind from the northwest making it downright chilly. But Thursday morning dawned clear and bright, with only a few high, wispy clouds drifting like cotton candy across the rich, light-blue of the sky. The air was almost balmy and filled with the promise of the prairie summer to come. There was no hint, that morning, of the cold, grim, Hell-spawned horror that would lie under that sun before the day had ended.

The buses from Lost Herd were scheduled to arrive at the college at nine that morning and I had made arrangements to be free for most of the time the kids would be on campus—not a difficult thing for me within the small, friendly, easy-going college. They were not there at nine, nor yet at ten and I was worried sick about Peggy by the time the two aged vehicles chugged and spluttered up the cursive drive, each trailing its inevitable cloud of thick, oily fumes.

Peggy and her twenty-three little second-graders were on the first bus, driven by blond, handsome Rudi Keilermann.

The second automotive antique was driven by plump, red-haired Irunn Gustafsson, leading her twenty-seven third-graders in a round of *Volkslieder.*

Olaf Bauer had outdone himself in preparations for the visiting children. Since most of them were farm kids and many would eventually be students at Buffalo Mountain Ag., he had set up a Cook's tour of all of the varied facilities and some of the classes, a cafeteria lunch, with the dairy herd and bison for dessert. The delayed arrival naturally forced him to reshuffle his schedule somewhat, but the program worked out just fine, with the children all suitably impressed throughout. But, at the end, they ignored the prize cattle to ooh and ahh and bombard poor, patient Olaf with their endless questions concerning the huge, shaggy, dark-brown bovines.

Doctor Wallace Churchill, the Administrator, had wired an inquiry to the Canadians regarding our five young *bison bison* and had received a return wire to the effect that none of the small herd seemed to be AWOL but, nonetheless, had included examples of the series of numbers which would be found tattooed inside the left ear of any Canadian-type bison.

The five shaggy strangers had proven amazingly tame and cooperative—which reinforced the suppositions that they were not truly wild. But when they were all chuted and examined, no man-made markings of any description were found.

The children were loaded aboard the buses a little after two PM, but then the third-grader bus refused to start. Two of our mechanics were hastily summoned from the college tractor garage. After extensive examinations of the grease-caked, oil-dripping engines of both buses, accompanied by exclamations and crudities that would have made even Wolff Knipsengeldt blush, the mechanics announced that, considering the abominable conditions of the engines, it was a divine miracle that either bus had even made it to the college and that the only way the one would make it off the campus would be behind a tow truck.

After some discussion, it was decided to put all the kids aboard the one operative bus, three instead of two to a seat. I offered to follow in my car and, since the bus was rather crowded, it was not difficult to persuade Peggy to ride with me.

With a roar and a clatter of loose parts, backfiring deafeningly and laying its usual smoke screen, the single, jam-packed bus swung around the drive and headed for the road back to Lost Herd.

Peggy had been sleeping when I had come in the night before and I had forgotten to tell her about the new seat belts earlier, so it took me a few minutes to explain to her how to fasten and tighten them. Then a student came running over to the car to bring Olaf the pipe he had left behind somewhere on the tour and to have a few words with the professor about something academic. By the time I finally got down to the highway, the bus was minuscule with distance on the straight, almost flat road.

Going a little faster than I liked to push my aging car, I took up pursuit, trying to at least close some of the lead. But young Rudi Keilermann seemed to think he was Raymond Mays, he was firewalling the bus as it started the long, looping curve around the flank of Buffalo Mountain. The mountain—all dark-green conifers and black rock outcrops—stood like a monstrous, shaggy-flanked beast in the midst of the flat or gently-rolling prairie lands and I suddenly realized how it had likely acquired its Indian name and legends: from this angle, its ridgecrest did bear a resemblance to a bison's silhouette—the glaciers of Pleistocene times had so carved it that the rounded peak took a sharp downslope on the long side and fell into a saddle on the other before rising back to another slightly lower round summit. Viewed imaginatively, this lone sentinel of the plains could easily be likened to a gigantic bison.

Nonetheless, I had closed the gap sufficiently to hear the sudden screaming of tortured rubber, followed almost immediately by a tearing, rending metallic crash!

"No! Oh, dear God, no!" screamed Peggy.

Not knowing just what lay ahead, I geared down as I rounded the mountain and started down the long, gentle slope into Slaughterhouse Valley, toward the bridge over Bloody Creek. All that was visible of the bus from that angle was the red-rust undercarriage and the smoking, still-spinning wheels. I could hear Peggy sobbing and Olaf muttering German prayers.

Then, as I neared the bridge, up the steep bank from the bed of Bloody Creek came the bison, a dozen or more of the huge beasts, all shining, curved horns and little red-glowing eyes. Each of the ton-weight monsters seemed to span the width of the road and I knew the Rambler would fold into itself like an accordion if it hit one. Nor was I the only one who saw them, for Olaf was leaning past me, pointing his finger at the animals while he shouted something incomprehensible in my ear.

I slammed on the brakes and it seemed for a moment that I might make it safely. But then the rear end fishtailed far, far to the right and both left wheels rose up and then it all was a kaleidoscope of the blue sky below and black macadam above and gut-wrenching terror for myself and for Peggy and Oh-God-take-me-if-you-must-but-please-spare-Peggy. The screams were as deafening as the grinding-tearing of rending metal and the bone-jarring, slamming thuds. And it seemed to go on forever, yet was over immediately.

I'll never know just how many times the little car rolled, but when I came to realize that I was alive, the Rambler was upright again and still on the roadway, just beyond the wrecked bus. The Rambler's hood was gone, along with the windshield, all the other windows and most of the roof . . . and poor old Olaf. I could see his grotesquely sprawled body in the middle of the road.

At first, I thought Peggy was gone, too, but she still was strapped safely beside me. As it developed, she actually had come out of it all with fewer physical injuries than had I, since the long-defective lock on her side of the seat-back had failed early-on and centrifugal force had held her prone, affording her body the added protection of the stronger sides of the car.

From far back the road, the broad, multiple skid marks showed the distance the bus had skidded before slamming over on its left side. The sliding bus had struck the strong, thick steel pole that held the state's **Slaughterhouse Valley—Lost Herd** sign at windshield level *and torn back almost the entire length* of the weak, rusty metal. The bus lay open like a discarded can of sardines and part of its contents spilled down the green, grassy slope into the old level of Slaughterhouse Valley.

And among those too-still little shapes, the bison moved. In twos and threes, the brown-and-black-nightmare monsters went from one battered small body to another, leaving in their wake . . . pure, screaming horror. The huge, primeval heads went down and when they arose, the small corpses lay stripped of both clothing and skin.

Other bison were grouped about Olaf, up the road. And then I saw a rider approaching—a white-haired, wrinkled Indian on a runty, big-headed, claybank horse. The pony-sized equine was devoid of saddle, only a faded blanket hung over his back and withers; and his "bridle" was a length of braided rawhide tied around his lower jaw. The old Indian bore no feathers or other ornaments, and his clothing was roughly fashioned of buckskin.

Though the oldster looked as if the wind would blow him away, he dropped lightly from his mount at Olaf's now bare and skinless body. The sun glinted on the blade of the curved knife he drew from a hide sheath. He bent and grabbed something that distance denied me sight of, and his knife moved downward in a swift blur. Then he remounted and rode on toward the bus.

I must have passed out then—I was seriously injured, although I was not then aware of the fact. But Peggy's terrified shrieks aroused me. My wrecked car was surrounded by bison. Still prone, Peggy was frantically working the chrome handle in a vain attempt to roll up the smashed-out window.

Then I thought of the old Colt revolver. I didn't think that even as massive a pistol as the Peacemaker would kill one of the shaggy behemoths, but the noise—with its big, .45-caliber cartridges and its shortened barrel, made a Hellacious racket—might panic the mammoth creatures into a long-distance run . . . away from us. Miracles still happen. The glove compartment had not come open during the demolition of the rest of the car, yet it opened easily for me.

One of the hideous, red-eyed heads had intruded over the edge of the buckled door on Peggy's side and, screaming mindlessly, she threw up her arms to fend it off. I saw the mouth open, the tremendous tongue come out and lick along the upper surface of her right arm, removing the skin almost from elbow to wrist. That was when I cocked, levelled and fired the big pistol, point-blank!

The bison just rolled one of those red hell-eyes at me and made to lower head and flaying tongue toward the now unconscious body of my wife. But, suddenly, the old Indian was there, sitting on his horse.

His lips moved in the shaping of words that could not have been English or any other language I spoke, yet I could clearly understand him.

"No, Children of The Mother, these two are not accursed of Her."

I wasn't fully conscious or rational for weeks and, of course, no one believed a word of my account of what happened. All of it was blamed on shock and my concussion. The various law-enforcement types were of the opinion that the fact I had a pistol and had fired a "warning shot" had kept the maniacs who had mutilated all the bodies from the bus and poor Olaf's away from me and Peggy. Nor could her story corroborate my own since her mind had mercifully blanked out the horrors of that day.

The coroner's inquest decided that the bus had been driven too fast and that the bodies had been mutilated by "person or persons unknown."

The copious cloven-hoofprints pressed into the rain-softened earth up and down the length and width of Slaughterhouse Valley were said to have been there before the accident, caused by a herd of reservation cattle surreptitiously driven by Indians from their own barren ranges of wiregrass to feed the night long on the verdant, state-owned roadsides before being driven back to the reservation before dawn. This was known to be fact because only the dirt-poor Reservation Indians did not shoe their starveling nags, and the prints of unshod horsehooves had been found here and there.

By the time I was released from the hospital in Regen, the county seat, thirty-five miles from Lost Herd, the summer was well along. So that she could more easily visit me during my protracted confinement. Peggy had gotten Wolff Knipsengeldt to teach her to drive and then had bought

181

Olaf Bauer's Bel-Air sedan from her instructor, who acted as agent in most of the used car sales in Lost Herd.

Old Wolff was, as well, the source of most of what follows, since he was the only townsperson who did not show acute discomfort whenever I came around and who did not change the subject, clam up, or walk rapidly away when an outsider broached the subject of the sinister tragedy in Slaughterhouse Valley.

Not only had the state police investigators come back to Lost Herd, but various federal officials, as well. The Governor, himself, had been in town for a few days, and most of his entourage had remained when he did leave—a mixed bag of experts in specialties ranging from forensic medicine and game management through highway engineering and psychology.

Within the seven days which followed the "accident," every square inch of land surface, every building, construction or excavation of any nature was covered and recovered by posses of townsmen and farmers under the sheriff and his deputies, two full battalions of National Guardsmen trucked up from the state capital, a busload of federal marshals and FBI agents, most of the male students and staff from the college and even a contingent of mounted Indians from Buffalo Mountain Reservation. They searched a fifteen-mile radius of Lost Herd, by day and by night. Crop dusters flew their light planes at almost treetop level, keeping in touch with the ground parties by radio.

A farmer some miles northeast of Lost Herd had a fine Holstein bull killed when the animal made the fatal error of charging a group of Guardsmen crossing his pasture one night; he fell under a hail of rifle and sub-machine gun fire. Several coyotes were shot, here and there; and a couple of deer poachers apprehended. A hired hand on Otto Kleist's dairy farm was determined to be an Army deserter, arrested, and returned to some post clear down in Texas. But his and those of the poachers were the only arrests ever made. No slightest trace was ever discovered of the maniac or maniacs responsible for the mutilations.

Wolff did say that, high up on Buffalo Mountain, a cave had been discovered, its mouth almost closed by an old rock slide all overgrown with trees that had stood there at least fifty years. Two skeletons were found far back in the cave. One was that of a small horse and the other that of a man.

Those forensic types still in Lost Herd determined that the horse had most likely starved to death, as there were no marks of violence on the desiccated skin stretched over the bones and since marks of equine teeth were found in the partially-chewed-away poles which had formed the creature's stall.

There was no question what had killed the man, what with a round hole half of an inch in diameter in the forehead and most of the back of the skull missing. What was questioned was why no skin was found stretched over the human bones, save on the hands, feet, and portions of the lower face. The dry, cool air of the cave had preserved the horse's skin, so why not the man's?

Another unanswered question was how, among a collection of rusty, antique pots and small hardware, had come to rest an antler-hilted knife. Its curved blade was bright and shiny, where it was not blotched with blood determined, by testing, to be of several different *human* types and no more than a few days old!

Wolff had only heard bits and pieces of my own story, third and fourth hand from people who did not believe it . . . or could not allow themselves to do so. When he asked me to tell him, I did; I told him all of it on the August evening he checked over the Bel-Air the last time. Peggy and I were to start the long drive east, to Ohio and the new positions we had accepted, the next day.

When I had finished, Wolff just stared at his bottle of beer for some minutes, then he shook his grizzled head and said, softly, "It's some things happens in this-here old worl', Franky, cain't nobody ever figger. So mos' folks jest swears them things dint never happen, nohow, an' the folks what see them things wuz teched or drunk or jest plain lyin'. They *has* to do thet way, Franky, elst they couldn' sleep nights. But jest 'cause them as dint *see* won't an' caint b'lieve, don't allus mean them p'culair things dint happun."

Arising and setting down his beer bottle, he took a big flashlight from a shelf and walked toward the door, saying

"C'mon, Franky. It's sumpin back in the junkyard you needs to see."

The Rambler had long-since been stripped of any usable parts and its crumpled, jaggedly ripped and scraped body was red with rust except in those rare patches where a bit of paint remained. Wolff lifted off the passenger side door and laid it atop the crumbled fender, then opened the glove compartment and shone his light in.

"Franky, look in the left-han' back corner, there. See that-there hole? Now, looky here."

From beneath the seat, he pulled a rumpled and water-stained brown paper bag, delved a hand into it, then shone the beam on that palm. Across the grimy palm lay about five inches of a broad, sharp-pointed horn. At the wider end, it was raggedly shattered.

"Is this-here yours, Franky, or Miz Peggy's?"

I tried to answer but couldn't and ended shaking my head.

Wordlessly, Wolff put his hand into the still-open glove compartment and stuck the pointed end of the piece of horn in the peculiar hole. It fitted perfectly.

"When I towed this-here car in," he explained, "I natcherly put it in the locked lot over there, so wouldn' nobody mess with it 'til after Dep'ty Kalb an' th' Sher'f an' all had done pokin' at it. But, since you's my frien', Franky, I figgered to clean out the trunk an' glove c'mpartmunt, cause—nothin' 'ginst Karl Kalb, y'unnerstan'—it's some dep'ties got sticky fingers.

"After I'd done got ever'thin out'n the trunk an' got the glove c'mpartmunt empty, I felt aroun' in there an' come out with thet. An' Franky, I purely had to pull to get'er out, too, she'd really dug in. How you reckon the end of some critter's horn come to be stuck th'ough there, enyhow, Franky?"

Again, I could picture the huge, shaggy, horned head of the monster bison, the red fires of hell flickering in its eyes. Again, I could feel myself jerking open the glove compartment to get to the old Colt, painfully cocking the hammer, then trying to force my tremulous hands to hold the heavy weapon level with a big, flaming eye. I figured, there in Wolff Knipsengeldt's junkyard, that it was entirely possible that the massive slug had missed the eye and struck the horn, propelling the splintered-off tip with sufficient force to imbed itself in the still-open glove compartment.

Neither Wolff nor I spoke as we picked our way between the rusty hulks and stacks of old tires, back to the grubby office and the bottles of warm beer, nor did we talk much as we finished that last beer together. But, after he had filled the Bel Air's tank, just before he extended his thick, grimy hand in farewell, he pressed the crumpled sack on me.

"Franky, most folks in town an'here'bouts cain' even stan' to think on *what* was done to them poor kids, much less *how* it mighta happund. That's why folks all wants you to think you dint see what really come down out there in *das Schlachthaustal*. It'll be the same wherever you goes, too, an' after while, you'll likely start wonderin' if they ain't right an' you wrong.

"Ever'time you start thinkin' like thet, Franky, you jest take out that there an' look at it, an' squeeze on it hard an' r'member that whutall folks says, you knows the truth . . . an' so does old Wolff Knipsengeldt, too."

I still have that old bit of horn. It's tucked away with a yellowed clipping from a Cincinnati paper, dated in early September of that year, a few weeks after Peggy and I came back east.

LOST HERD, N. DAK. (AP) This small farming community is once more in the news. On the first day of the current school year, yesterday morning, no children could be found in the yard of Lost Herd Elementary School, for the yard was crowded with a milling herd of buffalo, 53 of the huge wild cattle. No one here seems to know when or how they came into town, since residents did not see or hear them in the streets and none of the farmlands completely surrounding the town appear to have been recently crossed by so many large animals.

Deputy Sheriff K. S. Kalb states that five buffalo were found on the campus of a nearby college more than six months ago. Along with most other townspeople interviewed, Deputy Kalb thinks that the herd are part of a larger herd known to roam a park in Saskatchewan, which province borders on this state only bare miles north of Lost Herd.

Readers may recall that this little town was visited by tragedy last spring when 50 second and third grade children and three adults were killed in the wreck of a school bus two miles west of Lost Herd.

Famed action-adventure writer Robert Adams was born in Virginia in 1932. An expert in medieval history and fencing, he often manufactures medieval weapons at his own forge in his Florida home. He is best known best for his popular Horseclans series, nearly twenty novels set in a post-nuclear-war America sunk to barbarism, the most recent volume of which is The Clan of the Cats *(1988). Other titles are* Castaways in Time *(1979) and* Stairway to Forever *(1988), an adventure in time.*

Karl had to take care of his mother—no matter what happened to him.

SEVENTEEN

He Walked By Day

Julius Long

Friedenburg, Ohio, sleeps between the muddy waters of the Miami River and the trusty track of a little-used spur of the Big Four. It suddenly became important to us because of its strategic position. It bisected a road which we were to surface with tar. The materials were to come by way of the spur and to be unloaded at the tiny yard.

We began work on a Monday morning. I was watching the tar distributor while it pumped tar from the car, when I felt a tap upon my back. I turned about, and when I beheld the individual who had tapped me, I actually jumped.

I have never, before or since, encountered such a singular figure. He was at least seven feet tall, and he seemed even taller than that because of the uncommon slenderness of his frame. He looked as if he had never been warmed by the rays of the sun, but confined all his life in a dank and dismal cellar. I concluded that he had been the prey of some insidious, etiolating disease. Certainly, I thought, nothing else could account for his ashen complexion. It seems that not blood, but shadows passed through his veins.

"Do you want to see me?" I asked.

"Are you the road feller?"

"Yes."

"I want a job. My mother's sick. I have her to keep. Won't you please give me a job?"

We really didn't need another man, but I was interested in this pallid giant with his staring, gray eyes. I called to Juggy, my foreman.

"Do you think we can find a place for this fellow?" I asked.

Juggy stared incredulously. "He looks like he'd break in two."

"I'm stronger'n anyone," said the youth.

He looked about, and his eyes fell on the Mack, which had just been loaded with six tons of gravel. He walked over to it, reached down and seized the hub of a front wheel. To our utter amazement, the wheel was slowly lifted from the ground. When it was raised to a height of eight or nine inches, the youth looked inquiringly in our direction. We must have appeared sufficiently awed, for he dropped the wheel with an abruptness that evoked a yell from the driver, who thought his tire would blow out.

"We can certainly use this fellow," I said, and Juggy agreed.

"What's your name, Shadow?" he demanded.

"Karl Rand," said the boy but "Shadow" stuck to him, as far as the crew was concerned.

We put him to work at once, and he slaved all morning, accomplishing tasks that we ordinarily assigned two or three men to do.

We were on the road at lunchtime, some miles from Friedenburg. I recalled that Shadow had not brought his lunch.

"You can take mine," I said. "I'll drive in to the village and eat."

"I never eat none," was Shadow's astonishing remark.

"You never eat!" The crew had heard his assertion, and there was an amused crowd about him at once. I fancied that he was pleased to have an audience.

"No, I never eat," he repeated. "You see"—he lowered his voice—"you see, I'm a ghost!"

We exchanged glances. So Shadow was psychopathic. We shrugged our shoulders.

"Whose ghost are you?" gibed Juggy. "Napoleon's?"

"Oh, no. I'm my own ghost. You see, I'm dead."

"Ah!" This was all Juggy could say. For once, the arch-kidder was nonplussed.

"That's why I'm so strong," added Shadow.

"How long have you been dead?" I asked.

"Six years. I was fifteen years old then."

"Tell us how it happened. Did you die a natural death, or

188

were you killed trying to lift a fast freight off the track?" This question was asked by Juggy, who was slowly recovering.

"It was in the cave," answered Shadow solemnly. "I slipped and fell over a bank. I cracked my head on the floor. I've been a ghost ever since."

"Then why do you walk by day instead of by night?"

"I got to keep my mother."

Shadow looked so sincere, so pathetic when he made this answer, that we left off teasing him. I tried to make him eat my lunch, but he would have none of it. I expected to see him collapse that afternoon, but he worked steadily and showed no sign of tiring. We didn't know what to make of him. I confess that I was a little afraid in his presence. After all, a madman with almost superhuman strength is a dangerous character. But Shadow seemed perfectly harmless and docile.

When we had returned to our boarding-house that night, we plied our landlord with questions about Karl Rand. He drew himself up authoritatively, and lectured for some minutes upon Shadow's idiosyncrasies.

"The boy first started telling that story about six years ago," he said. "He never was right in his head, and nobody paid much attention to him at first. He said he'd fallen and busted his head in a cave, but everybody knows they ain't no caves hereabouts. I don't know what put that idea in his head. But Karl's stuck to it ever since, and I 'spect they's lots of folks round Friedenburg that's growed to believe him— more'n admits they do."

That evening, I patronized the village barber shop, and was careful to introduce Karl's name into the conversation. "All I can say is," said the barber solemnly, "that his hair ain't growed any in the last six years, and they was nary a whisker on his chin. No, sir, nary a whisker on his chin."

This did not strike me as so tremendously odd, for I had previously heard of cases of such arrested growth. However, I went to sleep that night thinking about Shadow.

The next morning, the strange youth appeared on time and rode with the crew to the job.

"Did you eat well?" Juggy asked him.

Shadow shook his head. "I never eat none."

The crew half believed him.

Early in the morning, Steve Bradshaw, the nozzle man on the tar distributer, burned his hand badly. I hurried him in to see the village doctor. When he had dressed Steve's hand, I took advantage of my opportunity and made inquiries about Shadow.

"Karl's got me stumped," said the country practitioner. "I confess I can't understand it. Of course, he won't let me get close enough to him to look at him, but it don't take an examination to tell there's something abnormal about him."

"I wonder what could have given him the idea that he's his own ghost," I said.

"I'm not sure, but I think what put it in his head was the things people used to say to him when he was a kid. He always looked like a ghost, and everybody kidded him about it. I kind of think that's what gave him the notion."

"Has he changed at all in the last six years?"

"Not a bit. He was as tall six years ago as he is today. I think that his abnormal growth might have had something to do with the stunting of his mind. But I don't know for sure."

I had to take Steve's place on the tar distributor during the next four days, and I watched Shadow pretty closely. He never ate any lunch, but he would sit with us while we devoured ours. Juggy could not resist the temptation to joke at his expense.

"There was a ghost back in my home town," Juggy once told him. "Mary Jenkens was an awful pretty woman when she was living, and when she was a girl, every fellow in town wanted to marry her. Jim Jenkens finally led her down the aisle, and we was all jealous—especially Joe Garver. He was broke up awful. Mary hadn't no more'n come back from the Falls when Joe was trying to make up to her. She wouldn't have nothing to do with him. Joe was hurt bad.

"A year after she was married, Mary took sick and died. Jim Jenkens was awful put out about it. He didn't act right from then on. He got to imagining things. He got suspicious of Joe.

" 'What you got to worry about?' people would ask him. 'Mary's dead. There can't no harm come to her now.'

"But Jim didn't feel that way. Joe heard about it, and he got to teasing Jim.

" 'I was out with Mary's ghost last night,' he would say. And Jim got to believing him. One night, he lays low for Joe and shoots him with both barrels. 'He was goin' to meet my wife!' Jim told the judge."

"Did they give him the chair?" I asked.

"No, they gave him life in the state hospital."

Shadow remained impervious to Juggy's yarns, which were told for his special benefit. During this time, I noticed something decidedly strange about the boy, but I kept my own counsel. After all, a contractor can not keep the respect of his men if he appears too credulous.

One day Juggy voiced my suspicions for me. "You know," he said, "I never saw that kid sweat. It's uncanny. It's ninety in the shade today, and Shadow ain't got a drop of perspiration on his face. Look at his shirt. Dry as if he'd just put it on."

Everyone in the crew noticed this. I think we all became uneasy in Shadow's presence.

One morning he didn't show up for work. We waited a few minutes and left without him. When the trucks came in with their second load of gravel, the drivers told us that Shadow's mother had died during the night. This news cast a gloom over the crew. We all sympathized with the youth.

"I wish I hadn't kidded him," said Juggy.

We all put in an appearance that evening at Shadow's little cottage, and I think he was tremendously gratified. "I won't be working no more," he told me. "There ain't no need for me now."

I couldn't afford to lay off the crew for the funeral, but I did go myself. I even accompanied Shadow to the cemetery.

We watched while the grave was being filled. There were many others there, for one of the chief delights in a rural community is to see how the mourners "take on" at a funeral. Moreover, their interest in Karl Rand was deeper. He had said he was going back to his cave, that he would never again walk by day. The villagers, as well as myself, wanted to see what would happen.

When the grave was filled, Shadow turned to me, eyed me pathetically a moment, then walked from the grave. Silently, we watched him set out across the field. Two mis-

191

chievous boys disobeyed the entreaties of their parents, and set out after him.

They returned to the village an hour later with a strange and incredible story. They had seen Karl disappear into the ground. The earth had literally swallowed him up. The youngsters were terribly frightened. It was thought that Karl had done something to scare them, and their imaginations had got the better of them.

But the next day they were asked to lead a group of the more curious to the spot where Karl had vanished. He had not returned, and they were worried.

In a ravine two miles from the village, the party discovered a small but penetrable entrance to a cave. Its existence had never been dreamed of by the farmer who owned the land. (He has since then opened it up for tourists, and it is known as Ghost Cave.)

Someone in the party had thoughtfully brought an electric searchlight, and the party squeezed its way into the cave. Exploration revealed a labyrinth of caverns of exquisite beauty. But the explorers were oblivious to the esthetics of the cave; they thought only of Karl and his weird story.

After circuitous ramblings, they came to a sudden drop in the floor. At the base of this precipice they beheld a skeleton.

The coroner and the sheriff were duly summoned. The sheriff invited me to accompany him.

I regret that I cannot describe the gruesome, awesome feeling that came over me as I made my way through those caverns. Within their chambers the human voice is given a peculiar, sepulchral sound. But perhaps it was the knowledge of Karl's bizarre story, his unaccountable disappearance that inspired me with such awe, such thoughts.

The skeleton gave me a shock, for it was a skeleton of a man *seven feet tall!* There was no mistake about this; the coroner was positive.

The skull had been fractured, apparently by a fall over the bank. It was I who discovered the hat near by. It was rotted with decay, but in the leather band were plainly discernible the crudely penned initials, "K.R."

I felt suddenly weak. The sheriff noticed my nervousness. "What's the matter, have you seen a ghost?"

I laughed nervously and affected nonchalance. With the best off-hand manner I could command, I told him of Karl Rand. He was not impressed.

"You don't—?" He did not wish to insult my intelligence by finishing his question.

At this moment, the coroner looked up and commented: "This skeleton has been here about six years, I'd say."

I was not courageous enough to acknowledge my suspicions, but the villagers were outspoken. The skeleton, they declared, was that of Karl Rand. The coroner and the sheriff were incredulous, but, politicians both, they displayed some sympathy with this view.

My friend, the sheriff, discussed the matter privately with me some days later. His theory was that Karl had discovered the cave, wandered inside and come upon the corpse of some unfortunate who had preceded him. He had been so excited by his discovery that his hat had fallen down beside the body. Later, aided by the remarks of the villagers about his ghostliness, he had fashioned his own legend.

This, of course, may be true. But the people of Friedenburg are not convinced by this explanation, and neither am I. For the identity of the skeleton has never been determined, and Karl Rand has never since been seen to walk by day.

Lawyer Julius Long took to writing fiction to supplement his income during the Great Depression. Until his death in 1955 at the age of forty-eight, he was a steady contributor of more than two hundred short stories. Nearly all his work was in the detective genré. "He Walked by Day" first appeared in Weird Tales.

Catesby Wran had to be hallucinating. After all, a ghost had to be the spirit of something that had died, right?

EIGHTEEN

Smoke Ghost
Fritz Leiber

Miss Millick wondered just what had happened to Mr. Wran. He kept making the strangest remarks when she took dictation. Just this morning he had quickly turned around and asked, "Have you ever seen a ghost, Miss Millick?" And she had tittered nervously and replied, "When I was a girl there was a thing in white that used to come out of the closet in the attic bedroom when I slept there, and moan. Of course it was just my imagination. I was frightened of lots of things." And he had said, "I don't mean that kind of ghost. I mean a ghost from the world today, with the soot of the factories on its face and the pounding of machinery in its soul. The kind that would haunt coal yards and slip around at night through deserted office buildings like this one. A real ghost. Not something out of books." And she hadn't known what to say.

He'd never been like this before. Of course he might be joking, but it didn't sound that way. Vaguely Miss Millick wondered whether he mightn't be seeking some sort of sympathy from her. Of course, Mr. Wran was married and had a little child, but that didn't prevent her from having daydreams. The daydreams were not very exciting, still they helped fill up her mind. But now he was asking her another of those unprecedented questions.

"Have you ever thought what a ghost of our times would look like, Miss Millick? Just picture it. A smoky composite face with the hungry anxiety of the unemployed, the neurotic restlessness of the person without purpose, the jerky tension of the high-pressure metropolitan worker, the uneasy resentment of the striker, the callous opportunism of the scab, the aggressive whine of the panhandler, the inhibited terror of the bombed civilian, and a thousand other twisted emotional patterns. Each one overlying and yet blending with the other, like a pile of semi-transparent masks?"

Miss Millick gave a little self-conscious shiver and said, "That would be terrible. What an awful thing to think of."

She peered furtively across the desk. She remembered having heard that there had been something impressively abnormal about Mr. Wran's childhood, but she couldn't recall what it was. If only she could do something—laugh at his mood or ask him what was really wrong. She shifted the extra pencils in her left hand and mechanically traced over some of the shorthand curlicues in her notebook.

"Yet, that's just what such a ghost or vitalized projection would look like, Miss Millick," he continued, smiling in a tight way. "It would grow out of the real world. It would reflect the tangled, sordid, vicious things. All the loose ends. And it would be very grimy. I don't think it would seem white or wispy, or favor graveyards. It wouldn't moan. But it would mutter unintelligibly, and twitch at your sleeve. Like a sick, surly ape. What would such a thing want from a person, Miss Millick? Sacrifice? Worship? Or just fear? What could you do to stop it from troubling you?"

Miss Millick giggled nervously. There was an expression beyond her powers of definition in Mr. Wran's ordinary, flat-cheeked, thirtyish face, silhouetted against the dusty window. He turned away and stared out into the gray downtown atmosphere that rolled in from the railroad yards and the mills. When he spoke again his voice sounded far away.

"Of course, being immaterial, it couldn't hurt you physically—at first. You'd have to be peculiarly sensitive to see it, or be aware of it at all. But it would begin to influence your actions. Make you do this. Stop you from doing that. Although only a projection, it would gradually get its hooks into the world of things as they are. Might even get control of suitably vacuous minds. Then it could hurt whomever it wanted."

Miss Millick squirmed and read back her shorthand, like

the books said you should do when there was a pause. She became aware of the failing light and wished Mr. Wran would ask her to turn on the overhead. She felt scratchy, as if soot were sifting down on to her skin.

"It's a rotten world, Miss Millick," said Mr. Wran, talking at the window. "Fit for another morbid growth of superstition. It's time the ghosts, or whatever you call them, took over and began a rule of fear. They'd be no worse than men."

"But"—Miss Millick's diaphragm jerked, making her titter inanely—"of course, there aren't any such things as ghosts."

Mr. Wran turned around.

"Of course there aren't, Miss Millick," he said in a loud, patronizing voice, as if she had been doing the talking rather than he. "Science and common sense and psychiatry all go to prove it."

She hung her head and might even have blushed if she hadn't felt so all at sea. Her leg muscles twitched, making her stand up, although she hadn't intended to. She aimlessly rubbed her hand along the edge of the desk.

"Why, Mr. Wran, look what I got off your desk," she said, showing him a heavy smudge. There was a note of clumsily playful reproof in her voice. "No wonder the copy I bring you always gets so black. Somebody ought to talk to those scrubwomen. They're skimping on your room."

She wished he would make some normal joking reply. But instead he drew back and his face hardened.

"Well, to get back," he rapped out harshly, and began to dictate.

When she was gone, he jumped up, dabbed his finger experimentally at the smudged part of the desk, frowned worriedly at the almost inky smears. He jerked open a drawer, snatched out a rag, hastily swabbed off the desk, crumpled the rag into a ball and tossed it back. There were three or four other rags in the drawer, each impregnated with soot.

Then he went over to the window and peered out anxiously through the dusk, his eyes searching the panorama of roofs, fixing on each chimney and water tank.

"It's a neurosis. Must be. Compulsions. Hallucinations," he muttered to himself in a tired, distraught voice that would have made Miss Millick gasp. "It's that damned mental abnormality cropping up in a new form. Can't be any other explanation. But it's so damned real. Even the soot. Good thing I'm seeing the psychiatrist. I don't think I could force myself to get on the elevated tonight." His voice trailed off, he rubbed his eyes, and his memory automatically started to grind.

It had all begun on the elevated. There was a particular little sea of roofs he had grown into the habit of glancing at just as the packed car carrying him homeward lurched around a turn. A dingy, melancholy little world of tar-paper, tarred gravel, and smoky brick. Rusty tin chimneys with odd conical hats suggested abandoned listening posts. There was a washed-out advertisement of some ancient patent medicine on the nearest wall. Superficially it was like ten thousand other drab city roofs. But he always saw it around dusk, either in the smoky half-light, or tinged with red by the flat rays of a dirty sunset, or covered by ghostly windblown white sheets of rain-splash, or patched with blackish snow; and it seemed unusually bleak and suggestive; almost beautifully ugly though in no sense picturesque; dreary, but meaningful. Unconsciously it came to symbolize for Catesby Wran certain disagreeable aspects of the frustrated, frightened century in which he lived, the jangled century of hate and heavy industry and total wars. The quick daily glance into the half darkness became an integral part of his life. Oddly, he never saw it in the morning, for it was then his habit to sit on the other side of the car, his head buried in the paper.

One evening toward winter he noticed what seemed to be a shapeless black sack lying on the third roof from the tracks. He did not think about it. It merely registered as an addition to the well-known scene and his memory stored away the impression for further reference. Next evening, however, he decided he had been mistaken in one detail. The object was a roof nearer than he had thought. Its color and texture, and the grimy stains around it, suggested that it was filled with coal dust, which was hardly reasonable. Then, too, the following evening it seemed to have been blown against a rusty ventilator by the wind—which could hardly have happened if it were at all heavy. Perhaps it was filled with leaves. Catesby was surprised to find himself anticipating his next daily glance with a minor note of apprehension. There was something unwholesome in the posture of the thing that stuck in his mind—a bulge in the sacking that suggested a misshaped head peering around the ventilator. And his apprehension was justified, for that evening the thing was on the nearest roof, though on the farther side, looking as if it had just flopped down over the low brick parapet.

Next evening the sack was gone. Catesby was annoyed at the momentary feeling of relief that went through him, because the whole matter seemed too unimportant to warrant feelings of any sort. What difference did it make if his imagination had played tricks on him, and he'd fancied that the object was slowly crawling and hitching itself closer across the roofs? That was the way any normal imagination worked. He deliberately chose to disregard the fact that there were reasons for thinking his imagination was by no means a normal one. As he walked home from the elevated, however, he found himself wondering whether the sack was really gone. He seemed to recall a vague, smudgy trail leading across the gravel to the nearer side of the roof, which was masked by a parapet. For an instant an unpleasant picture formed in his mind—that of an inky, humped creature crouched behind the parapet, waiting.

The next time he felt the familiar grating lurch of the car, he caught himself trying not to look out. That angered him. He turned his head quickly. When he turned it back, his compact face was definitely pale. There had been only time for a fleeting rearward glance at the escaping roof. Had he actually seen in silhouette the upper part of a head of some sort peering over the parapet? Nonsense, he told himself. And even if he had seen something, there were a thousand explanations which did not involve the supernatural or even true hallucination. Tomorrow he would take a god look and clear up the whole matter. If necessary, he would visit the roof personally, though he hardly knew where to find it and disliked in any case the idea of pampering a silly fear.

He did not relish the walk home from the elevated that evening, and visions of the thing disturbed his dreams, and were in and out of his mind all next day at the office. It was then that he first began to relieve his nerves by making jokingly serious remarks about the supernatural to Miss Millick, who seemed properly mystified. It was on the same day, too, that he became aware of a growing antipathy to grime and soot. Everything he touched seemed gritty, and he found himself mopping and wiping at his desk like an old lady with a morbid fear of germs. He reasoned that there was no real change in his office, and that he'd just now become sensitive to the dirt that had always been there, but there was no denying an increasing nervousness. Long before the car reached the curve, he was straining his eyes through the murky twilight, determined to take in every detail.

Afterward he realized he must have given a muffled cry of some sort, for the man beside him looked at him curiously, the woman ahead gave him an unfavorable stare. Conscious of his own pallor and uncontrollable trembling, he stared back at them hungrily, trying to regain the feeling of security he had completely lost. They were the usual reassuringly wooden-faced people everyone rides home with on the elevated. But suppose he had pointed out to one of them what he had seen—that sodden, distorted face of sacking and coal dust, that boneless paw which waved back and forth, unmistakably in his direction, as if reminding him of a future appointment—he involuntarily shut his eyes tight. His thoughts were racing ahead to tomorrow evening. He pictured this same windowed oblong of light and packed humanity surging around the curve—then an opaque monstrous form leaping out from the roof in a parabolic swoop—an unmentionable face pressed close against the window, smearing it with wet coal dust—huge paws fumbling sloppily at the glass—

Somehow he managed to turn off his wife's anxious inquiries. Next morning he reached a decision and made an appointment for that evening with a psychiatrist a friend had told him about. It cost him a considerable effort, for Catesby had a well-grounded distaste for anything dealing with psychological abnormality. Visiting a psychiatrist meant raking up an episode in his past which he had never fully described even to his wife. Once he had made the decision, however, he felt considerably relieved. The psychiatrist, he told himself, would clear everything up. He could almost fancy him saying, "Merely a bad case of nerves. However, you must consult the oculist whose name I'm writing down for you, and you must take two of these pills in water every four hours," and so on. It was almost comforting, and made the coming revelation he would have to make seem less painful.

But as the smoky dusk rolled in, his nervousness had returned and he had let his joking mystification of Miss Millick run away with him until he had realized he wasn't frightening anyone but himself.

He would have to keep his imagination under better control, he told himself, as he continued to peer out restlessly at the massive, murky shapes of the downtown office buildings. Why, he had spent the whole afternoon building up a kind of neo-medieval cosmology of superstition. It wouldn't do. He realized then that he had been standing at the window much longer than he'd thought, for the glass panel in the door was dark and there was no noise coming from the outer office. Miss Millick and the rest must have gone home.

It was then he made the discovery that there would have been no special reason for dreading the swing around the curve that night. It was, as it happened, a horrible discovery. For, on the shadowed roof across the street and four stories below, he saw the thing huddle and roll across the gravel and, after one upward look of recognition, merge into the blackness beneath the water tank.

As he hurriedly collected his things and made for the elevator, fighting the panicky impulse to run, he began to think of hallucination and mild psychosis as very desirable conditions. For better or for worse, he pinned all his hopes on the psychiatrist.

"So you find yourself growing nervous and . . . er . . . jumpy, as you put it," said Dr. Trevethick, smiling with dignified geniality. "Do you notice any more definite physical symptoms? Pain? Headache? Indigestion?"

Catesby shook his head and wet his lips. "I'm especially nervous while riding in the elevated," he muttered swiftly.

"I see. We'll discuss that more fully. But I'd like you first to tell me about something you mentioned earlier. You said there was something about your childhood that might predispose you to nervous ailments. As you know, the early years are critical ones in the development of an individual's behavior pattern."

Catesby studied the yellow reflections of frosted globes in the dark surface of the desk. The palm of his left hand aimlessly rubbed the thick nap of the armchair. After a while he raised his head and looked straight into the doctor's small brown eyes.

"From perhaps my third to my ninth year," he began, choosing the words with care, "I was what you might call a sensory prodigy."

The doctor's expression did not change. "Yes?" he inquired politely.

"What I mean is that I was supposed to be able to see through walls, read letters through envelopes and books through their covers, fence and play ping-pong blindfolded, find things that were buried, read thoughts." The words tumbled out.

"And could you?" The doctor's voice was toneless.

"I don't know. I don't suppose so," answered Catesby, long-lost emotions flooding back into his voice. "It's all confused now. I thought I could, but then they were always encouraging me. My mother . . . was . . . well . . . interested in psychic phenomena. I was . . . exhibited. I seem to remember seeing things other people couldn't. As if most opaque objects were transparent. But I was very young. I didn't have any scientific criteria for judgment."

He was reliving it now. The darkened rooms. The earnest assemblages of gawking, prying adults. Himself alone on a little platform, lost in a straight-backed wooden chair. The black silk handkerchief over his eyes. His mother's coaxing, insistent questions. The whispers. The gasps. His own hate of the whole business, mixed with hunger for the adulation of adults. Then the scientists from the university, the experiments, the big test. The reality of those memories engulfed him and momentarily made him forget the reason why he was disclosing them to a stranger.

"Do I understand that your mother tried to make use of you as a medium for communicating with the . . . er . . . other world?"

Catesby nodded eagerly.

"She tried to, but she couldn't. When it came to getting in touch with the dead, I was a complete failure. All I could do—or thought I could do—was see real, existing, three-dimensional objects beyond the vision of normal people. Objects anyone could have seen except for distance, obstruction, or darkness. It was always a disappointment to mother."

He could hear her sweetish, patient voice saying, "Try again, dear, just this once. Katie was your aunt. She loved you. Try to hear what she's saying." And he had answered, "I can see a woman in a blue dress standing on the other side of Dick's house." And she had replied, "Yes, I know, dear. But that's not Katie. Katie's a spirit. Try again. Just this once, dear." The doctor's voice gently jarred him back into the softly gleaming office.

"You mentioned scientific criteria for judgment, Mr. Wran. As far as you know, did anyone ever try to apply them to you?"

Catesby's nod was emphatic.

"They did. When I was eight, two young psychologists from the university got interested in me. I guess they did it for a joke at first, and I remember being very determined to show them I amounted to something. Even now I seem to recall how the note of polite superiority and amused sarcasm drained out of their voices. I suppose they decided at first that it was very clever trickery, but somehow they persuaded mother to let them try me out under controlled conditions. There were lots of tests that seemed very business-like after mother's slipshod little exhibitions. They found I was clairvoyant—or so they thought. I got worked up and on edge. They were going to demonstrate my supernormal sensory powers to the university psychology faculty. For the first time, I began to worry about whether I'd come through. Perhaps they kept me going at too hard a pace, I don't know. At any rate, when the test came, I couldn't do a thing. Everything became opaque. I got desperate and made things up out of my imagination. I lied. In the end I failed utterly, and I believe the two young psychologists got into a lot of hot water as a result."

He could hear the brusque, bearded man saying, "You've been taken in by a child, Flaxman, a mere child.

I'm greatly disturbed. You've put yourself on the same plane as common charlatans. Gentlemen, I ask you to banish from your minds this whole sorry episode. It must never be referred to." He winced at the recollection of his feeling of guilt. But at the same time he was beginning to feel exhilarated and almost light-hearted. Unburdening his long-repressed memories had altered his whole viewpoint. The episodes on the elevated began to take on what seemed their proper proportions as merely the bizarre workings of overwrought nerves and an overly suggestible mind. The doctor, he anticipated confidently, would disentangle the obscure subconscious causes, whatever they might be. And the whole business would be finished off quickly, just as his childhood experience—which was beginning to seem a little ridiculous now—had been finished off.

"From that day on," he continued, "I never exhibited a trace of my supposed powers. My mother was frantic and tried to sue the university. I had something like a nervous breakdown. Then the divorce was granted, and my father got custody of me. He did his best to make me forget it. We went on long outdoor vacations and did a lot of athletics, associated with normal matter-of-fact people. I went to business college eventually. I'm in advertising now. But," Catesby paused, "now that I'm having nervous symptoms, I've wondered if there mightn't be a connection. It's not a question of whether I was really clairvoyant or not. Very likely my mother taught me a lot of unconscious deceptions, good enough to fool even young psychology instructors. But don't you think it may have some important bearing on my present condition?"

For several moments the doctor regarded him with a professional frown. Then he said quietly, "And is there some . . . er . . . more specific connection between your experiences then and now? Do you by any chance find that you are once again beginning to . . . er . . . see things?"

Catesby swallowed. He had felt an increasing eagerness to unburden himself of his fears, but it was not easy to make a beginning, and the doctor's shrewd question rattled him. He forced himself to concentrate. The thing he thought he had seen on the roof loomed up before his inner eye with unexpected vividness. Yet it did not frighten him. He groped for words.

Then he saw that the doctor was not looking at him but over his shoulder. Color was draining out of the doctor's face and his eyes did not seem so small. Then the doctor sprang to his feet, walked past Catesby, threw up the window and peered into the darkness.

As Catesby rose, the doctor slammed down the window and said in a voice whose smoothness was marred by a slight, persistent gasping, "I hope I haven't alarmed you. I saw the face of . . . er . . . a Negro prowler on the fire escape. I must have frightened him, for he seems to have gotten out of sight in a hurry. Don't give it another thought. Doctors are frequently bothered by *voyeurs* . . . er . . . Peeping Toms."

"A Negro?" asked Catesby, moistening his lips.

The doctor laughed nervously. "I imagine so, though my first odd impression was that it was a white man in blackface. You see, the color didn't seem to have any brown in it. It was dead-black."

Catesby moved toward the window. There were smudges on the glass. "It's quite all right, Mr. Wran." The doctor's voice had acquired a sharp note in impatience, as if he were trying hard to reassume his professional authority. "Let's continue our conversation. I was asking you if you were"— he made a face—"seeing things."

Catesby's whirling thoughts slowed down and locked into place. "No, I'm not seeing anything that other people don't see, too. And I think I'd better go now. I've been keeping you too long." He disregarded the doctor's half-hearted gesture of denial. "I'll phone you about the physical examination. In a way you've already taken a big load off my mind." He smiled woodenly. "Goodnight, Dr. Trevethick."

Catesby Wran's mental state was a peculiar one. His eyes searched every angular shadow, he glanced sideways down each chasm-like alley and barren basement passageway, and kept stealing looks at the irregular line of the roofs, yet he was hardly conscious of where he was going. He pushed away the thoughts that came into his mind, and kept moving. He became aware of a slight sense of security as he turned into a lighted street where there were people and high buildings and blinking signs. After a while he found himself in the dim lobby of the structure that housed his office. Then he realized why he couldn't go home, why he daren't go home—after what had happened at the office of Dr. Trevethick.

"Hello, Mr. Wran," said the night elevator man, a burly figure in overalls, sliding open the grille-work door to the old-fashioned cage. "I didn't know you were working nights now, too."

Catesby stepped in automatically. "Sudden rush of orders," he murmured inanely. "Some stuff that has to be gotten out."

The cage creaked to a stop at the top floor. "Be working very late, Mr. Wran?"

He nodded vaguely, watched the car slide out of sight, found his keys, swiftly crossed the outer office, and entered his own. His hand went out to the light switch, but then the thought occurred to him that the two lighted windows, standing out against the dark bulk of the building, would indicate his whereabouts and serve as a goal toward which something could crawl and climb. He moved his chair so that the back was against the wall and sat down in the semi-darkness. He did not remove his overcoat.

For a long time he sat there motionless, listening to his own breathing and the faraway sounds from the streets below: the thin metallic surge of the crosstown streetcar, the farther one of the elevated, faint, lonely cries and honkings, indistinct rumblings. Words he had spoken to Miss Millick in nervous jest came back to him with the bitter taste of truth. He found himself unable to reason critically or connectedly, but by their own volition thoughts rose up into his mind and gyrated slowly and rearranged themselves with the inevitable movement of planets.

Gradually his mental picture of the world was transformed. No longer a world of material atoms and empty spaces, but a world in which the bodiless existed and moved according to its own obscure laws or unpredictable impulses. The new picture illuminated with dreadful clarity certain general facts which had always bewildered and troubled him and from which he had tried to hide: the inevitability of hate and war, the diabolically timed mischances which wreck the best of human intentions, the walls of willful misunderstanding that divide one man from another, the eternal vitality of cruelty and ignorance and greed. They seemed appropriate now, necessary parts of the picture. And superstition only a kind of wisdom.

Then his thoughts returned to himself and the question he had asked Miss Millick, "What would such a thing want from a person? Sacrifices? Worship, or just fear? What could you do to stop it from troubling you?" It had become a practical question.

With an explosive jangle, the phone began to ring. "Cate, I've been trying everywhere to get you," said his wife. "I never thought you'd be at the office. What are you doing? I've been worried."

He said something about work.

"You'll be home right away?" came the faint anxious question. "I'm a little frightened. Ronny just had a scare. It woke him up. He kept pointing to the window saying, 'Black man, black man.' Of course it's something he dreamed. But I'm frightened. You will be home? What's that, dear? Can't you hear me?"

"I will. Right away," he said. Then he was out of the office, buzzing the night bell and peering down the shaft.

He saw it peering up the shaft at him from the deep shadows three floors below, the sacking face pressed against the iron grille-work. It started up the stair at a shockingly swift, shambling gait, vanishing temporarily from sight as it swung into the second corridor below.

Catesby clawed at the door to the office, realized he had not locked it, pushed it in, slammed and locked it behind him, retreated to the other side of the room, cowered between the filing cases and the wall. His teeth were clicking. He heard the groan of the rising cage. A silhouette darkened the frosted glass of the door, blotting out part of the grotesque reverse of the company name. After a little the door opened.

The big-globed overhead light flared on and, standing inside the door, her hand on the switch, was Miss Millick.

"Why, Mr. Wran," she stammered vacuously, "I didn't

know you were here. I'd just come in to do some extra typing after the movie. I didn't . . . but the lights weren't on. What were you—"

He stared at her. He wanted to shout in relief, grab hold of her, talk rapidly. He realized he was grinning hysterically.

"Why, Mr. Wran, what's happened to you?" she asked embarrassedly, ending with a stupid titter. "Are you feeling sick? Isn't there something I can do for you?"

He shook his head jerkily and managed to say, "No, I'm just leaving. I was doing some extra work myself."

"But you *look* sick," she insisted, and walked over toward him. He inconsequentially realized she must have stepped in mud, for her high-heeled shoes left neat black prints.

"Yes, I'm sure you must be sick. You're so terribly pale." She sounded like an enthusiastic, incompetent nurse. Her face brightened with a sudden inspiration. "I've got something in my bag that'll fix you up right away," she said. "It's for indigestion."

She fumbled at her stuffed oblong purse. He noticed that she was absent-mindedly holding it shut with one hand while she tried to open it with the other. Then, under his very eyes, he saw her bend back the thick prongs of metal locking the purse as if they were tinfoil, or as if her fingers had become a pair of steel pliers.

Instantly his memory recited the words he had spoken to Miss Millick that afternoon. "It couldn't hurt you physically—at first . . . gradually get its hooks into the world . . . might even get control of suitably vacuous minds. Then it could hurt whomever it wanted." A sickish, cold feeling grew inside him. He began to edge toward the door.

But Miss Millick hurried ahead of him

"You don't have to wait, Fred," she called. "Mr. Wran's decided to stay a while longer."

The door to the cage shut with a mechanical rattle. The cage creaked. Then she turned around in the door.

"Why, Mr. Wran," she gurgled reproachfully, "I just couldn't think of letting you go home now. I'm sure you're terribly unwell. Why, you might collapse in the street. You've just got to stay here until you feel different."

The creaking died away. He stood in the center of the office, motionless. His eyes traced the coal-black course of

Miss Millick's footprints to where she stood blocking the door. Then a sound that was almost a scream was wrenched out of him, for it seemed to him that the blackness was creeping up her legs under the thin stockings.

"Why, Mr. Wran," she said, "you're acting as if you were crazy. You must lie down for a while. Here, I'll help you off with your coat."

The nauseously idiotic and rasping note was the same; only it had been intensified. As she came toward him he turned and ran through the storeroom, clattered a key desperately at the lock of the second door to the corridor.

"Why, Mr. Wran," he heard her call, "are you having some kind of a fit? You must let me help you."

The door came open and he plunged out into the corridor and up the stairs immediately ahead. It was only when he reached the top that he realized the heavy steel door in front of him led to the roof. He jerked up the catch.

"Why, Mr. Wran, you mustn't run away. I'm coming after you."

Then he was out on the gritty gravel of the roof. The night sky was clouded and murky, with a faint pinkish glow from the neon signs. From the distant mills rose a ghostly spurt of flame. He ran to the edge. The street lights glared dizzily upward. Two men were tiny round blobs of hat and shoulders. He swung around.

The thing was in the doorway. The voice was no longer solicitous but moronically playful, each sentence ending in a titter.

"Why, Mr. Wran, why have you come up here? We're all alone. Just think, I might push you off."

The thing came slowly toward him. He moved back until his heels touched the low parapet. Without knowing why, or what he was going to do, he dropped to his knees. He dared not look at the face as it came nearer, a focus for the worst in the world, a gathering point for poisons from everywhere. Then the lucidity of terror took possession of his mind, and words formed on his lips.

"I will obey you. You are my god," he said. "You have supreme power over man and his animals and his machines. You rule this city and all others. I recognize that."

Again the titter, closer. "Why, Mr. Wran, you never talked like this before. Do you mean it?"

"The world is yours to do with as you will, save or tear to pieces," he answered fawningly, the words automatically fitting themselves together in vaguely liturgical patterns. "I recognize that. I will praise, I will sacrifice. In smoke and soot I will worship you for ever."

The voice did not answer. He looked up. There was only Miss Millick, deathly pale and swaying drunkenly. Her eyes were closed. He caught her as she wobbled toward him. His knees gave way under the added weight and they sank down together on the edge of the roof.

After a while she began to twitch. Small noises came from her throat and her eyelids edged open.

"Come on, we'll go downstairs," he murmured jerkily, trying to draw her up. "You're feeling bad."

"I'm terribly dizzy," she whispered. "I must have fainted, I didn't eat enough. And then I'm so nervous lately, about the war and everything, I guess. Why, we're on the roof! Did you bring me up here to get some air? Or did I come up without knowing it? I'm awfully foolish. I used to walk in my sleep, my mother said."

As he helped her down the stairs, she turned and looked at him. "Why, Mr. Wran," she said, faintly, "you've got a big black smudge on your forehead. Here, let me get it off for you." Weakly she rubbed at it with her handkerchief. She started to sway again and he steadied her.

"No, I'll be all right," she said. "Only I feel cold. What happened, Mr. Wran? Did I have some sort of fainting spell?"

He told her it was something like that.

Later, riding home in the empty elevated car, he wondered how long he would be safe from the thing. It was a purely practical problem. He had no way of knowing, but instinct told him he had satisfied the brute for some time. Would it want more when it came again? Time enough to answer that question when it arose. It might be hard, he realized, to keep out of an insane asylum. With Helen and Ronny to protect, as well as himself, he would have to be careful and tight-lipped. He began to speculate as to how

209

many other men and women had seen the thing or things like it.

The elevated slowed and lurched in a familiar fashion. He looked at the roofs near the curve. They seemed very ordinary, as if what made them impressive had gone away for a while.

The winner of more awards in imaginative fiction than any other writer, including nine Hugos and four Nebulas, Fritz Leiber was born in Chicago in 1910. The son of a famous Shakespearean actor, he was educated at the University of Chicago and has been an actor, teacher, and editor. One of the founders of science fiction's Golden Age, he wrote such high quality novels as Gather, Darkness!, *in which future scientists create a dictatorship under cover of a fake religion, and* Conjure Wife (1941), *in which witchcraft is a science whose laws are not yet understood. His best supernatural stories are collected in* Night's Black Agents (1947).